Mending
My Heart

Mending
My Heart

The My Heart Series, Book 2

Kathleen Nelson Tellish

Studio of Books LLC
5900 Balcones Drive Suite 100
Austin, Texas 78731
www.studioofbooks.org
Hotline: (254) 800-1183

Ordering Information:
Special discounts are available on quantity purchases by corporations, associations, and others. For details, contact the publisher at the address above.

Printed in the United States of America.

ISBN-13: Softcover   978-1-964928-42-5
          eBook   978-1-964928-45-6

Library of Congress Control Number: 2025907416

DEDICATION

To all the healthcare and emergency services professionals. Thank you for your dedication to the safety and well-being of our communities.

ACKNOWLEDGEMENT

To my mother and father who allowed me to be the free spirit of the family. Rest easy knowing that I continue to do the things I want in my own way. My uninhibited imagination continues to bewilder those who know me. And after all, isn't that what being a free spirit is all about? You are loved and missed daily. You will always be in My Heart!

Table of Contents

CHAPTER 1

D r. Damon Parker finished the day shift in the ER, grabbed the first available elevator, and got off on the floor that housed the nursery. There was laughter coming from the room near the end of the corridor and he recognized Samantha's laugh. The florist delivered five bouquets of flowers earlier this afternoon. He carried an armful of flowers for the ladies and a new baseball mitt for Andrew. He knocked on the open door.

"Sounds like a celebration going on in this room ladies, and look, here is the new momma."

Walking over to Abbie, she stood, and Damon wrapped her in a hug and held out the biggest bouquet. Turning to the other ladies in the room, he handed each a smaller version of the bouquet that Abbie received. He said hello to Kate and Julie and asked how they had been doing since the wedding.

Stopping in front of Sam, he took her hand, pulled her to a standing position, and wrapped her in his arms. Abbie winked from across the room, and Samantha rolled her eyes.

"And last but not least, darlin, I hope these brighten your day."

Samantha didn't know if she should thank him or spout out a smart mouth answer, but she decided to be nice and did not embarrass him in front of her friends.

"Thank you, Damon. The flowers are lovely."

Damon turned toward Andy and gave him the new baseball mitt.

"This is for you, Andy. If you're ever in need of a break from all these ladies, give me a call and we'll toss the ball."

"That would be great, Dr. Parker. Sometimes they talk about things I don't understand. Dad says the prettier they are, the more they talk."

Everyone in the room laughed.

Damon shook Alex's hand, and the conversation turned to the new babies.

"Andy, I haven't seen those new sisters yet. Should we go to the nursery, and you can tell me who is who?"

"Mom and Dad haven't decided on names yet, Dr. Parker, and I don't think it is viewing time in the nursery right now."

"Let's see if I can fix that, Andy."

Damon walked over to the phone on Abbie's bedside stand and dialed a number. Everyone was quiet while Damon talked to the nurse.

"Afternoon, darlin. Dr. Damon Parker here. I understand there are three identical little beauties hanging out in the nursery that I haven't had the pleasure of meeting yet. Their brother is willing to introduce me. Can we get a quick peek? Thanks. Be there in a moment."

Damon hung up the phone and saw Samantha do another eye roll.

"Are you going too, Samantha?"

"Thanks, I'll pass this time, Parker. It is easier for you to get what you want from the nurses when you aren't toting another lady with you."

Alex smiled, but Abbie couldn't contain her laughter, and the others began laughing as well.

"I don't know why you find that funny, Abbie. Or the rest of you, either."

"Dr. Parker, we better go before someone gets in trouble with my dad. Do you want to go with us, Dad?"

"Yes, Andy. I'm not sure I should be here right now, either."

Andy stood up and ambled toward the door.

"Hey! You're walking, young man? When did that happen?" said Damon.

"The day my sisters were born. I can't go fast yet, but Sam is going to keep helping me with therapy. Someday I'll be able to run."

"Yes, you will, Andy. Congratulations on your accomplishments."

As soon as the men had time to get to the end of the corridor, Sam turned toward Abbie.

"Abbie. What do you find so funny?"

"Are you blind, Sam? That man only has eyes for you. He may know how to charm the nurses to get them to do what he wants, but he is not going to give up on you."

"Well, Miss Know-it-all, I've already agreed to date him. Well, not date, but I agreed to a bike ride and an occasional dinner."

"Have there been any more nights at his place?"

"What are you, Abbie? My mother?"

Julie spoke. "Are we going to have this same conversation again? I thought we settled the idea of getting whatever is needed to keep you happy?"

Samantha smiled and turned to Julie. "And who is keeping you happy, Julie?"

"I don't believe we were talking about me, Sam. We are consenting adults. Why does it matter?"

"I'm changing the conversation. Abbie, I'm going to your place and getting the pups this evening. Koko and Kody can stay at my house until the six of you get settled at your place. I'll ask Damon if I can use his truck to transport them to my place. Once you are back on your feet, we should look at getting a vehicle big enough to take everyone back and forth between the houses."

"My SUV is not being used right now, so you can use mine, Sam."

"Thanks, Abbie, but moving three baby seats from vehicle to vehicle all the time will be too much work. Once the seats are in correctly, it is easier to leave them alone. The car will stay cleaner too."

"Just take mine, Sam. There is not room for everyone to fit in to the SUV. I think I'm going to need a van. Dear Lord. The girls are not even a week old, and I've already turned into a soccer mom."

The guys returned, and Conor O'Brien walked in right behind Alex. Conor said hello to Dana first, then said hello to the other ladies. He gave Abbie a hug and gave her flowers and chocolates. There was a new game for Andy's X-Box®. Abbie and Alex thanked him for everything and for thinking of Andy as well.

Alex spoke up. "Julie, Conor's brother, Tobin, is a renowned orthopedic surgeon in Ireland. He is in route to the United States from Ireland to visit for a couple of weeks. I invited him over to the house. He is interested in moving to the states, and I thought maybe the two of you could grab time to discuss the requirements for getting licensed here."

"I'd be happy to do that, Alex. Kate and I are staying until next weekend, and I'd love to hear the latest treatments happening in Ireland."

"Damon, I have a favor to ask." said Samantha.

"Anything, darlin. What's up?"

"I'd like to get the pups this evening and keep them at my place for a while. Unfortunately, I can't take them on my bike and my car is too small as well. Could I borrow the truck?"

"I'll help with the pups, Samantha. I've nothing planned this evening."

"Thanks. Abbie, should we leave Kohl at your place so he can get to know the girls first? He'll keep the other two in line if they get too excited when they meet the girls."

"That sounds great. Sam."

"Damon, I don't want to rush you, but would you be willing to leave now? I'll cook dinner for us as payment for your help."

"Ready when you are, darlin. We need to drop off the bike and get the truck."

Samantha dropped her bike at the house, then they grabbed his truck, and went to Abbie's house. Kohl and the pups greeted them when they came through the door. Sam let the three outside, gave Kohl fresh water, and filled his food bowl.

"I swear the pups get bigger every day. How long until they are full grown, Samantha?"

"According to the breeder, a dog reaches adult status around two years old, but we should plan for them to weight around one-hundred-twenty pounds in one year."

Sam let the dogs back in and Damon sat on the floor. Koko and Kody went straight to him, and Kohl went to Sam.

"We don't need to take anything other than the dogs. I have duplicates of their belongings at my place. But, if you plan on eating dinner before midnight, let's get these two leashed and loaded."

Sam bent down to give Kohl a hug and explained she was taking the pups so that he could meet the new babies tomorrow. Kohl responded with a soft bark. She gave him a treat while Damon loaded the pups in the truck. The pups were walking back and forth in the back seat area and Damon gave the command to sit. They stopped pacing and sat.

"Well, look at that, Samantha. They listen very well."

"Their training has been going great, and the program receives new referrals every day. We may need to expand beyond one pool. Once Abbie gets rested and released to start doing work again, she and I need to have a serious discussion about expansion."

"She's going to be one busy lady, and those daughters are beautiful."

"Yes, they are adorable. She and Alex are lucky."

Damon pulled into the driveway. "Okay, boys. Let's get inside the house."

Samantha went to the kitchen while Damon went out to the backyard with the dogs. Earlier today, she had prepped food at the thought of asking Damon to dinner. Now he was here, and she was nervous because she was as bad as the rest of the women who couldn't resist him. She, too, was falling for him.

Sam took the steaks out of the fridge, so they would come to room temperature before putting them on the grill. All that would need done was to toss the salad and prepare the asparagus. There was a bottle of red wine for dinner, and she opened the bottle to let it breathe.

Damon walked into the kitchen with the dogs and smiled. Dear Lord, she was in trouble. How did she imagine she could resist him? He thought of trying to outbid her on the house when she and Abbie were with the realtor, but in all honesty, the house looked like it was built for him. He looked perfect here at her house. Reaching for the wine, she poured two glasses, and held out a glass to Damon.

"I opened a bottle of red wine, Damon. We can sit on the front porch and enjoy the wine until the steaks come up to room temperature."

They remained standing in the kitchen and took one sip of wine from the glass. Damon took both glasses and placed them on the counter. He picked her up and sat her on the counter as well.

"I know a great way to waste time while the steaks reach room temperature."

Placing a hand on each side of her body, he leaned toward her face. Closing her eyes, not sure of what to expect next, she moaned as he began kissing her neck. Resisting was not on her list of options, and she gave in and mimicked his moves, and heard him moan as well.

"Are you thinking of turning me away, darlin?"

"No, Parker. I am all in."

"There are two choices, Samantha. We can do this here or you can point in the direction of the bedroom."

Sliding off the counter, she stood in front of him, reached up to kiss him, and reached for his hand. The pups were asleep on the back porch, and she closed the door to the porch to prevent the two of them from getting into things while she and Damon were occupied.

Sam closed the bedroom door. Damon picked her up and carried her to bed. Piece by piece, they removed each other's clothing, exploring every inch of each other.

"One last chance to say no, Samantha."

Sam did not respond to his words. His lips felt warm and inviting, and they parted, allowing her tongue to slide inside his mouth. She couldn't concentrate on what he was saying. He tasted like wine. Deep, sweet, and dark. She heard her name again.

"You taste like heaven, Damon, and I told myself this is what I want right now. If you've changed your mind, now is your chance to stop."

"Let me show you what's on my mind."

Later, Damon tried to slip out of the bed, but Samantha grabbed his hand.

"Trying to sneak out?"

"No, darlin. I was going to finish dinner, unless you're ready for more of what is on my mind."

"After today, I'm certain I'll always be ready for more of what is on your mind, but I need food since I did not eat today. If you want me to keep up with you, then we need food."

"Good choice, because I need food, too."

Samantha set the table on the back porch while Damon worked his magic, as he called it, on the steaks. It was nice to have someone who liked to cook. When she was by herself, she fixed simple, whole foods. The pups were outside side chasing one another around the yard to keep them out of the kitchen while Damon was cooking.

Walking back into the kitchen to get the bottle of wine and the glasses she'd poured earlier, she smiled at Damon. She liked him in her house.

"Listen, darlin. You smile at me like that again, and we aren't eating until breakfast."

Sam chuckled. "You might be worth missing a meal, or two, Parker."

"Did you enjoy everything that was on my mind, Samantha?"

"If I didn't, would I have come back for seconds? Or was it thirds or fourths? I lost count."

"Dinner is ready, and we need to eat before we get busy doing other things. My plan is to keep us busy the entire night, but only after we have food. After we finish eating, if you are not opposed to keeping ourselves occupied throughout the night, I need to run back to my place for a change of clothes and my shaving kit. That will give our food time to digest."

"That sounds wonderful."

"Does this mean we are officially dating Samantha?"

"Why do we need to pigeonhole this into a term someone produced eons ago, Parker? Can't we enjoy one another without a name? If this thing last beyond the next few weeks, there is no need to worry that I'll be looking elsewhere for anything."

"Is that a promise, Samantha?"

"Lordy, Parker. I never took you for someone who needed reassurance in relationships. But yes, that is a promise."

"Good. I'm not looking for reassurance, Samantha. I enjoy hearing your sassy comments. Goading you makes you sassy, and I enjoy it."

"Parker, I need to know if you are bossy as well, because I've heard that Alex Montgomery will get bossy, and I want to prepare myself if that is just a learned behavior from working in the ER."

"We do get bossy at times, Samantha. Indecisiveness costs lives. Someone needs to oversee the ER. Unfortunately, that behavior can sneak into our daily lives if we aren't careful. We work to control it when out of the ER, but you are welcome to tell me if you see that happening with us."

'I understand that behavior, Damon, because I also spend my days telling people what to do. Guidance is what I call it when it relates to the patients. I get bossy too and expect you to call me out on that behavior as well. Now, get your belongings. Get several days' worth of belongings, Parker. Sometimes I prefer to try things out for a while to make sure I'm getting what I expected. I'll leave the front door unlocked."

"I guarantee you'll get what you are expecting."

Samantha cleaned the kitchen and took a shower before Damon returned. The dogs were asleep for the night. She turned the porch light on, and a lamp in the hallway. Her lingerie needed a serious update. Nothing like a new relationship to see everyday things in a different light. She settled on a tank top and a pair of shorts. This will do until she can find time to shop.

Damon pulled into the driveway and noticed Samantha walking back and forth in the kitchen wearing a tank top and a pair of shorts. He would bet his last nickel she was not aware of how gorgeous she appears to everyone around her, nor does she have one iota of how desirable she was to him.

What made her so different from everyone else he dated? He noticed her, but she never appeared to notice him, so he did not ask her out. Aware that his reputation was everything she said it was, he was honest with her when he told her nobody else was able to hold his interest for more than one date. Maybe two, but that was it.

Alex had said their group of friends were gorgeous and intelligent. When he met them at the wedding, he realized Alex had not exaggerated. Each of them was different, but stunning.

Samantha's coloring was darker, more toward the Italian look, but that was just a guess. Her eyes were the color of aquamarine gems. He had no idea of her heritage. Samantha's hair was shiny and silky but had no natural curls.

Abbie was blonde, and blue eyed, and looked like she was born to live at the beach. She had a head of curls and he had overheard her mumble about trying to keep them in place.

Dana's skin was a smooth chocolate color, with brown eyes and deep brown hair. She had curls like Abbie's. He did not know her well. She worked with Alex at the hospital in Charleston, before taking the open position in the ER here at Coastal.

Julie's hair was strawberry blonde, straight, and hung to her waist. Her green eyes went perfect with her hair. He met her a couple of times when she was visiting Abbie and Alex. She was a pediatrician and looked like she had the patience of a saint.

Kate was the petite one in the group, and he suspected she had long, brown hair, but it was usually piled on top of her head with a pencil sticking out and she wore dark-framed glasses that framed her hazel eyes. Stunning, intelligent, and devoted to one another to a fault.

Damon turned the truck off and walked in the front door. That smile of hers was his undoing. He locked the door. Samantha watched him come in and stopped at the entrance to the kitchen.

"I watched you from the driveway. Do you have any idea how beautiful you are, Samantha?"

"Do I need to call the police about a peeping Tom?"

"I'm being serious. Alex said your group of friends was the most stunning group of women he had ever encountered. I thought he was exaggerating. But when the five of you were together at the wedding, I decided he did not have the words to describe the five of you."

Damon took a step forward, and Sam met him in the middle of the hallway.

"I've heard people say I'm pretty, but I don't stand in front of the mirror, Parker. That's just foolish. Looks fade with time."

"You do not need a mirror, Samantha. Just stand in front of me and you will see your beauty in my eyes."

She rolled her eyes at him, but he scooped her up, walked into the bedroom, and kept the promise made to her earlier in the evening.

The pups were the only two in the house that would sleep tonight.

Damon and Samantha slept for an hour before the alarm jolted the two of them awake. After they showered, and got dressed, Damon walked straight to the kitchen to make coffee with his special brew and grinder. Samantha walked into the kitchen and watched the coffee making process.

"If you make that coffee every morning, I will grant you part of the garage."

"Seriously? You'll give space in the garage just for making coffee, Samantha?"

"If your bike or truck are parked in the driveway, the entire hospital staff will know we are sleeping together, so hide the vehicle, otherwise the rumor mill will be cranking."

"Samantha, I don't care who knows we're sleeping together. I'll park the truck at the end of the driveway with a sign in the front window and let them talk. Does it bother you if I don't put it away? If so, I'll be sure to put them both in the garage."

"I don't care either, Damon. I was offering you a choice, and you can still have one stall in the garage."

Damon's phone rang and he looked at the screen, He accepted the call, and turned on the speaker option.

"Good morning, Mother. How are you doing this morning?"

"Good morning, Damon. I'm well and so is Father. It has been a while since we spoke. Just checking to see how you are doing. Are you at the hospital this early?"

"No, Mother, I'm at Samantha's house."

"Oh. Who is Samantha? I don't believe we've met her."

"Samantha is my girlfriend, Mother. Would you care to say hello?"

"Good morning Mrs. Parker. This is Samantha. Thanks for calling this morning. Damon and I were enjoying a cup of the special brew coffee he makes before we go to work."

"Hello, Samantha. Do you work at the hospital with Damon?"

"I'm a physical therapist. The building I work in is on hospital property but run by a separate organization."

"Samantha has a doctorate degree in physical therapy, Mother, and recently developed an amazing hydrotherapy program. She and the co-founder are doing incredible work. The program is for children and adults alike. The neurosurgeons and orthopedic surgeons love the program and send referrals daily."

"That sounds like a subject your father might be interested in learning. Do you have time in your schedule for us to visit?"

"My schedule is full right now. Dr. Montgomery and his wife just had triplets, and I'm covering three extra shifts this week. We'll find time for you and Father to visit soon."

"That sounds lovely, Damon, and perhaps we can meet Samantha during that visit."

"I'm looking forward to meeting the two of you, Mrs. Parker. I'll remind Damon to check the schedule and call with dates."

"Samantha and I will be in touch soon, Mother, but we need to run, or be late for work. Love you."

"Love you, too, Damon."

Damon hung up and smiled at Samantha.

"Does that phone call count as meeting your mother, Damon?"

"Not in this lifetime, Samantha. I didn't give her the time to scrutinize your education, family crest, and DNA. Those are important things in the life of Abagail Parker."

"And what is your father's name?"

"Dr. John Parker, cardiothoracic surgery, retired."

"Does he eat meat? Because if not, he and Abbie will be best friends."

"Everything in moderation, or he wouldn't have any patients. But tell me, where was sassy Samantha during that phone call?"

"Hiding from Mrs. Parker. She's had more practice at being inquisitive. I need to brush up on that skill set before meeting her face, to face for the first time."

"Don't let her nosy behavior intimidate you. The nurses aren't the only ones I can get my way with Samantha. You're looking at an only child. Piece of cake."

"Noted. May I have another cup of that delicious coffee before it's time to go to work and pretend there was nobody in this house spending the night together?"

"Samantha. I don't care who knows. But if bothers you, please tell me. I will never embarrass you at the expense of others."

"I am not embarrassed that people know I am with you, Damon. I wanted to make sure we agree."

"We're good. Let's go for a bike ride this weekend. The weather is going to be good, and we won't go far. I want to spend time with you on the open road to blow off the stress of work."

"That sounds perfect. Will I see you after work today?"

"I heard you say you need to try out the merchandise for several days to make sure you got what you wanted. Are you denying me the opportunity to prove myself?"

"Absolutely not."

"Alright. I'll see you later today."

"I'm taking Koko and Kody to the therapy building today. I don't have too much on the schedule and there are new moves for them to learn. The three of us are going to walk this morning. Are you driving, or do you want to put the truck in the garage?"

"I'll walk with you. I want to get one more peek at those cute babies that belong to Abbie and Alex before they go home today. With the extra shifts this week, I might not be able to go if you want to visit."

"Will you have time to meet Conor's brother? Alex was planning a to get everyone together this week before Kate and Julie leave."

"I'll check and see what he's planning. There is a chance he might be at the hospital. If he dropped Andy off at school, he's most likely upstairs with Abbie. The parking lot is empty right now. I'll check in, then run up to the nursery."

"Okay. I need to go. I'll look for you later today. Go save lives, Parker."

Damon pulled Samantha into his arms and kissed her slowly. The slow kiss was caught by a group of nurses exiting the building.

"Well, get a look at that." The nurse said. "He never kissed me that way. Now I understand why nobody has seen him. Who's the lady with him?"

"That's Samantha from the therapy company." Said a nurse. "She and Dr. Montgomery's wife are best friends and put together the new hydrotherapy program. The two of them are also best friends with Dana, the director of nursing in the ER. The story is that there are a total of five friends in the group. All of them are super intelligent and gorgeous as well. In my opinion, the single ladies might as well give up. After that kiss, I'd say he's off the market for good."

Damon walked down the sidewalk toward the emergency room and approached the group. "Good morning, ladies. Susan."

"Good morning, Dr. Parker." The group replied.

"That was quite a kiss." Susan said.

"Samantha deserves the best of everything. Have a good day, ladies."

CHAPTER 2

Alex and Abbie arrived home with the babies, and Kate and Julie were there to welcome everyone home. Julie and Kate were staying at Dana's house this visit, three doors from Abbie's house, to be close by if Abbie needed help. They usually stayed with Samantha, but Dana was closer, and since they volunteered to stock the freezer with meals, being close by made sense.

Andy was at school today and was excited to get home and play with his sisters. He bragged to everyone this week, showing off pictures, and talking about the fun things he was planning to do together.

Damon Parker, and the other doctors offered to cover shifts for Alex this week so he and Abbie could get a routine established with the babies and the nanny, Ms. Helen. Unbeknownst to anyone, Damon was staying with Samantha this week, and because her house was across from the hospital, it was a quick walk to work.

Ms. Helen, the live-in nanny was available for as long as Abbie and Alex needed help. Her room adjoined the nursery. Abbie and Alex planned to be involved in every facet of care for the babies, but Alex needed rest so that he could react well during his shifts in the emergency room. Abbie agreed to hiring help but wanted to do as much on her own as possible. Once everyone developed a routine and the doctor okayed her to work again, Abbie and Samantha needed to discuss an expansion of the hydrotherapy program.

"You look good with a baby in your arms, Julie."

"That's why I chose pediatrics, Abbie. I love children, no matter what age, but I prefer caring for teenagers. Even though they can be contrary, they are generally well behaved and better interacting with me than with their parents. Keep that in mind when your four are teenagers."

"That sounds far away, but yet so close."

"Ms. Abbie. Don't fret. There's time to enjoy every minute." Said Ms. Helen. "Mr. Alex will doubtless spend time keeping the boys away from your girls and trying to keep the girls away from that handsome son. The two of you are great at making pretty babies."

"Maybe we should video them screaming, and crying, and puking all over us. That should keep the boys away."

"I doubt that would work, Ms. Abbie."

"I doubt it will either, Abbie. Have you looked in the mirror recently? How do you pop out three babies and look as though you've had twelve hours of sleep?"

"I owe it to this crazy hair, Kate. Even on the days I try to keep it under control, it still does its own thing, so when I do nothing with it, nobody can tell any different."

"Kate, you should wear your hair down, too." Said Julie. "And take that pencil out of your hair or one day these babies will stab you in the eye."

"I wear my hair down Julie, but you don't see it every day. And the pencil is a habit that I need to break, but the pencil comes in handy when I need to write down the calculations my brain is throwing at me."

"Speaking of looks, how do you think Samantha's dinner with Damon went last night?" Abbie asked. "Why is she trying to resist dating him? Other than my husband, Damon is one of the hottest looking guys in town. They make a good-looking couple, and I've told her she is wasting time she could be spending getting to know him better."

Julie laughed. "That Conor O'Brien is no lightweight when it comes to the looks department either. I get the feeling he is interested in Dana. I wonder if his brother is good looking, too. Good looks often run in families."

"Are you looking for a date if he is?" Kate asked. "You haven't admitted to any relationships recently. Abbie is out of the running, so it's up to the four of us to keep the excitement going."

"Look, Kate. Just because I am off the market does not mean there will not be hot stuff going on in this house. I just need to recover, then look out, Montgomery."

Alex came into the living room. "I overheard that declaration, Abbie, and I intend to hold you to that challenge. And if I remember correctly, you made a promise at the hospital, too. I still think you're incorrigible, and are the leader of the pack, but I love you, and I am looking forward to your recovery."

"Challenge accepted, Montgomery. I hope you're ready for more babies."

"I'll have Dr. Jeffers write a prescription for birth control, at least for a while. We can't have more babies until we have a place big enough to house everyone."

"Are you saying you want more babies, Alex?"

"I'm not saying no, but I need to recover from this recent batch we made and need time to collect enough sticks to keep the boys away from our daughters."

"Let's choose their names tonight, Alex. This can't go on much longer."

"I'm in agreement, Abbie. I need time to learn their names before chasing off the boys."

Abbie laughed, then stood and moved the baby she was holding to her shoulder. She whispered in Alex's ear again, and kissed him, then turned to walk back to her chair, but Alex put his arm around her waist and pulled her back to face him. He whispered in her ear, and she turned shades of red this time.

Kate chuckled. "We need to search for a couple of houses here, Julie. There are going to be enough babies living with these two to keep you in business until you retire."

"I like being here with everyone. I think I will research the pediatric practices here and see if anyone is looking at hiring another doctor. Can you leave your town and company, Kate?"

"I spend the day working on a computer. If I need to go into the lab, I could jump in the car and drive to the office. The company has apartments for staff right across the street from the lab, so moving should not be an issue. I'll check when I get back to the office."

"If you want help to find a practice, Julie, I can put the word out in the hospital. The pediatricians are in the ER frequently. One group has an office in the complex next to the hospital. This town is growing, the area needs more practitioners. This town was a good move for me and Andy."

"I think I'll take you up on that offer, Alex. Text me if you find a practice."

"Abbie, do you think you are feeling well enough to have our small group of friends over on Friday? I'm not asking you to do anything. I'll get all the food and drinks catered, and there will be enough people to take care of the girls. Ms. Helen can take the evening to do something she enjoys."

"Oh, Mr. Alex. I will not need an evening to myself. I can help around here. Your daughters are a joy to care for and easy to care for as well."

"Let's decide that later in the week, Ms. Helen. Damon is off on Saturday, and I am going to cover that shift, Abbie, if there is nothing planned. He and Samantha are going for a bike ride on Saturday, and he deserves the time to blow off the stress of the extra shifts he's covering for me. Julie and Kate will be leaving on Sunday. Friday seems like it would work best for everyone. I'll call Conor and ask if they are available, and we'll have time to meet his brother before Julie and Kate leave."

"Sounds good to me, Alex. I'm feeling great. It will be nice to have everyone together without worrying how loud the noise level is getting in the hospital. The children will be growing up with our friends, so we need to start them out young, and I agree Ms. Helen can have the evening to do something fun."

"Ms. Abbie. I'd love to stay here and meet your friends. They are like your family, and I will be seeing them often."

"The decision to up to you, Ms. Helen. You're welcome to stay."

The week flew by, and Alex arranged everything for Friday evening. Andy was excited that everyone would be spending time with his sisters. He wanted to show them off to everyone. Samantha and Damon arrived together, and Abbie raised her eyebrows at Sam.

"Don't start, Abbie. Remember, you are not my mother, and I met Damon's via phone this morning. When they come to town to visit their son, I need to try and control my sassy comments."

"I'm not saying a word. I'm happy you two are a couple. You complement each other. Alex said you two are going for a ride tomorrow. Any place special?"

"We're not going too far. We just want an open rode to ride and relax and find somewhere unique to grab lunch."

"Can you bring the dogs back here before you leave? Andy is missing Koko and Kody."

"Yes. I was going to ask you to take them tomorrow. I'm not sure how long we'll be gone, and I don't want them cooped up in the house the entire day."

"Drop the two of them off any time. You have the code for the door and the elevator."

The party was underway, and Andy and the girls were the center of attention. Ms. Helen stayed and thanked Abbie and Alex for allowing her to be included. The babies were spending time with everyone. Connor, and his brother Tobin, entered from the covered deck.

Alex and Abbie greeted them and introduced Tobin to the other guests.

"Julie, you need to get busy on that one. He's as hot as Alex and Damon. Are they twins?"

"Sam, we'll leave that up to you. Dana, when you were with Conor, did he say anything to you about having a twin?"

"There was no discussion of a twin, but they look the same. Every movement and gesture are the same. And for your information, Conor and I are not dating. You know as much about him as I do."

"Well, you need to do something to correct that, and soon. I'm going to ask, then I'll steer him your way, Julie."

Samantha walked over to Tobin.

"Welcome to the states, Tobin. How long are you in town?"

"It's Samantha, right?" Sam nodded. "I'm here for two weeks. There is so much I want to see, but I want to search for a practice here to join."

"Let me introduce you to Julie, the one in the blue sundress with the strawberry blonde hair. She's decided to look for a medical group here as well. Julie is a pediatrician. But if Abbie and Alex keep popping out babies in threes, she may need to hire on as a private doctor. You and Conor look very much alike. Identical twins?"

"Yes, we are, and he likes to remind me that he is twenty seconds older. I say he was in too much of a hurry to get out of the womb, so I stayed behind to pick up the brains he left when he was in such a rush to get out."

"That's funny, Tobin. The two of you are going to fit right into this group. We tease each other but will go to the ends of the earth to protect you. Let me introduce you to Julie, and you two can map out a plan to find a practice you can join."

Tobin invited Julie to the bar and poured two glasses of wine. They sat at a table on the deck and were still outdoors talking when Alex announced the food was ready. After filling plates, they returned to the deck. They talked nonstop, and the others picked up laughing through the evening.

Alex told everyone they had a surprise and asked them to come inside the house.

"We have decided on names for the babies." Everyone clapped.

"It's time you name your little ladies, Montgomery." Said Damon. "They need pretty names to match their pretty, little faces."

Kohl huffed to show his agreement with Damon, then walked over to stand by Andy.

Alex, Abbie, and Andy each held a baby.

Ms. Helen stood near Alex.

"With great pleasure, I am honored to announce the names for the newest members of this family." Said Ms. Helen.

"Will the person holding Isabella, please step forward?" Abbie stepped forward.

"Will the person holding Gabriella please step forward?" Alex stepped forward.

"That leaves Andy. Will the person holding Annabella please step forward?"

Everyone in the room cheered and congratulated the family. Dana and Samantha both took one of the babies to hold while Alex and Abbie said goodbye to their guest.

Damon shook Alex's hand. "Thanks again for covering a shift tomorrow. I'll drop Koko and Kody off in the morning. Excellent choice with the names too."

"Thanks, Parker. Enjoy the day on the bike."

CHAPTER 3

Damon slipped out of bed early and let Samantha sleep, made coffee, then walked out to the garage to check the bike before the ride this morning. After checking the tires and wheels, he checked the lights and controls, oil and other fluids, the chassis, and the stands. Next, he topped off the gas tank with the extra gas from a five-gallon container, then cleaned the seats and their helmets and adjusted the mirrors.

Returning to the kitchen, he brewed more coffee, filled a thermos, got two cups from the cupboard, and placed everything in the saddlebag. It was a surprise for Samantha for a midmorning coffee break.

Samantha was ready to go. Damon held out a mug of coffee and smiled.

"Dr. Parker, you are spoiling me for regular coffee. What am I to do when you go home and sleep in your own bed?"

"I have the perfect solution to the problem."

"Are you going to share that solution, or is this a guessing game?"

"Always make sure you are in the same bed as me, and you'll never need to worry about your first cup of coffee in the morning."

"Are we at that point, Damon? I want this to last. Moving too quickly makes me nervous."

"I want this to last too, Samantha. Let's take it one day at a time if that is easier for you. But I'm not planning to go anywhere."

"Good. I'm not planning to go anywhere either."

"Are you ready to ride?"

"Yes. Let get this day started."

Damon turned to the right onto Sea Mountain Highway, crossed the swing bridge, and took route seventeen south toward Charleston. There were interesting places to stop on the way south, and unique local restaurants as well.

The first stop was at Brookgreen Gardens. They strolled the grounds, enjoyed the botanical gardens and sculptures, and made new friends at the low country zoo. When they returned to the bike, Damon opened the saddlebag and handed Samantha a cup.

"What's this cup for, Damon?"

"Time for a coffee break. Let's sit on the bench under that tree and enjoy the coffee before we hit the road again. No snacks. We can stop for brunch soon. There is this restaurant that has cat head biscuits. If you leave hungry, that's your fault."

"What is a cat head biscuit?"

"Biscuits that are the size of a cat's head. They are a meal by themselves, but we can share if you think they are too big. The first time I ordered two. I couldn't eat two biscuits. The biscuits are served with fresh blueberry jam, and they are divine."

"Yum. That sounds delicious. Let's hit the road. The thought of them is making me hungry."

The line at the restaurant was out the door, so the hostess took Damon's name and handed them a pager. Next to the restaurant was a small handmade jewelry store. Damon and

Samantha perused the store. Samantha found a leather bracelet with three beads that she could tie on her wrist. The bracelet was able to withstand the water and chlorine. Samantha reached for her wallet, but Damon told her to put her money away.

"Is there a matching bracelet that fits my wrist?" Damon asked the salesperson.

"Yes. This one has strings that are a little longer. Let's see if it goes all the way around."

"That works. We will take both, please."

Damon tied Samantha's bracelet to her right wrist. "Think of me every time you look at the bracelet, and I'll do the same with mine. Can you tie it for me please? Promise to keep it on as long as we are together."

"I promise, Damon. And will you do the same?"

"I will, and I will not let anyone take this from me, Samantha."

The pager buzzed, and they were seated at a table near the window. They ordered eggs and biscuits. Samantha started laughing when they brought her order.

"I've never seen biscuits so big, Damon. I thought you were exaggerating. This is delicious. I may skip the eggs and just devour this biscuit. Between the butter and the jam, we may need a tow truck to get me back home."

"Let walk around town when we're done and walk off the excess calories from the biscuits. Charleston is a beautiful place to explore."

An hour went by, and they headed back to North Myrtle Beach. The ride back was slower due to traffic, but they enjoyed the slow pace of the ride. Damon took Ocean Blvd. once they got to North Myrtle, and they stopped to watch the waves. The beach was busy with tourists, and they took a walk toward the pier. The sun was scorching, and Damon shook his head at the number of people who were burnt from too much sun and too little sunscreen.

Getting back on the bike, Damon took Sea Mountain Highway back toward the swing bridge. The light at the swing bridge was green and as Damon entered the intersection, he noticed a truck barreling toward them. Unable to get out of the truck's path, Damon shoved Samantha from the bike, and the truck broadsided him.

It took Samantha a moment to realize what was happening when she realized the truck was going to strike Damon. Someone was screaming. She looked for Damon but didn't see him. Someone helped her up from the pavement. Where was Damon?

"Where's the bike? Where's Damon?" she asked the guy who helped her up off the road. "Where is he?" she screamed.

"He got hit by the truck. Are you okay? The police and ambulance are on the way. My name is Steve. I'm the bartender at the restaurant on the corner. Is there someone I can call for you?"

"Help me find Damon. He's an emergency department doctor. He can tell us what to do."

Samantha walked toward the truck and noticed Damon's leg sticking out from underneath the truck.

"Oh, no. No, no, no. Damon!"

Samantha threw herself on the ground and crawled toward the truck.

"Damon. Damon. I'm right here."

She grabbed his hand, and took out her phone with her other hand, and found Alex's cell number.

"Damon, wake up. Can you hear me?"

Alex answered his phone.

"Hey Sam. How's your ride going?"

"Alex," Samantha sobbed. "There's been an accident. Damon's unconscious and under a truck. I can't get him to wake up, Alex. Help me!"

"Sam, take a deep breath and listen to me. Is he breathing? And check for a pulse?"

"Let me check. He's breathing, but his pulse is weak."

"Do you notice any injuries?"

"Alex, I don't think I want to look."

"Sam, I need you to look at him. Is he bleeding?"

"Oh no, Alex. His left lower leg is bleeding. There's blood everywhere. His jeans are torn, and I see the bone showing. There's blood on his shirt as well."

"Okay, Sam. Excellent job. Is Damon wearing a belt?"

"Yes, Alex. Why?"

"I need you to remove his belt and place it around his thigh, above his knee. I need you to use it as a tourniquet. Try not to move him too much."

"I need help, Alex. Maybe Steve is still here."

"Who's Steve?"

"The bartender from the restaurant. He helped me up off the road."

"Yell for him, Sam. Get him to help you."

Samantha stood up and yelled for Steve, and he came running across the street in her direction.

"Steve. I need help to get his belt off so we can use it to make a tourniquet and put it on his leg."

"I can help you. What's your name?"

"Samantha. Or call me Sam. I'm on the phone with a doctor in the emergency department. We need to get his belt off now, Steve. Dr. Montgomery said not to move him too much."

"We can do this, Sam. Look at me. We can do this together."

"Okay."

Samantha wiped her face with her sleeve. She was having trouble seeing past the tears and the sweat on her face. Steve unbuckled Damon's belt and pulled it out from beneath his back. Damon moaned in pain.

"Damon, open your eyes and look at me."

Damon barely opened his eyes.

"Samantha, are you alright?"

"I'm good Damon. Alex is on the phone. We need your belt to make a tourniquet. You have an injury to your lower leg and you're bleeding. The ambulance should be here soon. Alex will have everyone you need waiting for you in the emergency room."

"Put Alex on speaker, Samantha." She did as he requested.

"Alex don't let them take my leg. Do you and Samantha understand what I'm telling you?"

"We understand, Damon, but I can't make that promise. You'll be here soon, and then we'll know what is going on with your leg. We'll do everything we can."

Damon nodded.

"Samantha, can you hold my hand? If I can feel your hand, everything will be okay. Promise me you won't let go of my hand."

Damon's eyes fluttered shut, and Samantha started sobbing again.

"I'll hold your hand, Damon."

"Sam, the ambulance is here. We need to get out from under the truck so they can help Damon."

"No. He told me to hold his hand, and that's what I'm doing."

"Sam, Sam!" Alex was trying to get her attention. "Sam, you need to let the ambulance and fire department do their job. The sooner they can get to him, the sooner they can get the two of you to me. Are you injured, Sam?"

"I don't know if I'm injured, Alex."

"Okay. Where are you, Sam? Where did the accident happen?"

"Just on the other side of the swing bride."

"Okay, Sam. I will be waiting. The ambulance will have Damon here soon."

The police officer demanded her to get out from under the truck.

"I can't. I made Damon a promise."

Steve was pleading with Sam to get out and let the medics and firemen get to work. He told her she was impeding the care Damon needed. She crawled out from the truck once the police officer threatened to arrest her.

Steve stood beside Sam and walked with her to the sidewalk.

"Hold onto my hand, Sam. Can I give you a ride to the hospital?"

"Thanks for the help, Steve. I could not have done this without your help. I'll ride in the ambulance with Damon."

The police officer talked with Samantha while they worked on getting Damon out from under the truck. The truck driver tried to run away, but bystanders stopped him, and the police had him in handcuffs, sitting in the back of the cruiser.

The fire department used airbags to lift the truck enough to get Damon out from under the truck. They were moving toward the ambulance doors, and Samantha turned and gave Steve a hug.

"I've got to go. I'll find you once they take care of Damon."

Alex hung up the phone and searched for Dana.

"Has anyone seen Dana?"

"I think she is in her office."

Alex knocked on the door.

"The door is open."

Alex took a deep breath. "Dana, there was an accident on the far side of the swing bridge. Two victims. They should be here soon. I want only your best nurses and you in the room."

"Okay, Alex. What happened?"

"Truck vs a motorcycle. Male patient trapped under the truck with a severe leg injury. The female does not appear to be injured. If so, it sounds minor. We need to get blood up here and I want the x-ray department here as soon as they bring him through the door. I'm going to call the orthopedic surgeon and make him aware they are on the way. Call the operating room and get a surgical suite for ortho on hold as well."

"What else, Alex?"

"The victims are Damon and Samantha."..

Dana stood, then sat down in her chair.

"Dana, I need you to hold it together until we get Damon treated. It hasn't been long since we did this with Tom. Speaking of which, don't call any of the others. They are at my place, and I will go home and tell them in person when I have the details and have Damon off to surgery. Abbie has done well so far, but I want her to hear everything from me."

"I understand Alex. Let me get things moving. I need to make the staff aware that Dr. Parker is coming in via ambulance."

"Sam told me she is fine, but she may be in shock. Damon was conscious for just a minute or two. He tried to get me and Sam to promise not to let anyone amputate his leg. I told him I could not make that promise. He asked Sam to hold onto his hand, and she was on the speaker phone when the police and fire department arrived. She refused to get out from under the truck, and the police officer threatened to arrest her. She's going to give us a tough time, I'm sure. There was a guy named Steve that helped her up off the street, and he helped her under the truck to get Damon's belt off to use as a tourniquet. If he shows up, put him in the private waiting room. Get her examined while I am checking Damon, then find someone to stay with her. Better yet, have someone call the restaurant at the intersection of Sea Mountain and Little River Neck Road and get Steve up here. He was able to reason with her at the accident scene. Maybe he can be the voice of reason here as well."

CHAPTER 4

Samantha jumped out of the ambulance as soon as the forward motion stopped and stood near the door as they unloaded the gurney. Alex came through the ambulance doors and went directly to Sam.

"How are you, Sam? What hurts?"

"Go get Damon, Alex. I'm okay."

"You need to get checked. Where's the helmet you were wearing? Do you remember if you struck your head? How fast was the truck going when it struck the bike?"

"I don't know where the helmet is, Alex. When I noticed Damon under the truck, I must have thrown it. I wasn't on the bike when Damon got hit. I think he must have seen the truck coming because he shoved me off the bike before he got hit."

"Okay, Sam. One of the physician assistants will do an exam, but I want x-rays done. No argument."

Samantha nodded, and the tears started again.

"Come here, Sam." Alex wrapped her in a hug. "We are not having another outcome like Abbie and Tom. Do you understand me?"

Samantha nodded but couldn't speak.

"Okay, Damon's out of the ambulance. Find me when you are done."

"Can you find his phone? I need to call his parents. He keeps it in his back pocket."

"I'll find it. Now go, so I can update you before he goes into surgery."

Sam waited until the gurney was next to her and grabbed Damon's hand and ran beside the gurney.

"I'm right here, Damon. I'm not going anywhere. I'll call your parents. Alex will take care of you." She leaned over and kissed his cheek. "I'll see you soon."

Dana waited for Samantha to enter the building. She hugged Samantha, and they held on to one another.

"We are not having another Tom and Abbie episode. Do you understand me, Sam?"

Samantha nodded. "Alex told me the same thing."

"Let's get you into an exam room so you can get back to Damon. Alex gave me orders before you got here, so everything is already on the computer, and they are waiting for you. Alex asked me not to call Abbie, Kate, and Julie. He is afraid of how Abbie might react if we call her, so he is going to the house to tell her, then he will bring them back here to be with you."

Sam nodded. She was shaking and her teeth were chattering. She had a bluish tint on her lips, and she swayed before sitting on the gurney to change into an exam gown.

Dana recognized signs of shock from the traumatic event, gave Sam supplemental oxygen, got her vital signs, and called out to the nurse practitioner, and they proceeded with her exam. The x-ray department was ready for her, so Dana asked the nursing assistant to stay with Sam during her scans.

"I'm going to check on Damon, Sam. I'll fill you in when you are done. It won't take long."

"Can you find his phone, Dana? I'll need to call his parents. His facial recognition is setup, so just hold the phone up to his face to open it."

"I'll find it Sam. Let's wait to call them until Alex is free and can speak with them about his injuries."

"I will. His father is a cardiothoracic surgeon, retired, but he will have questions, and his mother sounds as though she can be intimidating. It might be best if Alex did the talking."

"Got it, Sam. I'll let Alex know Damon's father is a physician."

Alex began a head-to-toe assessment as soon as Damon was wheeled into the room.

Damon's helmet was on and had a crack on the left side of the helmet. He removed the helmet and checked his head. There were no open wounds. The x-ray technician was standing by for orders.

"We need a skull x-ray and then a head CT. It looks as though the damage is on his left side. Add ribs, hips, femur, and lower leg films to that list."

Dana walked into the room.

"Did orthopedics call back?"

"Not that I'm aware of, Dr. Montgomery. I'll try again. Samantha is in x-ray. She was showing signs of shock, but we got warm blankets and oxygen on her, and I started an IV."

"Good call, Dana. Thanks."

Dana picked up the phone in the trauma room and made her phone call.

"Dr. Montgomery, the orthopedic surgeon is busy in the OR with a surgery that is not going as expected. His other two partners are out with COVID. Who do you want me to call next?"

"Get Conor O'Brien on the phone and ask if his brother is available. Better yet, get him on the phone and put him on speaker phone. We'll have the x-ray results back in a couple of minutes, and I'll have better information."

"Hi Dr. O'Brien. Dana in the ER. I'm good. Dr. Montgomery needs to speak with you. I'm putting you on speaker. We are in trauma room two with a patient and other staff member. Go ahead, Dr. Montgomery."

"Hey Conor. Sorry to bother you. Is your brother available? Dr. Damon Parker and his girlfriend Samantha were involved in a motorcycle accident this afternoon. He arrived here minutes ago. There is a significant injury to his left leg, and my orthopedic surgeon is engaged in a difficult case in the OR. I was hoping Tobin might look at is his injury."

"He's right here, Alex. I'm handing over the phone."

"Tobin O'Brien here. What's happening, Alex?"

"I need an orthopedic surgeon, ASAP. If I get clearance through the board and the ethics committee, are you willing to fix Damon Parker's leg? I think I can get emergency authorization. I know that's a big ask, but I'll make up for it."

"We are in the parking lot. I just picked up Conor from his shift. We'll be there as soon as I turn the car around and park. What room?"

"Trauma room two. There are x-rays for you to look at, and CT is ready for him once he is stable enough to move."

"Great. Be there in a second."

"Dana, call the hospital CEO and tell him the OR situation and that we are treating Dr. Parker, and I will talk to him."

Tobin and Conor entered the room. Tobin looked at the films.

"I need the CT scan done, Alex, and I'm glad you have blood hanging. Let's get antibiotics on board as well. There's road grime on that wound. Did you get consent from his family?"

"Not yet. As soon as we get clearance for you, I need to call his family. His father is a cardiothoracic surgeon. He will understand everything you tell him. Samantha is in x-ray and CT now. She is in decent shape. Apparently, Damon noticed the truck coming at them and shoved Sam off the bike. She's going to be sore, but it does not appear as though she has any major injuries. She crawled under the truck and found help to get a tourniquet on Damon's leg."

"Dana, did anyone find Steve from the accident scene? Samantha should be here soon, and I do not want her by herself."

"I can stay with her, Alex. If Tobin is going to do surgery, I will spend time with all of you for a while."

"I'll check with security to see if he's arrived, Alex."

Dana walked to the private waiting room and found Steve. He was sipping a coffee and watching the news.

"Hi Steve, I'm Dana, the director of nursing for the emergency department. I'm best friends with Samantha. Thank you for helping her and Damon this afternoon at the accident scene. Dr. Montgomery asked if you could stay with Samantha for an hour. We are busy taking care of Dr. Parker, and we thought you might keep her company for a short while."

"I'm happy to do that for her. How is she?"

"She is getting x-rays done and should be here soon. Do you need something else to drink? Do you want something to eat?"

"Thank you for offering, but I'm okay. I'll wait for Samantha if you need me to stay."

"Dr. Conor O'Brien may be along to sit with her for a while. We are bringing her best friends in too, but it might be an hour until Dr. Montgomery is able to pick them up and bring them to the hospital. Will you need a ride back to your restaurant?"

"No, thank you. I'll call my roommate."

"Great. This is a private waiting room, so the only people who will be in this room have a connection with Samantha and Dr. Parker. Any of them can get you whatever you need, but I will be back to check on you as well."

Dana walked back to trauma room two and Alex was inserting a chest tube on Damon's left side to help re-inflate his collapsed lung which appeared to have occurred from a broken rib. His breathing was easier now, but he was still unconscious. The nursing assistant came into the room to tell Dana that Sam was back from her test and getting dressed.

"I'm going to talk to Sam. Did you find Dr. Parker's phone?"

"Yes, it was in his pocket."

"He uses facial recognition, so before he goes off to CT, I will get his phone opened."

"Radiology is waiting for Damon, Dana. I'm going to wait in the CT suite so that I can l check the films as soon as possible. I'm hoping to get permission from the Board and the Ethics Committee soon, then I'll call Damon's parents."

"Do you think they are going to okay your request?"

"I hope so. He's the only chance we've got right now."

"I'm going to put Sam in the family waiting room and get the phone number for you. We'll be waiting for you when you're done. Will you let her see him before he goes to surgery?"

"Yes. Otherwise, I'll be in trouble with Abbie and the rest of your group. Once I talk to Sam, I'll go to the house and get them. The nanny will manage the girls, and Andy is a tremendous help, too."

Alex met Dana and Sam in the hallway as they were pushing Damon to the CT suite. Alex noticed the tears start again and took her hand.

"Sam. Damon hasn't regained consciousness, so the first thing we are looking for is a head injury. We are getting CTs of his head, chest, hip, femur, and his leg. The orthopedic surgeon is in the OR with a difficult case and his partners are out with COVID, so I've asked the board to grant Tobin O'Brien permission to do the surgery on his leg. I'll stay in the room with him during the CT. I'll watch everything that is going on, and I will be right there if he needs any other physicians or tests. Once the scans are done, we'll call his parents together."

Sam nodded. She took Damon's hand and kissed his cheek. She whispered something in his ear.

"Okay, let's go. Sam, I'll return soon."

Dana took Sam's hand and walked her to the waiting room.

"Steve. What are you doing here?"

Steve walked over and took her hand. "Dr. Montgomery asked if I could stay with you while they were taking care of Dr. Parker. I didn't want you to be alone."

Steve smiled at her, and she hugged him. "You have the best smile, Steve. Has anyone ever told you that?"

"I hear people say that often. Come over here and sit with me. Can I fix you a cup of tea?"

"Yes, please. That would be great. I can't get warm."

"I'll get you a blanket and that tea, Sam. You stay here with Steve, and I'll be right back."

Dana returned to the waiting room with blankets and the dietary department was right behind Dana with coffee, tea, soft drinks, water, and snacks. Everyone was in for a long night and more food and drinks could be ordered as needed.

Before long, Alex was back and sat beside Sam.

"Okay, Sam. Here's everything that Damon is dealing with right now. There is a small amount of swelling and a small blood clot, the size of a nickel, on the left side of the brain. The neurosurgeon looked at the scans and felt there was no immediate need for surgical intervention. He'll watch that area closely and will call if there are any changes. The left lung has re-inflated. The fractured rib is stable. He is having trouble breathing, so he's on a ventilator for a day or two. Once he regains consciousness, we can remove the vent. Tobin was granted permission to do the surgery. Were you aware he is renowned orthopedic surgeon in Ireland?"

"I overheard someone discussing that at your house."

"Good. Damon is aware of Tobin's skills, and I'm comfortable asking for his assistance with the surgery. Tobin ordered antibiotics and fluids, and I gave Damon one unit of blood so far. Labs have been ordered twice a day so that we can be aware of changes. There is road grime in the wound, so Tobin will watch for infection and treat it if needed. Are there any questions you need answered, Sam?"

Sam shook her head no, and Alex assured her he would be close by.

"Let's call Damon's parents. I'll do the talking, but they may want to speak to you, too. Do you think you can do that, Sam?"

Sam nodded.

Alex dialed the number, and Mrs. Parker answered.

"Damon darling. I didn't expect to talk with you twice in a week."

"Mrs. Parker. This is Dr. Alexander Montgomery. I work in the ER with Damon."

"Damon speaks highly of you, Dr. Montgomery. Why are you calling on his phone?"

"I'm sorry I need to do this over the phone, but Damon and Samantha were injured in a truck vs. motorcycle accident this afternoon. Is your husband there?"

"Yes. He is here. How is Damon?"

"Alive, but in critical condition."

"And Samantha?"

"Samantha is doing okay. She's here beside me."

"Just a moment while I get my husband."

Alex took Sam's hand again.

"We are both here, Dr. Montgomery."

Alex explained the events leading up to the accident and the injuries Damon sustained.

"I need consent for the surgery from you. He is in pre-op, and they will start once I get your permission. He'll be in surgery for a while. I'll call with updates."

Damon's father spoke.

"We give our consent, Dr. Montgomery. We'll get our things together and be on our way. It's a three-hour drive."

"I'll let security know who you are, and they will bring you to the private family waiting room. We'll be here with Samantha."

Samantha stood and paced.

"Sam, I'm going after Abbie, Kate, and Julie. Conor is going to stay with us as well. I won't be gone long, and Steve will be here, too. The OR has my cell phone number and will call me with any updates. We are likely in for a long night. Is there something you want me to pick up for you?"

"I don't believe so, Alex. Thank you for everything you've done. I cannot do this without you and the others. Damon trusts you, and so do I, but I might need the courage to get through meeting his parents face-to-face."

"We'll be right here beside you." Alex gave her a hug and left to get Abbie.

CHAPTER 5

Abbie, Kate, and Julie were in the living room, each with a baby in their arms. Ms. Helen was napping in her room, and Andy was not home from school yet. Abbie heard the elevator moving.

"Sounds as though Alex is home early. I wasn't expecting him for another couple of hours."

"Maybe it was a slow day, and he got out early."

Abbie stood and greeted Alex as he exited the elevator.

"Hey love. You're home early."

Alex reached out and took Gabriella from Abbie's arms. He kissed her, took her hand, and walked to the sofa.

"Julie, Kate. How was your day?"

"We had a good day, Alex. Kate and I spent a couple of hours on the beach, while mama here spoiled these little girls."

Alex grinned at his daughter, and Abbie saw a tear form in the corner of his eye.

"What's making you teary-eyed this afternoon, Montgomery?"

He stood with the baby and faced the three ladies.

"There's no other way to put this than to be direct. There's been an accident. A truck struck Damon and Samantha earlier this afternoon near the swing bridge."

Abbie was on her feet instantly. "No! No, no, no! You're wrong, Montgomery! They were going for a ride down the coast for lunch."

"Abbie. Let me finish."

Abbie swiped tears from her face, and Julie and Kate were on their feet as well.

"Sit down please, and I will fill you in on everything."

The three of them sat together on the sofa.

"Damon and Sam were about to enter the intersection at the bridge. Damon had the green light and was entering the intersection. A truck blew through the red light. Damon must have seen the truck heading for them, and he shoved Samantha off the bike. She landed on the street, but other than a couple of areas of bruising, she is okay. Steve, a bartender at the restaurant at the bridge, helped Sam to get up off the street. That's when she noticed Damon came to rest under the truck. Sam crawled under the truck and called me. He was unconscious and had a severe leg injury. Steve helped her get Damon's belt off and use it as a tourniquet. Once they arrived at the ER, I had Sam get x-rays and a CT of her head. Everything with her is good. She is going to be sore, but there were no major injuries."

"And Damon?" Said Julie.

"Damon is unconscious and has a small bleed the size of a nickel on the left side of his brain. There is minimal swelling right now, and the neurosurgeon does not believe that surgical intervention is necessary. He'll check with scans to make sure the swelling does not increase. Damon has a fractured rib which caused a collapsed lung. I inserted a chest tube, and the lung has re-inflated. He suffered a severe injury with an open fracture to his lower leg and was undergoing surgery when I left the hospital. I did not have an orthopedic surgeon available, so I got permission from the board and ethics committees to have Tobin O'Brien do the surgery. Damon's parents are on the way. Why don't you three grab your things and let's wait with Sam?"

"I need to see if Ms. Helen is okay with taking care of the three girls."

"Andy will be home soon, Abbie. He is a tremendous help with them, and she can always call us if she needs us to come home."

"Let me go check, and I'll be ready to go in a minute. Can you change diapers for her while I get ready?"

"Of course. I will do whatever I can to spend time with them, even if it means changing diapers."

"Alex, Kate, and I just had showers after we came in from the beach, so I am ready. I'll help with the girls. We made bottles earlier, so Ms. Helen should be okay with their formula until we get back. What time are you expecting Damon's parents to arrive?"

"Another two hours or more. Damon won't be out of surgery before they get here. We need to keep an eye on Sam, though. She was showing signs of shock when she arrived in the ER. Dana ran fluids and got her under a warm blanket. She had a cup of tea. I don't want her too far out of our sight this evening."

"I can stay at the hospital with her tonight. You and Abbie need to get back here to rest. You two have enough on your plates right now. More than likely, Abbie will give us a tough time leaving tonight."

"Has she always been this stubborn?"

"Yes, she has, but she had a tough fight growing up, so we try to overlook the stubbornness."

"I'm glad she has you to lean on, Julie."

Ms. Helen came into the nursery. "Mr. Alex, it's my job to change their diapers. Get, I'll finish here."

"I've got this Ms. Helen. It gives me a chance to see their little faces before we leave. If you need us, do not be afraid to call me. Andy will be home soon and will pitch in wherever you need him. I smell amazing scents coming from the kitchen, so Abbie must have dinner prepared in the slow cooker. That girl could be a chef."

Julie chuckled. "We had an extended period of trial-and-error teaching ourselves to cook, but we do well now. The slow cooker was the easiest way for us to get dinner after our classes without slaving over the stove."

"I'm ready, Montgomery. Let me kiss my babies, then let's go. Sam might have Conor and Steve with her, but she needs the three of us as well."

Alex's phone pinged with a text message from Connor. "Going okay in the OR. Sam fell asleep on the sofa in the waiting room."

"We are on our way now. See you soon."

Julie drove her car to the hospital so Alex and Abbie could leave when they were ready. As Alex and Abbie approached the intersection near the swing bridge and accident site, Abbie noticed Sam's helmet laying on the grass beside the road.

"Alex, that's Sam's helmet. Can we stop and get it? I know she'll need a new one, but I don't want to leave it here."

"I'll pull into the hotel parking lot. We can't stop on the road. I'll get it for her, and that will give me a chance to see if there is any damage. She couldn't remember what she did with it once she saw Damon under the truck."

Alex parked and retrieved the helmet.

"How do you get over seeing someone you love under a vehicle, Alex?"

"I have no idea, love. I hope I never have to find out."

Alex took Abbie's hand, and they were silent the rest of the drive to the hospital.

Julie and Kate were waiting in the parking lot of the ER. Alex used his ID to open the door. Samantha was still asleep on the sofa when they opened the door to the private waiting room, but her eyes popped open, and she stood.

"What's going on, Alex?"

"Everything's okay, Sam. Damon is still in the OR, and Abbie, Julie, and Kate are here to keep you company. The last word from Tobin was good. Everything is going well in the OR, but it's going to be awhile. I thought you might want your friends with you."

"Thank you, Alex. I appreciate your thoughtfulness, and I need them with me."

Dana was still in the room, and the five of them did one large group hug. Steve introduced himself.

"Connor. Let's walk over to the operating theater and check in on Damon's progress. Steve, do you have the stomach to watch surgery in progress? If so, you are welcome to join us."

"Thank you, Dr. Montgomery. I'd love to join you."

Samantha was surrounded by her friends. She gave them a detailed description of the events of the day, starting from the time they pulled out of the driveway. She kept her emotions in check until she tried to describe finding Damon beneath the truck. The five of them were crying now, and they consoled one another. The phone rang, and Julie answered.

"Hello."

"Julie, it's Alex. The surgery is going well. His vital signs are stable. Tobin said it's going to be a couple more hours at least. Update Sam, please. The three of us will be there soon. We're giving Steve the lowdown on how things work around here."

"Thanks, Alex. Take your time. We aren't going anywhere."

There was a knock at the door. Kate opened the door to find two North Myrtle Beach police officers.

"May I help you?"

"I'm officer Todd, and my partner is officer Smith. Were here to speak to Samantha D'Alessandro."

Samantha stood and wiped the tears from her face.

"I'm Samantha."

"Sorry to bother you, but we have questions regarding the accident. It shouldn't take long. How are you doing? Are you injured?"

"I'm good. Thank you. A little sore, but no actual injuries. My x-rays and scans were normal."

"We're glad to hear you're okay. How is Dr. Parker doing?"

Sam looked toward the police officers and the tears started flowing again, and she shrugged. Julie stepped forward.

"I'm Dr. Julia Baxter. I'm friends with Samantha. We just had a report from the operating room. Samantha, sit here. Officers, take a seat, please."

Everyone sat and Julie gave a report to the officers.

Officer Todd thanked Julie for the information and turned his attention to Samantha.

"We had Dr. Parker's bike towed to Pete's body shop. Do you have access to any insurance information or a copy of his license?"

Dana spoke up next. "My name is Dana Williams I'm the Director of Nursing for the ER. I'm a good friend of Samantha's as well. I have Dr. Parker's wallet and his other belongings. Give me a moment and I will give his wallet to Samantha. I'll be right back."

"Does Dr. Parker have any next of kin?"

"His parents are in route and should be here in a couple of hours. Their names are Dr. John Parker, and Abagail Parker. Dr. Montgomery spoke with them earlier. They are aware of the accident and his condition, and that Damon was going to surgery."

"Here is my card. Call me when they arrive."

"Did you find the guy who caused the accident, Officer Todd?"

"Yes, we did, Ms. D'Alessandro. He's under arrest. We are waiting for lab results and an update on Dr. Parker's condition before we charge him. We'll keep you updated."

Julie took charge.

"Thank you, Officer Todd, and Officer Smith. We appreciate the information. One of us will call you. By the way, let me introduce you to Abbie Montgomery, Dr. Montgomery's wife, and close friend of Samantha, and Dr. Katie Gill, another close friend of Samantha. She goes by Kate. Dana should return in just a moment with the information you need."

"We'll wait at the nurse's station. Samantha, we hope you and Dr. Parker recover with no lasting complications from your accident."

Samantha nodded and looked at her watch. She paced back and forth across the room. Abbie approached her and wrapped her in a hug.

"What do you need, Sam? I can't help unless you talk to me."

Samantha shrugged. "I want him to walk through that door with that lazy smile of his and call me darlin. I want to go home with him. He belongs in that house with me. I was wrong, Abbie. He's precisely what I need, and I'm afraid I'm going to lose him."

"I understand your fear, Sam. When Tom died, I had no idea what to do next. Without you, I could not have survived. Now I'm here for you and so are Dana, Kate, and Julie. We'll get through this together. We are not leaving you."

"You need to go home to your babies, Abbie. I will be fine here. Julie and Kate will be with me."

"I am staying until Damon is out of surgery and in the ICU. Alex will be here as well. Damon's parents should be here soon. Alex will talk to them. I know you're scared. I am too, but we will be right beside you, Sam."

Sam nodded.

Julie, Kate, and Dana left the room to stretch their legs and get dinner ordered for everyone in the room, and to have the dietary department refresh the drinks and snacks. Julie and Kate were planning to stay through the night if Samantha insisted. If she agreed to stay at home, which was across the street, they'd stay there with her in case Damon's condition worsened and they needed to return.

There was a knock at the door. The security officer opened the door and introduced Dr. and Mrs. Parker.

Samantha stood and wiped her face with her sleeve, stood straighter, and walked across the room to greet Damon's parents. Abbie sent a text to Alex telling him Damon's parents had arrived. Alex text back.

"I'll be right there to update everyone."

Samantha faced the Parkers.

"Dr. and Mrs. Parker, I'm Samantha. I'm sorry we had to meet under these circumstances. Dr. Montgomery is on his way back from the OR theater to update us on Damon's condition. Let me introduce you to one of my best friends, Abbie Montgomery. Her husband is Dr. Alex Montgomery."

Dr. and Mrs. Parker hugged Samantha.

"Please call us John and Abagail, Samantha. And you too, Abbie. It's nice to meet Damon's friends."

"Thank you. Kate, Julie, and Dana went to order dinner and fresh coffee. Everyone will be back soon. Alex will be here in just a moment to update you on Damon."

Samantha turned to the Parkers. "Where are you staying while you are in town?"

"We haven't made reservations yet, Samantha, but Abagail and I were considering the hotel near the bridge. That's the closest one in the event we need to come back to the hospital."

"I live just across the street. I have three extra bedrooms, each with a sitting room and a private bathroom. Why don't you stay with me? You'd be more comfortable there and close enough to walk back and forth?"

"That's a lovely gesture, Samantha, but we don't want to impose."

"You won't be imposing, John. There is room for you to relax. There is a large covered front porch and a covered back porch. I could use the company, and we could get to know one another. You're welcome to stay as long as you want."

"Abagail, I'll leave the decision up to you."

"Her offer makes sense, John. With the limited visiting hours in the ICU, we will be in and out of the hospital two or three times a day. If we find it doesn't work for either of us, we can always get a hotel."

"It's settled then, Samantha. We appreciate your offer and will try not to get in your way."

"I work in the building next door, so I will be close if you need something, and I will be close enough to visit with Damon, too. Julie and Kate will be here tonight and will be leaving tomorrow afternoon. They may stay at the house tonight if I decide to go home. Everything depends on Damon's condition over the next few hours."

"And where do you live, Abbie?"

"Alex and I have a place on the beach, John. Once Damon stabilizes, we'd love to have you over to meet our family."

"Are you the one who just had the triplets?"

Abbie smiled. "That's me. We have a seven-year-old as well. His name is Andy, and he is in love with his little sisters."

The door opened and Alex, Connor, and Steve entered the room. John and Abagail stood.

"I'm Dr. Alex Montgomery, Dr., and Mrs. Parker. I'm sorry we had to meet under these conditions. Please have a seat, and I'll fill you in on Damon's condition."

Alex introduced Conor and Steve.

"Meet Dr. Conor O'Brien. His brother Tobin O'Brien is the one who is performing Damon's surgery. This is our new friend, Steve. He was at the accident scene and helped Samantha up off the road and helped her under the truck to get a tourniquet on Damon's leg before the ambulance arrived."

Abagail stood and hugged Steve. "Thank you for helping Damon and Samantha. How can we ever repay you?"

"I'm glad I was there to help."

The door opened again, and Kate, Julie, and Dana walked into the room.

Alex noticed John smile and he looked toward Abagail.

"Let me introduce you to our friends and Abbie's best friends. Dana Williams, Nursing Director of the ER, Dr. Julia Baxter, pediatrician, and Dr. Katie Gill our genius physician friend whose practice involves DNA research and other things I'm sure has not yet been revealed."

Damon's parents stood and greeted everyone.

"Okay, everyone take a seat and I'll give you an update."

"Damon's surgery is progressing. There was significant bone damage and splintering, which caused the initial bleeding. Tobin is attempting to piece the bone together. There is muscle damage as well, but he feels that is insignificant in the overall recovery. His concern is infection and the ability to save his leg. Additional surgery is a possibility."

John Parker spoke. "Would it be best to amputate the leg now to prevent complications?"

"I considered that option when I saw his leg, John, but Damon awoke for a brief minute under the truck and insisted that Samantha and I promise to not let anyone amputate his leg. I told him we couldn't make that promise, but I'd like to honor that request for as long as possible. Tobin O'Brien is one of the best surgeons in the world. If he says he can save Damon's leg, I guess it's worth a try. That doesn't mean there won't be complications."

Abagail Parker was on her feet. "There will be no one cutting off his leg, John, so you can just forget that idea. I don't care how many years of experience you have in medicine. I'm not giving my permission."

"Abagail, we can discuss this later and review the options, but if it's necessary to save his life, then it might be necessary."

"Not happening, John. There is nothing more to discuss."

CHAPTER 6

Abbie's phone rang, and Ms Helen's name was on the screen. When she answered, it was Andy.

"Hi Mom. How's Doctor Parker and Sam? Ms. Helen told me they were in a minor accident this afternoon and you are with them at the hospital."

"How's my sweet boy this afternoon? Did your day go well at school?"

"I had a good day and walked to my classes. For the last couple of classes, I used my walker. My teachers and classmates are proud of me."

"We are proud of you, too. Sam is doing okay and is sitting here beside me. Doctor Parker is in surgery, getting his broken leg fixed. Doctor Tobin O'Brien is fixing it for him, and Doctor Connor O'Brien is waiting in the room with us."

"Is he going to stay in the hospital?"

"He may be here for a few nights, but we will be home by nightfall. How are your sisters doing?"

"They are good too, Mom. They are trying to smile at me. I love to hold them, and I can't wait until they can play. Ms. Helen told me they will be into everything before I know it."

Abbie laughed. "That is true. You'll need to hide things you don't want them to see. Keeping up with the three of them will keep us busy. Do you want to say hello to Sam and tell her how you got around the school today?"

"Yes, please."

Abbie handed the phone to Samantha.

"Hi Andy. How are you today?"

"I'm good, Sam. How are you feeling? Did you get hurt on the motorcycle today?"

"I have a couple of bruises. Dana and your dad checked me out to make sure everything was okay. Do you think we can do a couple of therapy sessions this week? We haven't seen you at the pool since your sisters were born. I think we could use a play date. What do you say?"

"That sounds fun. Koko, Kody, and Kohl are doing good here. They love the babies and lay next to them to make sure they are okay. As soon as they make a sound, the dogs are standing at the crib to check on them and let us know if they need anything. Ms. Helen said they are the best-behaved dogs she has ever seen. Kohl hasn't huffed at her once. He still huffs at Mom and Dad all the time. I walked to my classes today except for the last two, and I used my walker. I did not use my chair."

"That's great news, Andy. I am so proud of you. I think Doctor Parker might need to use that wheelchair."

"He's very tall, Sam. I don't think he's going to fit in it. Do you think the hospital will give him one for tall guys?"

"I'll check on that for him. Do you want to say hi to your dad?"

"Yes, please. I hope you are feeling better soon, Sam."

"Thank you, love. I'll get with you later this week. Here's your dad."

Sam handed the phone to Alex and looked at Abbie. "Thanks for letting me talk to him. That was a piece of normalcy I needed this afternoon."

"You're welcome. You can always find a distraction at our house. I'm not sure normalcy is what you'll find, but if you need something to keep you busy, I can keep you busy. Let's look at your afternoon schedule tomorrow and get Andy back in the pool. He would not be where he is without your help, Sam. I can't tell you how much that means to us."

"This program was your idea, Abbie. I just had the skills to help it get underway. We are getting busy, and we need to consider getting more space. I'm not sure how we do that."

"We could look at buying property and building a larger complex. I noticed there's a large piece of property on the same side of the road as your house right at the intersection. I'll investigate that before someone else buys it out from under us."

"Abbie, that means we need to expand staff. Does that mean we need more dogs?"

"I don't believe we need more dogs. I was considering expanding the square footage of the therapy suites. The lack of space makes it impossible to offer underwater treadmill and other advanced therapies."

"Remember, Sam, we will be looking at a year or two before everything has a license, is built, and is ready to go. There is room on that property for other medical facilities. Julie or Kate might want space for their practices. Both are looking for homes here. It's a great space for other practices that can refer patients to the program. We can talk to Connor and Tobin as well. Cardio and orthopedics are our two biggest referrals."

"You keep coming up with ways to spend the money Tom left for you."

"The project will pay back the investment. We've proven the program is working. The community is growing and there will always be a need for therapy, and we need to consider building the complex."

"Abbie, I agree."

"I'll work on preliminary plans and call the realtor. Once Damon is stable, we can invite everyone to dinner and discuss the options. I'll talk with Alex and get his opinion as well. That complex will not put a dent in that trust fund. Mr Walker can draft the legal papers for me. I need to get wills and custody forms, and personal stuff done, as well. I know I can trust him to make sure we are covering everything that needs to be done."

Tobin opened the door to the private waning room and walked in. Samantha was on her feet. Dr. and Mrs. Parker stood as well. Alex introduced Tobin to the Parkers. Tobin took a chair to the front of the room and sat where everyone could see him and hear what he had to say.

"Sit please, and I'll run through the surgery. Damon will be transferred to the ICU soon. There was a significant amount of bone damage to his leg, and I did the best I could to piece it back together. He is going to need a long recovery and a good therapist. I suspect Samantha will know what will work best for him. The therapy pool will be an effective way to begin his recovery before getting him back to a weight bearing status."

"We are getting another CT scan before he goes to the ICU so I have a solid understanding of any further surgical interventions that he might need. The neurosurgeon ordered another CT of his head to check the swelling. I ordered a chest x-ray to check his left lung, as well as a pelvic x-ray. The results should be back soon. Obviously, there's concern for infection and we will do our best to cut the risk of sepsis. I put a drain in place, and we can get wound cultures if needed. Once the drainage is minimal, we can remove the drain."

"We will get that tube out of the lung as soon as possible. I feel certain the vital areas are covered. We may find an incidental injury, but if so, it will be minor. I checked every extremity and noted bruising, but nothing else looked broken. I doubt we will find injuries on the pelvic CT, either. He's young and healthy, and I am hopeful his recovery will go smoothly. What questions do you want to ask me?"

Mrs. Parker spoke. "When can we see him, Doctor O'Brien? And we want to put Samantha's name on the visitor list. We realize she is not family, but she needs to visit with him and talk to him."

Mrs. Parker took Samantha's hand. "Damon needs her. In the last five years or so, she has been the only one he has introduced us to, and that tells his father and I that the two of them have something special, and he is intrigued with her. We want her involved and informed as though she extends us."

"That's not a problem, Mrs. Parker. I will get a shower and return if there is nothing else."

Samantha stood. "Tobin, I am so thankful you were here today and willing to step in when Damon needed you. Dinner is here, and you are welcome to eat. It's the least I can offer you right now, but I thank you for your skills and kindness."

"Thanks, Samantha. I'll take you up on that food."

"He never turns food away, Sam." Connor interjected. "So, the rest of you better fill your plates before he gets back, or you'll most likely starve."

"Funny brother. After you make your plate, I will be happy if there's any left. I'll be the one who starves if you're involved. I'll check in with the ICU, Mrs. Parker, and they'll call the waiting room when they get Damon ready. It shouldn't be much longer."

Doctor Parker stood up and shook Tobin's hand. "I'll repeat what Samantha said, we cannot thank you enough. I have a wide circle of friends in the medical association. Alex told me you might be interested in moving here from Ireland. I'll do everything I can to help make that a reality for you, Tobin."

"Alex is correct. I am looking to move. It is tough to tease Conor from across the seas, and after being here on vacation, I'd love to make a permanent move."

Abbie stood next. "I'm in the preliminary stages of a new project I'd like to discuss with every one of you present in this room. Once Damon stabilizes, Alex and I plan to invite you over to our place at the beach. You can see the kids, and I'll scrape together something delicious for dinner. Now get showered so you can eat."

"Spoken like a true mother. I'll be right back."

Everyone filled a plate and left food for Tobin. Julie stood beside Abbie. "What are you up to now, Abbie? What plans are you putting in place?"

"I can't say just yet. Something is coming together in my brain, but it might involve you if you're interested. I notice how you look at Tobin. Before one of the nurses gets their claws in him, consider that he is moving here. Besides, I need a good pediatrician for the kids, and maybe one of you will get married and give my kids playmates one day."

"Sounds like you are making big plans, Abbie. Are you sure you've recovered enough to take on an enormous project?"

"Yes. It will take time, and I will have help around the house. Ms. Helen is perfect for us and does not appear to be worn out by the babies. I did not expect them to be such good sleepers, and that is helping us stay sane as we figure out how to manage everything."

"If you can stay sane through teething and the terrible twos, you might deserve a medal."

The phone rang, and everyone stopped talking. Alex answered the phone.

"Dr. and Mrs. Parker. That was the ICU. You and Samantha are allowed to visit for ten minutes. There's a buzzer outside the entrance to the unit. Ring it and they will let you in."

Samantha held Abagail's hand, led the way to the ICU, and pushed the buzzer. The nurse let them in, introduced herself, and led them to room six. Samantha stopped short of entering the room. The sight of Damon took her back to the accident scene, and she froze in her tracks. The only thing she could imagine was his body lying under the truck, and she realized what he had sacrificed for her by pushing her off the back of the motorcycle. His body was bruised and swollen and there were tubes and IV lines running everywhere. If they had both been on the bike when the truck struck, one of them would have been dead. Damon had done what he could to give them both a chance to live.

His parents approached the bed, and Samantha noticed his mother's hands shaking. His appearance shocked them both as well, and she noticed Abagail wiping tears from her face as she took his hand and spoke to him as only a mother can when their child is ill. Damon was in worse shape than Samantha expected.

Damon was hooked up to a ventilator that breathed in for him to give his lung a chance to stabilize. His leg was being elevated and stabilized in a position that help reduce swelling while still permitting the extra fluids to drain from his leg. The head of the bed was raised at a thirty-degree angle, and he looked peaceful. His skin color was pasty white. He lost blood at the accident scene and during the surgery. He was receiving a blood transfusion, and Samantha was sure he'd need more units of blood within the next forty-eight hours.

She scanned the room and noted the machine used to watch his vital signs, IV poles, and a suction machine on the wall above his bed. There was a variety of other equipment, including medicines, syringes, and dressing materials. He was in the direct line of sight to the nursing station.

Samantha had not been to the ICU in years. During her training, it had been part of the curriculum, and she enjoyed learning. She was aware that his nurse is crucial in providing medications and treatments to keep him alive. She'd be their liaison between the doctors who provided care and the vital judgment needed to work in such a fast-paced, team-based environment. She was thankful for Alex, Connor, and Tobin as part of his team. They'd be there to keep her informed and answer her questions.

Abagail and John turned and noticed Samantha still standing outside of the room. Abagail walked out and took her hand.

"Are you ready, Samantha? John and I will be right beside you."

Samantha looked at them as she walked into the room.

"He sacrificed himself to save me. There was no way we were both going to survive that accident. He realized that and put himself in harm's way for me. How do I live with that?"

John put his arm around her. "Samantha, we will figure this out together. We might need to take it day by day, or minute by minute, but we will do this together."

Samantha walked to the side of the bed and took Damon's hand in her.

"Damon, I'm holding your hand. You asked me not to let go. I am not letting go, and you need to not let go either. I was wrong when I said this couldn't go anywhere. You are exactly what I need. I want to look at that sexy smile of yours and hear you call me darlin. I want your custom coffee every morning, and I promise to learn to make it so that you can enjoy a cup as soon as the doctor approves you to sit up and drink. You can take the whole garage as soon as you get back on your feet. I promise to help you get through every single minute of your therapy. I realize what you sacrificed for me, love, and I will do the same for you. We have a long road ahead of us, and I plan to be there every step of the way. Just don't let go."

The nurse came into the room to check on Damon and told them their time was up for today. Samantha thanked her, and they walked back to the private waiting room in the ER. The room was silent when they entered. Tears were running off Sam's face and instantly her crew was around her. She was sobbing and broken by Damon's consideration of her and his current condition, and they held on to her through the grief.

Alex and the other men realized that these ladies had a bond that nobody could break. They'd protect and care for those in their lives no matter what happened along the way.

Steve smiled at the group and considered himself lucky to have the opportunity to meet such an elite group of people. It was time for him to go. He sent a text to his friend Charlie to pick him up at the hospital.

CHAPTER 7

"I am going to stay at my house tonight. It looks as though we have a long road ahead of us, and we need to get rest."

"Kate and I have our things with us. You can ride over to the house in my car, and the Parker's can follow us. Abbie and Alex, you two need to go home to your children, and we'll check in with you before we leave tomorrow."

"John and I want to thank you for your friendship with Damon, and the work you did to save him from his injuries. We can never repay you for the knowledge and kindness you have shown to him and to us today."

"Alex, can you bring the dogs to the house tomorrow, please? We have appointments scheduled for Monday, and I want to introduce them to the Parkers and let them get acquainted."

"Sure, Sam. I'll be here checking on Damon tomorrow and can drop them off. Text me tomorrow and let me know what time works best."

There was a round of hugs, and everyone agreed to talk the next day. The Parker's followed Julie across the street and carried their things into the house.

"Samantha, this house is amazing. How did you find such a lovely southern home?"

"I had a one-bedroom apartment, but it was not big enough to house three enormous dogs. Abbie noticed this was for sale and called a realtor she had used with an earlier house search. The foundation that funds the hydrotherapy program owns the house, and I pay rent. Damon fell in love with it and tried to buy it out from under the foundation, but he was too late. The owner accepted the offer and signed the contract."

"Damon loves the garage and parked his truck there yesterday. His bike is in Pete's garage, which is right down the road. The police had it towed there after the accident. We need to check in with them this week. John, I'll let you oversee that business. His wallet is with his belongings. You need to call the police officer as well. Let me get his card for you. He wanted to speak with the two of you after you arrived. There is a library on the main floor where you can meet."

Samantha handed John the card. "I'll call them now. Abagail, do you want to listen to the call? I can put them on speakerphone, and we can use the library."

"Get them on the phone and let me know if they are stopping by or just want to discuss the accident on the phone."

"Abagail, let me help you with your luggage and you can choose what room you want. Kate and I will only be here for one night. Each of the rooms has a balcony and splendid views, but I want you to choose."

"Thank you, Julie. John will get the luggage. Let's have a look at the rooms."

Kate and Samantha took a stool at the kitchen island.

"Sam, is there something I can get you?"

"I don't think so, Kate. Thanks for staying tonight. I'm sad that you need to leave tomorrow. Are you and Julie serious about moving here?"

"Yes, Sam. We've been here so often since Tom died that it makes sense to move. My company will be fine with me moving, and I can go to the office if they need me. Julie is more interested in Tobin than she is letting on, and she can find a practice to join or start one of her own."

"Abbie is making plans to expand the hydrotherapy program. There is a property near the intersection that is for sale. There is enough room to build a new building for therapy, and room to build other medical buildings. Because of its location to the hospital, there should be no problem finding groups to lease space in the building."

Kate chuckled. "Who would imagine she had an interest in building new programs, and new buildings as well?"

Sam chuckled too. "Tom's trust fund is so massive; she could build a whole town and still have money to spare. I give her credit, though. She is doing remarkable things for the neighborhood, and Kohl was her inspiration for the innovation. She will probably sign for the property on Monday. If she does not follow through with the buildings, she can always sell the land at a profit."

"Alex has been good for her. He keeps her challenged and motivated, but calm and reasonable."

"I agree Kate. There was an abundance of convenience in her relationship with Tom, but she and Tom made a great couple. I realize she is still trying to figure out who Tom was and where the money was made. I'm sure she'll find a nugget of information one day that will lead her to the answers she has been searching for these months. It still amazes me he could hide this from us."

"I say she needs to do an ancestry test. It will put her on the path to finding his family history and how they became so wealthy."

"Perhaps she's afraid to find out, or since she is the only one left, it doesn't matter to her any longer."

"Perhaps, Sam. But mark my words, she will gather us together one day and announce that she has discovered his family and how they amassed such a fortune."

"I'm certain she will figure it out someday. She is full of surprises lately."

John and Abagail put away their belongings in their room, came back downstairs, and finished their call with the local police. Sam asked if they had everything they needed, and Abagail said they were set.

"I was considering having a glass of wine and relaxing on the front porch for a while before turning in for the night. Would anyone like to join me?"

Everyone agreed that was a great idea. Samantha poured the wine, and they walked outside to the porch. A soft breeze carried the essence of newly cut grass as the sun was setting. The traffic was a distant hum in the backdrop, and the porch swing produced a soothing creaking sound as John and Abagail swung back and forth. The rocking chairs that Samantha, Kate, and Julie settled in kept rhythm with the swing.

Everyone in the group was quiet this evening, contemplating Damon's recovery and the events that led up to them being in the same place. Sam swiped away tears that were rolling off her face, and Julie reached out and took her hand. Sam interrupted everyone's thoughts with talk of the dogs.

"John and Abagail, I need to fill you in on our dogs, who will arrive tomorrow. They are large and as gentle as can be, but I don't want you to be afraid."

"We'd love to meet them, Samantha. Wouldn't we John?"

"Absolutely."

"The three of them will be here tomorrow. Kohl is the oldest and belongs to Abbie. Her late husband Tom was a coast guard rescue swimmer and Kohl was the rescue dog attached to his coast guard unit. Kohl is a local hero and loved by the community. Abbie and I trained him to be a therapy dog after Tom died in a helicopter crash. For a long time, Kohl refused to go back into the water. Abbie and I worked with him, and he slowly began to enter the pool. Once Abbie and I put together the hydrotherapy program and presented it to the board and the physicians at the hospital, we got so many referrals, we realized we needed more dogs. Koko and Kody came from the same breeder as Kohl, and their personalities are remarkably like Kohl's."

"How large are they, Samantha?"

"Well, John, Kohl is a thin, one hundred fifty pounds. Koko and Kody are one hundred fifteen and one hundred twenty pounds. They are just under a year old, so they will still grow over the next year. I imagine they will top out at the one hundred fifty range as well. Kohl is tall and his head is at the same height as my waist when I am standing, and the other two are nearly as tall."

"Are people frightened by their size?"

"Abagail, most people are not. We always get questions when they are out in public, but they are incredibly gentle. Abbie and Tom taught Kohl to ride a paddle board, so when they are on the beach, they always draw a large crowd. The breed loves children, and they keep watch over Abbie's triplets to make sure they are okay."

"That's amazing."

"They love Damon, Abagail. The first time he met them, we were in the therapy pool teaching them new maneuvers, and Damon stopped to say hi. He put on his trunks and stepped into the water. They swam right up to him and followed him around the pool. Damon swan the perimeter and back and forth, and they were right beside him every inch of the way. They love when he stays here, and Damon plays in the backyard with them."

"We're looking forward to meeting them tomorrow. Will they be involved in Damon's therapy?"

"Most likely. Once Tobin and I put together a plan of care, I will know more. I'm uncertain how long Tobin will stay. He was supposed to be here for a couple of weeks. He plans to move here, but I'm not sure what the timeline is for a permanent move."

"I have contacts, Samantha. I will do whatever is needed to help with the move. He is an excellent provider, and the community will be lucky he is part of the medical staff."

"Julie and Kate are planning on moving here as well."

John smiled. "What's your motivation for the move?"

Julie spoke up first. "Our group has been friends since college. We met while enrolled in the same classes. We are always back and forth from our houses to Myrtle Beach. Since Abbie and Alex had the babies, Kate and I want to be more involved in their lives. I can find a group to join here, and Alex has offered to check in with the pediatric groups to see if any of them are open to another partner."

"I'm sure your friends will be glad you are closer. And Kate, what research are you doing?"

"I've been working on a project that involves artificial intelligence and the impact on the patients."

"Anything specific you can discuss?"

"I am researching the impact artificial intelligence has on early diagnosis and personalized treatment. There's research on drug development, and remote monitoring options as well."

"That's certainly interesting and important work. When I started in this field, we were required to tote enormous books around to find information and put together treatment plans. The world certainly has changed in the last forty years."

Kate chuckled. "It has, and it will change rapidly over the next forty years. I can't even imagine what medicine might be like once we have the same number of years under our belt as you."

"It will be an interesting evolution for sure."

Samantha stood. "I'm going to bed. I'm not trying to be a poor hostess, but it has been an emotional day, and I'm sore and need to take a dose of ibuprofen and rest. Just wake me if any of you need something. Visitation for the ICU starts at 11:00 am. I'll see you in the morning. I hope everyone gets much-needed rest. Julie, what time are you and Kate planning on leaving tomorrow?"

"I planned to leave around 2:00 pm. And you Kate?"

"I was planning to leave around the same time. I have flexibility as well, so if you need me to stay later, Samantha, just let me know."

Samantha gave everyone a hug and the others were off to their rooms as well. Samantha showered and crawled into bed. Achy from her contact with the road, she found a comfortable position. The bed carried Damon's scent from his stay, and she wondered how she might keep that scent with her. It comforted her. She closed her eyes and reflected over the ride she and Damon had experienced. She opened her eyes and realized it was morning. How did the night pass so quickly?

Samantha reached for her phone to check the day and time. The house was quiet. She dialed the ICU number to check on Damon. The nurse gave her an update. No actual change in his condition. He had not regained consciousness.

Samantha got up, showered, dressed, and went to the kitchen to make coffee. She found Damon's coffee beans and grinder and hoped she could replicate his recipe. She put the beans in the grinder and left it on the setting he used previously and pressed the button. The grinder started and the smell of the coffee beans caused her mouth to start watering for a cup of coffee immediately. The grinder shut off automatically. It must have a timer built in that he set.

Samantha poured the coffee grounds into the coffee press and boiled water in her teapot. Slowly, she poured the water over the grounds the way she had watched Damon do the same task. She noticed he timed the process, but she had not paid attention to his exact timing. She estimated the time at five minutes. That was the same time she used when brewing her looseleaf tea. She poured the coffee into her favorite cup and took a sip. Not awful. It was stronger than Damon had made. He either used fewer beans, or less time. She needed to experiment.

Samantha heard the stairs squeak and John came around the corner from the hallway.

"Good morning, Samantha. Did you get rest?"

"Good morning, John. Yes, I did. I was just trying to make Damon's special brew, but something is not right. Would you like to try a cup?"

"I'd love a cup but let me tell you a secret. I know the recipe for Damon's secret brew. He's been making this for years. I don't think he knows I have the recipe. We'll keep this between us for now. Even his mother doesn't realize I am aware of how to brew it. She usually says something is different, but I've observed him measure the beans by the ounce, and the exact volume of water he uses. His brew time is four and a half minutes. Anything less is too weak, and additional time makes it too strong."

"Well, let's drink a strong cup of his brew, then we'll try again. I could drink this coffee all day long. He made a thermos full and took it on our ride yesterday. We drank it in Brookgreen Gardens under the shade of a live oak. It was terribly romantic."

"Damon's a decent guy, Samantha. He's my son, so I am somewhat biased, but he is a brilliant doctor and a great friend. He will always treat you right."

"Thanks, John. By the way, I called the ICU this morning. There has been no change in his condition. He is running a low-grade fever and has not regained consciousness. There is drainage from the wound, but his circulation appears to be good right now. There is still edema in the lower extremity, but that's it. The nurse said the three of us could visit at the same time."

"I appreciate the update, Samantha."

"Did you get enough rest last night?"

"The doctor in me ran through every scenario that could go wrong, and the father in me tried to reassure the doctor that everything would be fine. I realize he is in excellent hands, and the entire hospital staff will do everything they can to help in his recovery. Still, it is difficult for the father in me. Do your parents live nearby?"

"No. When I was a child, my parents divorced. My father chose not to stay in contact with me or my mother. My mother remarried years ago, and they live on the west coast. It's difficult to travel that far when I'm working. We talk periodically, but I've been gone for years, and we've grown apart."

"I'm sorry, Samantha. Let's try that coffee again. I could use another cup and I heard Abagail up and moving. She'll want coffee as well."

"That sounds good."

Samantha's phone rang. "Excuse me, John. It's Abbie. I'm going to take this call."

"Hey, Abbie. How are you?"

"I'm all right. How are you? Did you get rest?"

"Yes, I did. I talked to the ICU this morning. There has been no change in his condition."

"Alex called as well. I'm sorry there has been no improvement, but it does not sound as though there are any further complications."

"No. That's a good thing. What are you up to today?"

"Alex was going to bring the dogs up around one o'clock. I considered bringing the kids and lunch as well. You have a lot on your plate, so I made meals for you that you can put in the freezer and heat up when you are too tired or busy to cook."

"That sounds great. Can you fit in one vehicle?"

"No, but Alex is going to park the SUV at the hospital after he drops off the dogs, and I'll bring the van. I'll run him to work in the morning."

"I'll check my schedule and see when I can fit Andy in after school this week. You can pick the days that work best. Kate and Julie are up as well. I'm going to see if anyone wants breakfast, and I will see you this afternoon. Julie will doubtless call you to see what you made for meals. By the time I get back from the hospital, I'll have enough food for the entire month."

"I'm sure. See you soon."

CHAPTER 8

Samantha and Julie fixed breakfast and cleaned up the kitchen. At 10:45 a.m., Samantha, John, and Abagail went outside and walked to the hospital across the street. Families of the patients in the ICU were waiting in the ICU waiting room when they arrived. The nurse called each family when it was their turn to enter the ICU and gave an update of the patient's condition.

Damon's nurse called for his family, and the three of them entered the ICU suite. Samantha became sick to her stomach at the thought of Damon's condition. She held back and walked behind John and Abagail. She crossed her arms in front of her to keep anyone from seeing her hands shake.

Damon was lying on his right side with all the IVs and tubes in place. The nurse gave an update from her call this morning. His temperature was now higher than this morning, but nothing to worry over. Samantha noted a small bag of antibiotics running through his IV line. Tobin had made it clear yesterday that infection was a concern because of the large amount of road debris present in the wound.

Abagail took Damon's hand in hers and wiped tears that ran down her face with her opposite hand. She whispered to him. John held on to his left hand and bent over to place a kiss on his forehead. Samantha stood, wishing her mother could be here. She needed her support, but the distance between them prevented that support from being within her reach. Her crew was always there for her, but she missed the love and support of her mother. She needed to be the stronger person and reach out to her mother. Watching John and Abagail with Damon made her miss the closeness she once had with her mother.

Abagail turned from Damon's bed and noticed Samantha standing outside the cubicle. She walked out into the corridor and took Samantha's hand.

"Damon needs you, Samantha. John and I promised him yesterday that we would support the two of you. Go be with him. Our time is limited, and we promised to share that time with you."

Samantha nodded, and they walked into the cubicle.

John nodded, kissed Damon's forehead again, and turned to leave the room.

"Damon, it's me. I'm right here holding your hand. You're doing okay, and your friends and staff at the hospital are praying for you. Your parents are staying at the house with me, so we are just across the street."

"Thank you for looking out for me yesterday. Everything happened so fast that I did not realize until you came out of surgery yesterday what you had sacrificed for me. I can never repay you for saving my life, but I promise you, I will be right here as you heal, no matter what it takes. We have a long road ahead of us."

"How does someone fall in love so fast, Damon? And I'm not asking that because of the accident. Even before then, I realized you are my heart. You are what I have looked for in a partner. I'm not sure if you can understand what I am saying to you, but I will be here until every part of you has recovered, until every wound has mended."

The nurse entered the cubicle to let them know they had just two minutes left to visit. Samantha kissed Damon's cheek and stepped back to let his parents back into the cubicle. When their two minutes expired, they walked together toward the door and across the street to the house.

Damon's nurse repositioned him in the bed and straightened his covers. She checked his IV lines and turned the light out in the room so that he might rest. Intensive care units were busy places. Patients sometimes lost track of time and had difficulty determining day from night. Right now, he needed rest.

Damon heard someone moan. He tried to open his eyes, but they were not cooperating. He was unsure of where he was at that moment. Maybe he was dreaming. Was that Samantha's voice he was hearing? Or was it his mother's voice? Why couldn't he tell who was speaking to him? He was tired. His head hurt. So did his chest and his leg. He must have the flu because he felt hot. It was most likely a fever, and every part of his body hurt. He thought he smelled his father's cologne. He needed sleep. He was too tired to figure out what was going on. He gave up and drifted off to sleep.

"Samantha, what time are Abbie and Alex arriving?"

"Around 1:00 pm, Abagail."

"John and I are going to rest in our room. Do you need help with anything, Samantha?"

"No, Abagail. Enjoy your rest. I may stretch out as well. Kate and Julie know where everything is in the house. Just ask if there is something you need."

Kate and Julie had prepared drinks and set the table for lunch, then went outside to sit on the front porch. They sent Samantha off to her room.

Samantha fell asleep instantly and woke up when she heard Andy talking with Julie and Kate on the front porch. She freshened up in the master bath and pulled her hair into a high bun. When she walked out the door to the porch, Andy stood up and smiled at her. He walked over to her and wrapped her in a big hug.

"Sam, I'm sorry Dr. Parker is not well. I made him a get-well card. Could you bring this to him when you go to the hospital later today, please? Dad said he is not allowed to have flowers in the ICU, but the nurses might let me give him a card and they might put it where he will see it."

"Thank you, Andy. I am sure Dr. Parker will love it, and yes, I will take it to him later today when I visit."

"Can you tell him to get better soon? We are planning to play catch, and I haven't had time to use my new mitt that he bought for me."

"I will tell him that as well, Andy."

"Mom said you and I might do therapy this week. Do you know what days?"

"Let's look at my schedule before you leave today."

"Thanks, Sam."

"Where's your dad and the dogs, Andy?"

"They were right behind us. Dad helped mom and I get my sisters in their seats. He should be here soon."

John and Abagail came out the front door. Samantha introduced them to Andy.

"Andy, I'd like you to meet Dr. John Parker and Mrs. Parker. They are Damon's parents."

"Nice to meet you, Dr., and Mrs. Parker. I'm sorry Dr. Parker got hurt in the accident and I hope he gets better soon."

"Thank you, Andy. You may call us John and Abagail. Are these your new sisters?"

"They sure are. Do you want to meet them?"

"Yes, please."

"This one is Isabella. She likes to cuddle with me. She smiles all the time. Well, she cries sometimes when she is hungry or needs her diaper changed, but otherwise she is happy. This one is Annabella, and she likes to sleep. She likes to be held as well, and she likes our dogs, too. Gabriella is here, and she gets grouchy sometimes when she is tired or hungry. As soon as you feed her, she just smiles."

"They are incredibly beautiful little girls, and you are a wonderful, handsome older brother. You look very much like your father."

"People tell me I look like dad. Mom says I'm going to break hearts when I get older. I'm not sure what that means, but Dr. Conor O'Brien is a heart doctor, so maybe I will ask him what she means."

"I'm sure he will tell you how to avoid breaking hearts. He's nearly as handsome as you, and I bet he broke hearts when he was young."

"Oh, look. Here comes dad with the dogs. I'll introduce you to them, too."

Alex stopped in the driveway and let the dogs off their leash and told them, "No running."

Kohl led the way and trotted the rest of the distance to the porch. He went straight to Samàntha, and she laid Kohl's head on her lap. She bent to whisper in his ear, and he looked up and smiled at her.

Koko and Kody looked around and noticed John and Abagail. They walked toward the two of them and sat at their feet. Andy walked over to the dogs and introduced them to the Parkers. Both dogs lifted their paws to shake hands with the Parkers.

Their size frightened Abagail, but John shook their hands and talked to both Koko and Kody.

"Dr. Parker, Sam and I are going to do therapy this week in the pool. Maybe you and Mrs. Parker can watch my therapy session, and you can see how the dogs help people with their therapy. Kohl loves the water and likes to show off to everybody. He and I are best friends, and he's helping me learn to walk again, and we thrilled the doctors with my progress."

"Thank you for the invitation, Andy. We'd love to watch your therapy session. Samantha, can you tell us the date and time, please?"

"Abbie and I will check the schedule after lunch. I think I'll head inside and get lunch on the table."

"Samantha, can the dogs and I play in the backyard until lunch is ready?"

"Yes, Andy, you may. We'll tell you when it's time to eat."

John stood. "Andy, may I join you and the dogs for a round of catch?"

"Sure, Dr. Parker. That will be fun. Dad, do you want to join us?"

"I join you in just a minute or two."

Alex filled the dogs' food and water bowls. He wanted to take the girls outside with him, but Abagail, Kate, and Julie would not give them to him.

"Go outside, Alex. You get them every day. Kate and I need our last-minute snuggle time with your girls before we go home this afternoon."

Abbie smiled at him and blew him a kiss. He shook his head and opened the back door.

"How are you and Abagail doing, John? How's Damon?"

"We're okay, Alex. Damon has a low-grade fever, but no other major changes. The doctors were to schedule CT scans today, according to the nurse. We'll learn more on our visit later today. He's not tried to wake up yet, but that might change as well. Thank you again for everything you have done for him."

"I'm sorry we are in this spot, John. Damon and I have become friends since I started at the hospital, and he and Samantha appear to get along well."

"I'm worried about his fever, Alex. I've said nothing to Abagail, but I still think he may need his leg amputated. She is adamant that saving his leg is necessary, but I'm more realistic when considering his overall health. I pray Tobin can keep the infection at bay."

"John, I have concerns as well. Damon appeared to be aware there might be an issue, or he wouldn't have asked me to promise not to amputate. I clarified with him that we may not be able to save it. But we'll keep an eye on the progress before making a rash decision."

"I agree with you, Alex, but I believe Abagail and Samantha will team up against us. Do you know how long Tobin is planning to stay?"

"He planned to stay for two weeks but while Conor and I were in the operating theater during the surgery, Conor thought he might extend his stay by a couple of weeks. I'd love to see him stick around until Damon is stable, awake, and able to make his own decisions."

"He's as stubborn as his mother and has always had her wrapped around his little finger. She will default to his wishes, even if she does not agree with him."

Abbie walked outside to the porch and announced lunch was ready. Andy came in and washed up and told the dogs to rest on the back porch. Abbie had made a vegetarian lasagna, as well as a salad, and fresh rolls. She was unsure of John and Abagail's food preferences and decided this meal was an excellent choice for everyone.

Abagail took one bite of the lasagna and moaned. "Abbie, this is the best veggie lasagna I have ever eaten."

"Thanks, Abagail. Kate, Julie, Dana, Sam, and I taught ourselves to cook when we were in college. We have our favorites we made then, but I lean more toward a plant-based diet than the others. Alex is tolerant of my cooking, but I will include meats he enjoys. Andy's favorite foods are burgers and fries. I suspect he will expand his food choices as he ages and gets more of the foods I cook."

Alex chuckled. "Not only are they beautiful, but they also cook like trained chefs. But they are bossy too, so don't let them fool you. They don't have too many flaws, but they have some."

The ladies started talking at once to defend themselves against Alex's comments. John looked at Abagail and smiled, and they noticed Andy roll his eyes.

"Dr. and Mrs. Parker. They talk this way all the time, so you might need to get used to it. Dad says the prettier they are, the louder they talk, and sometimes he makes me leave the room, because he says they are out of control."

John tried not to laugh, and Abagail hid her laugh behind her napkin. "Thanks for the warning, Andy. If you have any tips on what we need to do, just let us know."

"Dr. Julie says they are adults, and they should just do what makes them happy."

Alex looked over at Julie and Abbie and raised his eyebrows, then shook his head. He was going to remind them again that

Andy's little ears heard everything they said, and his little mouth had no filter, so unless they are willing to be embarrassed in front of a crowd of people, they need to be more aware of who is listening.

"We'll see how that works out for them, Andy. In the meantime, if you need someone to hang out with during one of their conversations, call me. I'm sure we can find something to keep ourselves busy."

"Thanks, Dr. Parker. I'll get your cell number from Sam."

They finished lunch, cleaned up the dining room and kitchen, changed and fed the girls, and settled out on the front porch again. Abbie and Samantha reviewed her schedule and put Andy on the schedule for two days this week and three days next week. The dogs lay on the porch near Abagail. Although she was apprehensive, she warmed up to their size. Kate and Julie gathered their belongings and packed their cars. They said goodbye to everyone and gave one last group hug to Samantha and Abbie.

Kate turned back to Samantha before getting in her car. "I'll set up a call for tomorrow after the last visiting session. That will be easier than calling everyone. In the meantime, call if you need us."

Samantha blew her a kiss and wiped tears from her face once again.

The evening visitation period neared, so Alex and Abbie gathered their children and their belongings and got everyone settled into the van.

"John, I'll reach out to you tomorrow. Sam's going to put my cell number in your phone. Call with questions, and if I don't have the answer, I'll do my best to get it for you."

It was a nice evening when it was time to leave for hospital visiting hours. Samantha and the Parkers walked to the hospital.

The nurse let them in and gave them an update. Damon's fever was higher than it was earlier today. She had medicated him an hour ago and planned to check it again soon. He still had not opened his eyes or made any sign that indicated he was aware of events happening around him.

Samantha hung back again and let his parents go first. When it was her time, she took his hand and gave him a synopsis of the day and everyone who gathered at the house. The dogs looked for him, and she told them he would be home soon.

Damon tried to open his eyes. He thought he heard Samantha's voice again, but why was she so far away? No, it was his mother speaking. Why was he so exhausted? Every part of his body hurt, and he couldn't find the energy to figure it out. He needed to get himself awake and needed something for a headache, and he thought he could smell his father's cologne again. He was so hot. If he could just get awake, he could get medicine and turn on a fan. He smiled when he remembered riding down the highway with Samantha. They cruised on the open road, and the breeze cooled him. He was no longer overheated. He glanced at the sky. The sun was out and there were no clouds. It must be the sun beating down on him that was causing him to overheat. They could stop at a local fuel station and grab a bottle of water. Sam had ibuprofen in her purse, as she always prepared for the unexpected. She was beautiful, and just what he needed. If he could wake up, everything would be perfect.

CHAPTER 9

Samantha woke up on Monday morning to her alarm. Rarely did she need to set an alarm. Typically, she was already awake and ready to go by 6:00 a.m. She was still a bit sore from her fall off the bike and exhausted from the emotional turmoil of Damon's injuries. One way or another, she would make it through the day.

She looked forward to seeing Andy tomorrow, but her patients today were challenges. They expected her to do the work and lacked the patience needed to recover from their injuries. Everyone wanted to swim with the dogs, and they did not comprehend when she tried to explain the differences in therapy.

The hydrotherapy program had taken off, and when she and Abbie had finished their first trial period and had proven to the board and therapy company that the hydrotherapy program was effective in reducing pain, and improving range of motion, both of which lead to improved outcomes, they were off and running.

She finally got out of bed, showered, and dressed. John was up and, in the kitchen, making coffee. As soon as she smelled the coffee, she felt the tears starting. She missed Damon and wanted him to be here with her.

John noticed the tear in the corner of her eye but said nothing. He lifted his arm and held out his other hand with a cup of steaming coffee for Samantha and gave her a hug.

"I know how you are feeling, Samantha. Neither Abagail nor I are sleeping well, and the exhaustion is catching up with us, too."

"I'm sorry, John. I am not trying to make this any more difficult on either of you, but I am concerned that he is still not awake."

"Your concerns are valid, Samantha. Let me text Alex and see if he can get us more information. Are you going to do the 11:00 o'clock visit today?"

"I have a client, but I should be able to make the 3:00 p.m. visit. Could you stop in and give me an update after this morning's visit?"

"Of course. I am hoping the CT scans show improvement. Since we did not receive a phone call during the night, I hope that his fever is at baseline, and we'll see additional improvements today as well."

The dogs were standing at the back door, and Samantha let them inside. She gave a round of hugs and filled their food and water dishes.

"Thanks for letting the dogs out this morning, John."

"My pleasure. It is nice having them here to greet me in the morning. They brighten my day. They have outstanding personalities. Kohl is definitely the leader of the pack."

Samantha chuckled. "He is the alpha dog, but he is the sweetest of the group, or it might be because we have been friends longer and know each other so much better."

Samantha grabbed leftovers out of the refrigerator and tossed them into her lunch bag. She picked up two pieces of fruit and added those as well. She was not hungry, but she needed to eat to sustain her energy for the long days ahead.

"Alex is going to check in on Damon and call me in a while. I need to exercise this morning, so if it is okay with you, I'll join you and the dogs on your walk to the hospital. Does the sidewalk go the entire way around the building?"

"It does, John. The staff uses it to get steps in on their breaks."

"I'll send Abagail a text message. I don't want her to worry about where I've gone off to this morning. I'll be happy if I can get in a couple of miles at least and try to get back to normal."

The dogs appeared eager to get moving and sat facing the door, waiting for Samantha. They walked to the therapy building and John promised again to fill Samantha in on Damon's condition as soon as he received the information.

Alex and Andy gathered their backpacks and kissed Abbie and the three girls goodbye.

"What's on your agenda today, Abbie?"

"Not too much. Sam and I need to look at a bigger place for the hydrotherapy program. There are so many referrals that we can't accommodate. I'm going to check around while the girls take their nap and see what is out there."

"What are the chances of a building with a pool or pools being available?"

"My guess is zero. We may need to consider building a new therapy complex."

"Are you sure you are ready and able to take on a project of that size, Abbie? There are tons of regulations that go into building a medical building. You may have a tough fight on your hands."

"Are you saying it's a lousy idea, Montgomery?"

Alex sighed inwardly. Every time she used his last name while talking with him, she began to feel defensive. It was a leftover defense mechanism from her foster home days.

"No love. I am not saying it's a lousy idea. I'm warning you that the regulations are outrageous, and you need to be prepared to fight city hall, as the saying goes."

"I will be well prepared to fight, Alex. Have a good day and see if you can get Damon to wake up and open his eyes."

"That's a tall order, Abbie, but I will see what I can do."

Alex dropped Andy off at school and checked into the ER. There were only four patients this morning, so he told the nurse practitioner he was going to the ICU to check on Dr. Parker.

Catherine, the ICU nurse, waved to Alex from Damon's cubicle, and he walked over to room six.

"How's it going this morning? Damon's father asked me to check in and to give him an update."

"Sorry, Dr. Montgomery. I have been terribly busy this morning and have not had time to give his parents a call. Unfortunately, his fever is up, and his breathing is rapid and shallow. The lab was here and drew blood cultures, and X-ray is scheduled to do a portable chest x-ray to see if he's developing pneumonia. I don't think this antibiotic works. I called Dr. Tobin O'Brien, and he said he was coming in. He should be here any time. Dr. Parker is still unconscious. We have been talking to him and asking him questions related to Dr. D'Alessandro. We thought hearing her name might wake him up, but no such luck. Respiratory therapy did a breathing treatment, but it made extraordinarily little change in his breathing."

"Were the CT scans of his head, chest, and leg completed yesterday?"

"CT was not working yesterday. My understanding is they got the part they needed and are up and running again. I need to get him stabilized before sending him over to get that done this morning. There will be no respiratory arrest today on my shift if can be avoided."

"I am in complete agreement with you. Let me give them a call and see how backed up they are over there. I've got a feeling that my shift in the ER is going to be affected by this backup as well."

"I'm sorry I don't have better news for you, Dr. Montgomery. I'm aware you and your wife are good friends with Dr. Parker and Dr. D'Alessandro. I'll give his parents a call."

"I'll call them Catherine. You have enough to keep you busy. They will be in for the 11:00 a.m. visit. It would be great if we can get things moving in a better direction by the time they arrive."

"I hope so, Dr. Montgomery."

"Thanks for everything you are doing for him and thank the other staff as well. I'm here until 3:00 p.m., if you need anything at all. I hope your day gets better."

As Alex exited the ICU, Tobin and Conor O'Brien walked up to the door.

"Hey, Alex. What's happening in there?"

"It seems Damon is developing a fever and shortness of breath, but I'm not sure where it originates. It might be from the leg wound or if he could be developing pneumonia. The CT scanner was out of commission yesterday as well, and they did not get the repeat scans that were ordered. The nurse is hoping to get him stable before sending him over this morning."

"Not what I wanted to hear. I'm going to check in on him and I'll catch up with you later. Is Samantha working today?"

"She planned to work today. Dana is in the ER this morning. She will know where she is if you want to speak to her."

"Sounds good. I'll see you shortly. Thanks for checking in on him this morning."

Alex left the ICU and walked back to the ER, preparing himself for questions from Dana. She would ask for an update as well. He liked having her as his director of nursing, but her friendship with Abbie and Samantha put him in a tough position. HIPAA guidelines prevented him from providing her with information, so she would need to get the information from Damon's parents or Samantha, since they had given her permission to receive the information they received. The five of them were aware of the laws. He did not need to remind them of the rules. They were going to need to rely on Samantha's or Damon's parents for updates.

The ER activity was slow, so Alex walked over to the coffee pot. He missed the early morning banter with Damon. Abbie, Samantha, Dana, Kate, and Julie were equivalent to sisters, and they shared nearly everything that went on in their lives. If one of them was sick or going through a tough spot, they essentially dropped everything to help one another. Damon had become somewhat of a brother to him. Alex fit into the group that the ladies had developed. Once they learned to trust him, he became one of their group members. They did the same with Damon. Tobin and Conor were on the precipice of becoming part of the group as well.

The one thing he and Abbie rarely spoke about was his parents. Abbie was raised in a foster home, so she only had her foster parents. He became estranged with his parents after the accident that killed Maria, and he decided to hit the road with Andy. They were angry with him because he chose to take Andy from them soon after Maria died. Maria's parents were angry with him as well. Both sets of parents would be thrilled to know there were three identical little girls who had recently joined the family. He needed to find a way to make amends and let his parents get to know their grandchildren.

He had not discussed calling his parents with Abbie. He doubted she would have any issues with meeting his parents. They were not awful people, just angry that he decided to move his life in a direction with which they did not agree. They did not recognize how Maria's death had affected him. He did not recognize how her death had affected him until he met Abbie. She was the catalyst that changed everything for him and Andy.

Alex vowed he would go to his grave knowing that Kohl was solely responsible for Andy being able to walk again, and Andy was the reason that Kohl had begun to heal after Tom's death. They were meant to be together. He would never admit to Abbie that he believed the run in with Kohl on the beach was fate. Most people did not believe in fate. He believed in it extraordinarily little this past year, but that dog was put in his path for a reason. Sure, Kohl huffed at him occasionally, but he was forever thankful for that morning on the beach.

Dana entered the doctor's area and asked after Damon. Alex shrugged his shoulders.

"You know HIPAA regulations prevent me from telling you what is going on with him, Dana. Tobin is going to talk to his parents once he figures out what is going on, then someone will inform Sam as well. Tobin should be here shortly. Be patient. We'll know soon enough. He has a tough, long road before him. Despite our best efforts, there will be challenges along the way. Damon is lucky to be alive, and if he had not shoved Sam from the bike, I agree with Sam that one of them most likely would not have survived."

"When did she make that statement, Alex?"

"After she saw him in the ICU the night of the accident. Once she had the chance to understand the extent of his injuries, she knew that Damon's actions that night were done to save both from being killed in the accident. She knows he sacrificed his life for her, and that is something that not everyone can understand, or live with, Dana. If he survives, they have a long road ahead of them. Right now, she is trying to come to terms with the fact that he cared for her enough to give up his life for her. If he survives, they both need to figure out if they can live with that decision."

Dana stood silently and nodded her head. "Working in the emergency department is a tough job, Alex. We pray every day that the next person coming through that door is not one of our loved ones. Sometimes our friends are closer to us than our families. These events either bring us closer together or break us. None of us knows what's coming next. I will do everything I can to help the five of us and our friends survive this tragedy."

"Can I ask you something, Dana?"

"Sure, Alex, what's going on in that brain of yours?"

"How often do you talk to your parents?"

"Not as often as I should. What about you?"

"Same, Dana. Not as often as I should."

"Maybe it's time to get rid of old habits, Alex."

"I agree with you, Dana. By the way, do you know if Sam is working today?"

"She is supposed to be working. Why do you ask?"

"Tobin asked. He is planning to talk to her after he figures out what is going on with Damon."

"Thanks, Alex. I think I'll call my parents tonight after my shift. We certainly are not able to predict what the next minute is bringing us."

"That sounds like a great idea, Dana. I hope they are doing well."

Dana walked back to the nurse's station and noticed Conor O'Brien leaning on the counter.

"Hey Dr. O'Brien. What brings you in today?"

"Two things, Dana. Are you free to grab dinner this evening? Things have been crazy busy at the hospital, I need to relax this evening, and I'd like to spend time with you."

"Dinner sounds great. Anywhere in particular?"

"I was thinking of something overlooking the ocean. Casual, and laid back. I'll pick you up around 7:00 p.m."

"That sounds perfect. I'm looking forward to it. Thanks, Conor. What was the second thing?"

"Is Samantha working today? I did a cardiology consult on Damon. I just want to let her know everything is fine."

"She is. Let me text her and see if she is free."

Dana sent the text.

"She's free, Conor. Once you enter the building, make a right and you will see her office on the left."

"Thanks, Dana. You will probably see Tobin come through here next. He will want to update Samantha as well. See you this evening."

Damon tried to open his eyes, but they would not cooperate. He felt as though he was going through a tunnel. He could hear people talking but could not recognize the voices. He needed to call Samantha and check on her. It felt like forever since he'd talked to her. He thought he overheard Alex asking a nurse questions. Someone had an infection. She rattled off the things she had done to find the underlying cause of the issue. She seemed to be knowledgeable. Fever, rapid shallow breathing, blood cultures, and CT scans. The test he would order to decide what the next steps should be in the patient's plan of care.

Wait! Did he hear the nurse refer to Samantha as Dr. D'Alessandro? He chucked to himself. Sometimes he forgot that

Samantha was a doctor as well. She was beautiful and kind. He was falling in love with her, but it might be too soon to tell her. He loved her dogs, too. They were big and slobbered frequently, and they loved Samantha.

He laughed when Kohl huffed at Alex. It was Kohl's way of dismissing Alex, and sometimes he did the same thing to Abbie.

They had the cutest little girls. Would he and Samantha have little girls one day as well? Samantha was very independent; he was not sure if she was even interested in having children. He needed to introduce her to his parents. His mother was never going to settle for just a phone call, but he knew she'd settle for either grandsons or granddaughters. She would not be fussy when it came to his babies.

Sometimes he wished he had siblings. He often felt like Alex was becoming like a brother to him. They worked very well together and laughed at the crazy things Abbie and Samantha thought up on a normal day. How they concocted the hydrotherapy program he could never figure out, but they managed to convince the hospital board, so good for them. The program was doing extremely well.

This tunnel was sucking his breath right out of him. He was having trouble breathing. How did he get into a tunnel? He felt overheated again as well, and he was too dang tired to figure it out. He bet Samantha could tell him where the tunnel was located. If he could just find his phone, he could call her and find a way to get out.

CHAPTER 10

John had just completed a two-mile walk around the hospital when his phone rang. Alex's number appeared, and John hoped Alex had good news. He was concerned with the bleeding on the left side of Damon's brain.

"Hey Alex. Thanks for checking back in with me."

"Good morning, John. I'm afraid I don't have good news."

John received a report from Alex of the issues Damon was facing this morning, including treatments completed, and those still outstanding.

"That's genuinely concerning, Alex. Thanks for the update. I'll give Samantha and Abagail an update face-to-face. This isn't something I should tell them over the phone. In your opinion, is the leg the issue? I'm wondering if an amputation might still be the answer."

"I'm not sure where the infection originates. I say let's wait for the test results. Tobin stopped in the ER and said that he may need to go back on a ventilator if his oxygen saturation drops any further. It was an encouraging idea to take him off the ventilator early this morning, but it looks like he is going to need it a bit longer. Are you okay with that?"

"Sure, Alex. Whatever he needs."

"Tobin ordered a pulmonary consultation. The group we have is excellent, but if you'd like to consult with a different outside group, that will be fine with everyone."

"Nobody has given me a reason to search elsewhere, Alex. For now, I'll trust your judgement. I'll stop next door, and update Samantha."

John walked the remainder of the way around the building and entered the therapy complex. Samantha was in her office and had just poured a cup of coffee. She had finished her notes on her last client when John knocked on her door.

"John, come in. Can I get you coffee? It doesn't match Damon's, but it's caffeine."

"No more coffee for me this morning, but I'll take a bottle of water if you have one available."

She reached into her refrigerator and grabbed a bottle. "Any update on Damon's condition?"

John nodded while taking a drink of water. "I'm afraid I don't have good news, Samantha."

"What's wrong, John?"

John filled her in on the events of the morning and the outstanding test. Just as he finished explaining the details, his phone rang.

"It's Tobin. I need to take his call."

Samantha had no time to respond or ask questions before John's phone rang. She walked out to the corridor and paced while John was on the phone. She overheard him say, "I understand. No, you have our permission. Thanks. We'll be in at 11:00 a.m. We'll see you then."

John turned toward Samantha, and she noticed his hands were shaking. She was going to be sick. She was instantly aware that something was happening with Damon.

"John, what's happening? That call was regarding Damon, correct?"

"His breathing has worsened, and he his chest x-ray is showing left lower lobe pneumonia. Tobin spoke with the pulmonologist, and they added an antibiotic, but he needs to be intubated again, Samantha. He is struggling to breathe, and his vital signs are elevated. I need to go to the house and update Abagail on his condition."

Samanta nodded her head to show she understood but said nothing. She was trying to process the information John had given her, and this was news she was not expecting.

"Will you be okay here by yourself? Do you want me to call someone for you?"

"I'll be okay. I'll call Abbie, and my next client will be here in a couple minutes. Go update Abagail on Damon's condition."

"I'll be in to update you after the 11:00 a.m. visit. Call me if you need something."

Samantha nodded again and reached for her phone. She found Abbie's number and hit the send button.

Abbie answered on the first ring. "Hey, I've been thinking of you. How are things this morning?"

Samantha began spewing out all the information from John's visit and Abbie barely understood her through the tears.

"Sam, stop. Stop talking. Where are you?"

"I'm standing in my office."

The dogs could hear her distress and came to stand by her side. Kohl leaned into her, and she rubbed his big head. Koko and Kody sat next to Kohl, the three of them acting as her protectors.

"Okay. Sit down, Sam, and start over again. I need to understand everything you are saying, but I can't understand you through your tears. Start with John and tell me what he said."

Sam moved to her chair, sat, and started over again, and this time Abbie was able to comprehend what she was saying.

"Okay, Sam. Listen to me. This is not to be unexpected because of his lung injury and the chest tube to help re-inflate the lung. It's not working at full capacity yet and so his risk of pneumonia was extremely high. You know this, Sam. You need to take each issue into consideration and how it affects his recovery."

"I understand, Abbie, but I'm just so overwhelmed. I have a patient scheduled, and I needed to hear your voice. I need to go splash water on my face and get ready for the session. Can I call you when I'm done with this patient?"

"Absolutely. The girls are napping, and Ms. Helen and I are just sitting here folding laundry and talking. You call whenever you need."

"I worry you might be busy with the babies. I don't want to interrupt you."

"Listen, Sam. I have this mother thing figured out and I am getting good at holding babies and doing all the other things I need to get done. Ms. Helen and I work like a well-oiled machine. And you know that if I am busy, I will tell you and call you back as soon as possible."

"Thanks, Abbie. We'll talk soon."

"Call me as soon as you get another update."

Samantha hung up the phone. She freshened up in the ladies' room and put on a smile as her next patient came through the door. The dogs started wagging their tails at the patient but did not move from her side. They noticed her change of tone, but still felt her distress and did not want to leave her alone. She gave them a command to lie down, and they obeyed, but watched her closely during the time she was with her patient.

Samantha noticed John and Abagail enter the building and they waited in the corridor on a bench until she had finished with her client. Both had grim looks on their faces when they walked into her office.

The dogs joined them in the office and sat at Abagail's feet. She reached over and tried to pet each of them. She spoke to them, but her voice was quivering. Kohl licked her hand and Abagail tried to smile at him, but it was a wasted effort.

"Good morning, Abagail. The look on your face tells me there's been no improvement, John. Please tell me things aren't worse."

"There's been no further decline, but too soon to notice improvement, either. The vent has eased his breathing, and the plan is to get him off it as soon as possible. They haven't completed the CT scans yet either. They are waiting for him to stabilize before they complete the scan. I wish I had better news, Samantha."

Samantha nodded her head.

"I doubt there will be any major improvement in the next twenty-four to seventy-two hours, and I understand you are both as disappointed as I am. I want him to open his eyes and tell me he is okay. I am still overwhelmed by the extent of his injuries. Even though Alex was clear on everything that was happening the day of the accident, I was in shock and not fully comprehending everything that happened to Damon."

"I called Abbie right after you left, John, and she helped bring me back to reality and reminded me that as a doctor, I understand how the body reacts to injuries. I just didn't want to face reality with Damon. It's barely forty-eight hours since the accident. It feels like this has been going on for a long time."

"We understand, Abbie. John and I were just talking about the three-hour drive here. It seemed to take hours longer than it should have, and the past two days have felt like weeks. We appreciate you letting us stay with you. It is more convenient than staying in a hotel. How can we ever repay you?"

"No repayment necessary, Abagail. I'm grateful to have the company right now. That's payment enough. I'll be able to make a visit this afternoon. I have a client soon and want to take the dogs out before he arrives. You two rest and I'll catch up with you soon."

"We can take the dogs back to the house with us, Samantha. We aren't planning to go anywhere. They can relax in their own place, and I can play catch with them in the yard to keep the four of us occupied."

"Are you sure, John? Because they are used to being here, but I don't have hydrotherapy this afternoon, so they might enjoy the extra time at home."

"I need something to occupy my time, Samantha, and they help me get in some exercise in as well."

"Okay. Let me get their leashes. I appreciate your offer and they will be glad to have that playtime. They are fine to leave in the house when you come back over for visitation. I'll meet you in the waiting room outside the ICU at 3:00 p.m."

"By the way, tomorrow afternoon Andy will be here for his therapy session with Kohl. He'll be here after school. When we finish the afternoon visitation with Damon, we can meet back here, and you can watch how the dogs interact with Andy and get a better understanding of how the hydrotherapy program works."

"We're looking forward to it."

Samantha finished the session with her client and locked the office door. She entered the hospital and walked slowly toward the ICU. Alex waited for her in the corridor as she approached the waiting room.

"Please tell me you are just here to say hi. I can't take too much more unwelcome news, Doc."

"I just wanted to check in on you, Sam. Abbie wants an update about how you are doing. She'll see you tomorrow. She's going to pick up Andy from school and bring him for his appointment. I'll stop over after my shift."

"I'm hanging in there, Alex. I did not realize the extent of his injuries until I observed him in the ICU that first evening. And even though I knew there might be complications, I was praying his recovery might go smoother."

"There have certainly been bumps, Sam, but overall, with the condition of his leg and the injury to his lung, he's been hanging in there. Are you feeling, okay?"

"Still a bit sore, but the anti-inflammatories help, and I put together a stretching routine for myself as well. I will say I am glad to be able to go to bed at night."

"I'm sure you are, and the emotional toll adds to the exhaustion. I won't keep you any longer, Sam. I'm sure you are eager to visit him, and I'm glad you're doing well. Abbie will be happy that I have an update for her."

"I'm sure. She acts like my mother sometimes."

Alex chuckled. "Maybe with four kids of her own, she'll stop that behavior."

"Don't put money on that one, Alex. I'm sure you'll lose."

"Here comes Dr. and Mrs. Parker. I'll say hello to them, and I will see you tomorrow."

"Thanks for checking on me, Alex. I appreciate everything."

Samantha hugged Alex and leaned against the wall to wait for the Parkers. The nurse called their name, and they once again trudged into the ICU corridor to Damon's room.

Nothing had changed with Damon's condition in the past few hours. He still had a fever, and the ventilator was assisting his breathing. Samantha let the Parkers go into the cubicle first as she had been doing. It visibly shook Abagail at the sight of Damon on a ventilator again. John did his best to explain everything and to comfort her at the same time. As a cardiothoracic surgeon, John was used to seeing patients on a ventilator and tried to separate his concern from his son, like he had done with others he had experienced on a ventilator, but he was struggling too.

Abagail soon left the room and let Samantha be with Damon.

"Samantha, seeing him on the ventilator again is too much for Abagail right now. We'll meet you in the waiting room when you're done."

Samantha nodded her head and reached for Damon's hand. She stood silently to compose herself before she started talking to him. She closed her eyes and listened to the sound of the ventilator. The rhythmic hissing and whoosh of the machine helped her calm her nerves and rapid breathing.

She talked to Damon about the three dogs and told him about Abbie's plans to build a new therapy complex. She informed him his father was going to Pete's Garage to look at his motorcycle and check the condition it was in after the accident. He planned to have it repaired if possible, and if not, he would bring it back to her place and store it in the garage.

She told him Andy made a get-well card for him and told him where she put it up on the wall so he could see it once he gained consciousness. She described to him Andy's observation of his little sisters and how much he enjoyed taking care of them. The dogs loved them too. Andy waited patiently for him to get better so they could play catch with the new mitt he bought for him. His dad enjoyed playing catch with the dogs and he and Andy were planning on a game of catch after Andy's therapy appointment tomorrow.

She chuckled when she explained that his parents were getting used to the size of the dogs, and described how his mother was apprehensive at first, but was finally warming up to the three of them. Both of his parents were stopping over tomorrow to watch Kohl and Andy during their therapy session. His dad was extremely interested in how she and Abbie put together the program, and he wanted to understand the details.

Samantha told Damon she had figured out how to make his special brew and she could not wait to make it for him once he received permission to drink coffee again. She talked of their trip to Brookgreen Gardens and the bracelets they bought in Charleston. She was still wearing hers, and she had given extremely specific instructions to Alex and the other physicians that his matching bracelet was not to be removed, either.

The nurse came into the cubicle to tell her visiting hours were over for the afternoon. She kissed Damon's cheek, told him she loved him, and would come back to check on him later that evening and kissed him again.

Damon smelled Samantha's perfume. It smelled warm, and sexy, and comforting. It smelled like her. He was struggling to get his eyes open and decided she must have slipped into bed next to him, and he smiled, knowing she was close by his side.

He was still overheated but could breathe easier. His leg was killing him, and his head and chest hurt, too. He would ask Samantha to bring him two anti-inflammatory capsules. He heard her mention his special brew of coffee, and his mouth watered. He would love to have a sip of coffee right now. It might help relieve his headache.

Damon wondered if the air conditioner stopped working. Perhaps that's why he was so hot. He had not tried to make his special coffee brew as an iced coffee, but he planned to do that as soon as he began feeling better. If he had a way to get a cold coffee right now, that might help cool him off. He loved the south, but dang, there were so many days the humidity was suffocating, and today was one of those days.

Damon wanted to get better so he and Samantha could go for a ride on the bike. He loved having her on his bike. He loved feeling her next to him and the way she liked to wrap her arms around his middle. Their headsets let them talk if they wanted, without needing to shout at one another. Most of the time, they were quiet and listened to the music or just the sounds of the world around them as they made their way down the highway.

Damon admitted to himself that he was falling in love with her. She called him a player and refused to date him at first, but she finally came around, and he was so happy that she did. He wanted this to be a permanent thing for them and hoped she had the same feelings. Suddenly, he felt lightheaded. Had someone had given him pain medication via an IV? He knew that feeling. What the heck was happening?

There was no change in Damon's condition at the evening visitation. Samantha talked about their friends and her workday. She hoped that hearing her voice might make Damon open his eyes. But that was not happening this evening.

When visiting hours were over, and she and the Parkers made their way back to the house, everyone was quiet. Sam grabbed a bottle of water out of the fridge and took the dogs to the back yard to chase the ball. Kohl was quieter this evening too, and Samantha wondered if he was noticing her emotions. She would need to try harder when he was around. Tomorrow will be a good day. Her schedule was lighter, and Andy would be at the pool after school for his session.

The dogs wore themselves out, and Samantha let them inside and gave them all fresh water. The Parkers had retired to their room when they returned from visiting Damon. She was weary too and went to her room to get ready for bed. The dogs followed her, and she decided to let them sleep on the floor in her room tonight. Kohl would rest easier if he could be near her, and there was no harm in letting them sleep near her on occasion.

She slid into bed and reached for a book on her nightstand. Reading helped her to relax. She barely made it through two pages, and she was having difficulty holding her eyes open. She laid the book on the nightstand, and her phone pinged with a text message. It was Alex letting her know he had checked on Damon and there was no improvement, but no decline either. She thanked him. No decline was a small victory, and she would take the small victories.

John was awake and, in the kitchen the next morning. This was becoming their routine. He had coffee ready for her and handed her a cup. The dogs were still outside. She had not heard them get up and leave her room. She had not shut the door to the bedroom last night in case Kohl decided to move to his own bed.

"What are you up to today, John?"

"I am going to go to Pete's garage and check on Damon's bike. Do you know where the keys to the truck are? I thought I would use it in case I am able to bring the bike home."

"I think he leaves them on the floorboard when it is in the garage."

"Abagail wants to go with me, but I am not sure what condition the bike is in. This has been affecting her more than I expected."

"Well, he is your only child, and I have heard mothers are often more sensitive to these types of situations. I hope I never need to find out."

"I hope that for you as well, Samantha. He's always been a bit of a daredevil, especially during his teen years, but he settled down when he went to med school."

"There was nothing he did that put us in jeopardy on Saturday, John. We have gone on a couple of other rides, and he always obeys every rule. The Myrtle Beach area is a tough area for bikers. The traffic is horrible during tourist season, and people will cross over four lanes of traffic with no regard to anyone else, just because they don't want to miss a turn. Add alcohol to that mix, and it can be a deadly combination. It's sad that so many vacations are ruined because of that combination. The locals know the risk of an accident is high during the season, and therefore try to be more tolerant of the increased traffic. If we could find a way to keep intoxicated drivers off the roads, the number of deaths would plummet. Unfortunately, Damon and I were hit by a local who thought he could make it home without getting caught."

"Abagail and I are going to take a walk on the beach this morning after we get back from the garage and visit Damon. We need to get out of the house for a little while."

"That sounds like a good idea."

Samantha called for the dogs and got their leashes on and grabbed her lunch from the fridge.

"Will you stop in and give me an update, John?"

"Absolutely, Samantha. See you around 11:20 am."

Samantha had an early client who helped pass the time. Before she knew it, John and Abagail were knocking on her door.

"Wow, I lost track of time. How's Damon?"

"His fever is down, and they repeated the chest x-ray. It is already showing improvement. The pulmonologist is hoping they can wean him off the ventilator tomorrow and see how he does. The drainage from the leg wound has decreased as well, and his nurse said there was less swelling on his leg measurements this morning."

"Thank you for the good news. We all needed to hear something positive. Maybe he will open his eyes soon too. Did you get his bike this morning, John?"

"The bike cannot be repaired, Samantha. I called his insurance company and gave them the information about the accident, then called Officer Todd to send the accident report to them. I took photos. I'm not sure if you really want to see them, Samantha. They are quite disturbing."

Samantha looked toward Abagail and saw tears in her eyes. "I'll look, John, and I am sure Damon will want the photos as well."

John took his phone out of his pocket and pulled up the photos. Samantha gasped when she saw the first photo. The bike was so mangled, she could not imagine the force that struck Damon. Again, she wondered how he had survived.

There was a knock at her door and Samantha looked up and saw Dana standing in the doorway.

Dana took one look at Samantha and noticed her pale skin and shaky hands.

"What's happened now, Sam?"

Samantha just held out the phone to Dana and did not say a word. Dana hesitated to take the phone. She had no idea what Sam was looking at but when she saw the photo she gasped as well.

"Is this Damon's bike?"

Sam nodded her head. "I crawled under the truck to help him. I did not even wonder where his bike was or what condition it was in. Once I saw him after the surgery, I knew he was lucky to be alive based on his injuries. Now that I've seen the photo, I have no idea how he survived."

"Sam, there are things about all this that we may need to try to block from our minds. We can't dwell on the horrible things that happened. We need to concentrate on the fact that you both survived. Sure, Damon has a fight ahead of him, but you are here to help him on that journey."

"I have a client in five minutes, then I am going to visit Damon, and come back here to work with Andy. Abbie is bringing the babies, and Alex is coming too. I need to finish paperwork and prep for my client. Can you close the door on your way out?"

Samantha turned her back to everyone and sat at her desk. John and Abagail got up and returned to the house, and Dana returned to the ER.

Dana searched for Alex and found him in the physician section.

"Alex, are you busy?"

"No, Dana. What's up?"

"Did you see Damon's bike after the accident?"

"No. The police had it towed to Pete's garage after the accident. Why do you ask?"

"I walked over to see Samantha during my lunch break and when I walked in, she was standing there as white as a sheet. I asked her what had happened, and she showed me a photo of Damon's bike."

"How bad was it?"

"I can't even explain it. Let me see if I can get a copy of the photo. Better yet, she had John's phone. Why don't you text him? Tell him I mention it and you want a copy for injury purposes."

"I'll do that, Dana."

"That's not the only problem, Alex. I told her we can't concentrate on the horrible things that happened. They both survived and Damon was lucky to have her to help with his therapy. She immediately said she had a client and that Abbie, and the kids were coming and to close the door on our way out."

"It's been a long week, Dana. Actually, it's only been five days. Stress does weird things to people. Don't take it personally. She will come around. She may be suffering a little survivor's guilt. Even though Damon survived, to her, the situation may feel different. She can see him, but he cannot respond to her or open his eyes or speak. Seeing that picture may have been too much. I'll talk to her this afternoon. She may need to see a therapist."

Samantha finished with her client, finished paperwork, and walked to the ICU. The Parkers had not yet arrived, but as she turned the corner to the waiting room, she literally ran into Alex.

"I'm sorry. Alex? What are you doing here?"

"I understand you saw a photo of Damon's bike, and your reaction concerned Dana."

"What? Do they both think they are my mother? Every time they don't understand something, they question me or run to you."

"They do it because they love you, Sam. Dana described your skin color as 'white as a sheet.' You may be suffering from survivor's guilt, and before you start having too many symptoms, I would like to recommend a therapist friend of mine. Abbie, Andy, and I used her to get our heads on straight. She's great. What do you say? Can I send her info?"

"You didn't see the photo, Alex. The damage to the bike is unbelievable."

"John sent me the photo, Sam. I was shocked as well. But when I look at the bike and compare Damon's injuries, they are significantly less than I would have expected had I seen that photo first."

"I just want to hear his voice and have him tell me he is okay."

"I know how you feel. Remember all the times I asked you why Abbie couldn't call me herself. I just want to hear her voice. But I needed to be patient. Give him time to heal and he will wake up. Trust me. I know he is injured, but his body is letting him rest and heal. I promise he's going to wake up."

"I'm going to hold you to that, Doc."

"Here come the Parkers. I'll see you this afternoon. Maybe since you will be in the water, I can get time with my daughters."

"Thanks, Alex. You know I didn't trust you at first. I thought maybe you were trying to take advantage of Abbie, but I was wrong. She trusted you and I learned to trust you as well."

"I'm glad we are on the same team, Sam. Tell Damon I said to get out of that bed. He's missing all the good stuff."

"I'll tell him, Alex."

Samantha and the Parkers followed their usual routine. They went in to see Damon first. She watched from the corridor. She looked at the monitors and his vital signs looked stable. He was still pale, but he no longer had any blood transfusion in progress. His color was slightly better, or else she was used to seeing him so pale. There was little drainage from his wound, which was a good sign. His leg was still swollen but not as much as it was initially.

The Parkers walked out of the cubicle, and she walked in. She took Damon's hand.

"Hey, Damon. I'm here love, and still holding your hand. Alex said to get out of this bed because you're missing all the good stuff. The dogs miss you as well. Andy is scheduled for a therapy session this afternoon, and you are missing an opportunity to swim with the dogs. His little sisters are developing their individual personalities, and he has a sweet way of describing how they react to their surroundings."

"Abbie is making plans to purchase a piece of property. I'm probably not supposed to be telling you about this, but she wants to build a new therapy building. We are getting so many referrals and we don't have the room to fill the request. Do you know anything about building a medical building? If so, Abbie could use your help. Perhaps I can make a list of the things I would like to have that I don't have access to now, and a list of pros and cons. Abbie loves list. That will make her happy. Do you know what would make me happy, Damon? I would be happy if you could wake up and look at me. I miss your smile. I know you need to heal, but I miss you. The nurse is coming in and she is going to tell me I need to leave. Please get better so I can take you with me. Rest well, my love. See you tomorrow."

Damon smiled to himself. He heard Samantha call him love. When had she started doing that? He was still so tired. She must be leaving for work. He was having a tough time concentrating on what she was saying. He realized he did not feel overheated, and he was not struggling to breathe. His chest and head still hurt, but his leg was throbbing a little less than it was earlier. This had to be the worst case of the flu he ever had, because it was kicking his butt. He had patients who complained of being exhausted. This must be what they were talking about. He was so tired he still could not get his eyes open. It had been a long day, but if he could get rest tonight, he might feel better in the morning. He decided not to fight his body's need for rest, and went back to sleep.

Abbie walked into the therapy department with Andy and the girls. The dogs ran to greet them, and Kohl leaned into Abbie while she showed him love. Koko and Kody smothered Andy with kisses. The girls watched the dogs and Samantha stooped down to greet the girls.

"I'm going to get changed, Mom. Can I take the dogs with me?"

"Sure, but don't be too long. We need to stay on schedule so that Sam can visit with Damon."

Alex finished his shift and walked to the therapy building. Andy, Sam, and Kohl were in the pool. Andy said hello to his dad and Alex sat next to Abbie. He kissed her and reached for Isabella. Abbie had Gabriella and Annabella on her lap. Alex spoke to the three of them and Gabriella tried to smile at him. Alex looked at Abbie.

"Thank you!"

"For what, Alex?"

"For all of this. My entire life has changed because of you. I am the happiest I have been in my entire life."

CHAPTER 12

Today's plan for Andy's forty-five-minute session was for Samantha to help him find the courage to let go of Kohl for short periods, and kick his legs to help strengthen them, as Koko and Kody followed closely. Andy laughed every time he could swim on his own. Kohl stayed close by his side, and he was always within Andy's reach.

Abbie was so proud of Kohl and Andy's success. She planned to call the marketing company tomorrow to get a video of Andy swimming independently and walking independently as well. She and Sam needed to put together a targeted list of questions that spoke to Andy's plan of care and his successful completion of his therapy to bring in more referrals. She was to meet the realtor tomorrow as well, to look at the site she had in mind. The appointment was at 1:00 pm. It was nap time for the girls, and she hoped Samantha and Alex had free time to join her.

She had a very rough drawing of her conception and needed guidance from others in the medical field. The areas on the ground floor would be the pools, lockers and dressing rooms, storage, office space, restrooms, waiting rooms, snack bar, and laundry services. The second floor consisted of the standard therapy rooms, office space and storage, and included waiting rooms, snack machines, and restrooms.

Sam needed to review the layout and Abbie welcomed her recommendations, although she was not sure what Alex thought of this idea for expansion. When she mentioned it to Alex, he said it was an enormous project, and questioned her on her willingness to put up with bureaucratic interference.

Her ace in the game was Kohl. He'd proven himself repeatedly, and Kody and Koko were nearly as impressive as Kohl. But Abbie believed she could make this a success, and she had made a vow to use the money Tom had left her to improve lives. She'd do everything she could to provide modern therapy services to people whose lives could be improved because of the talents of her sweet Newfoundland dogs.

Andy completed his session and Alex accompanied him to the changing room in case he needed help to get dressed. Andy did not want to admit that the fun he was having was therapy. He was having fun with his best friend.

Samantha changed as well. Abbie and her family were going out to dinner at a restaurant near the hospital and had asked her to join them for dinner. She hesitated at first but gave in when Andy begged her to go with them.

Abbie smiled. "You need a break, Sam. Damon was stable today, and you are visiting him this evening. His parents need time for themselves as well. And we miss you."

"I said yes, Abbie. I miss you as well."

"Good. I am going to send you a rough draft of a floor plan I put together. I am probably missing a million things. That's where your expertise is needed."

"I will have a list for you. You love making lists, Abbie, so it should make you happy. I'm going to ask for everything I don't have at the therapy department and look for the new-fangled stuff out on the market. We need to discuss a budget, and go back through, and we can decide what is necessary. It will be like making a Christmas list as kids."

"I never had a Christmas list. I'll help you fill that list until it looks like the ones in the Christmas advertisements."

"Abbie, I'm sorry. I hadn't considered that you never made a Christmas list. I'll let you make the list instead."

"Sam, I'm not a child any longer. I do not need a wish list. We need items that will provide the needed services. We could buy everything we want, but that is wasteful. We need to consider the necessary items and pick a handful that we can splurge on that other facilities don't currently use. How does that sound?"

"That sounds perfect, Abbie. Now, let's go. Andy is doubtless starving by now, and so am I."

"Andy wants burgers. Are you okay with that choice?"

"Sounds good to me."

Samantha relaxed over dinner and tried hard not to laugh at Andy's descriptions of everything on the menu. She asked for a large order of fries that she and Andy would share, and he gave her a high five.

She helped Abbie and Alex feed the girls while they waited for their food, and Andy asked Sam how long it might be before he could start running.

"Where are you planning to run to, love?"

"I'd like to run with my dad. He runs every day so it must be fun, and I want to run with him."

Alex turned to glance at Andy.

"Are you serious, Andy? You want to run with me?"

"Sure Dad. You run every day, and I want to run with you. I bet Kohl will like running with us, too. Mom said he likes to run on the beach with her. I also want to learn how to ride the paddleboard with Mom, too, so that Kohl and I can ride. But you better stand back, Dad. He might get you wet and sandy again."

Abbie and Alex laughed. "Well, Andy. I will be okay if Kohl gets me wet again. The two of us got off to a rough start, but I'm sure he and I are friends now."

"He has not huffed at you or Mom lately."

"He is busy keeping Kody and Koko in line and watching over your sisters. He's too busy to huff at us."

They devoured their burgers and dropped Sam back at her place on their way home.

It was nearly time to visit Damon, and the Parkers were sitting on the front porch.

"Give me five minutes to freshen up and I will be ready to go. Did you find somewhere good for dinner?"

"We found a place overlooking the ocean and ordered appetizers to share. We brought desert back with us and brought a piece for you as well."

"Thank you. That was very generous of you. I'll be right back."

They walked the short distance to the hospital and waited their turn to enter the ICU. They recognized the families now and asked after their loved ones.

When they entered the ICU and Damon's cubicle, they noticed the ventilator was gone. Abagail and Samantha smiled at one another. This was a step in the right direction. Samantha read the monitors and noticed John doing the same thing. Everything appeared stable. Now they needed to wait for him to open his eyes.

Samantha held back while Damon's parents spent the first five minutes with him. She saw his finger twitch and wondered if he was trying to move his hand, or if it was a reflex from his mother holding on to his hand. She watched intently but did not observe any further movement.

John and Abagail stepped out to give her time with him. When she picked up his hand, he moved his fingers.

"Damon, it's Samantha. Open your eyes for me."

She waited, but there was no sign he had heard her. She tried an unorthodox method.

"Listen, Parker. I'm tired of standing here waiting for you to answer me. Open your eyes and look at me. How many one-sided conversations do I need to have with you.? This routine is getting boring. So, answer me or I'm going to let go of your hand."

Samantha did not see Abagail smile at John, but they were both silently cheering her stance with Damon.

He did not open his eyes, but he whispered, "Don't let go."

Samantha's eyes turned weepy. "What did you say, Parker?"

And he whispered again, "Don't let go."

"Okay. I won't let go, but I need you to open your eyes and look at me, Damon."

"Tired."

"I realize you're tired, love, but can you open them for a moment?"

Samantha felt John and Abagail standing right beside her.

"So tired."

"Try really hard and I will let you go back to sleep."

"Promise?"

"I promise. I will not make you stay awake for more than a moment."

Damon's nurse was standing in the room now as well.

"Please, Damon. I will not stand here and keep begging you, though. You've been asleep for a long time, and it's beyond tine for you to wake up."

"Headache."

"Okay, I'll get you something for your headache."

"Leg hurts."

"Okay, love. I'll take care of that for you. Look at me for a moment, and I'll let you go back to sleep."

Damon sighed inwardly. Why is she insisting that he look at her? Did she not realize what he told her? This conversation was nearly as awful as the one they had when she insisted, she wouldn't date him.

Damon opened his eyes and looked at her. Standing next to her were his parents. What were they doing? Why were they staring at him? He glanced around the room but did not recognize where he was. He looked back at Samantha.

"Where am I?"

"You are in the ICU at Coastal, Damon. Your parents are here with me."

"What happened?"

"We had an accident on the bike?"

"When?"

"Last Saturday."

He closed his eyes again. The light from the hallway caused his head to hurt more.

"What is today?"

"It is Wednesday evening."

"Wow! Need sleep."

"Alright, love. The nurse went to get you medicine. Can you say hello to your parents? You don't have to open your eyes again. They've been worried about you, love."

"No, too tired."

John and Abagail reached for his other hand and Abagail spoke first.

"You don't need to talk, Damon. We'll visit you tomorrow. Your father and I are staying with Samantha, so we are right across the street. The nurse is here with your medicine. We are so glad you are doing better."

"You need to rest and heal, son. But we are glad you could open your eyes for a moment and say a couple words. We love you."

"I will be back tomorrow, love. The nurse is giving you the pain medication now. Sleep well, love."

Damon squeezed her hand, and she kissed his cheek.

They thanked the nurse for allowing them extra time with Damon.

"My pleasure. We are glad he is responding. He gave us quite a scare, and everyone prayed for him. You can rest easier tonight. We are repeating the CTs tomorrow to check how things are progressing. I'll call Dr. Tobin O'Brien and tell him Dr. Parker woke up for a minute or two. Dr. D'Alessandro, are you going to call Dr. Montgomery, or do you want me to call?"

"I'll call him when I get home. If I don't report to Abbie, she will not be happy. Thank you again."

They walked home with more hope this evening. They realized he was not out of the woods, but he understood what they were saying and that showed there may be minimal brain damage. Damon needed a thorough cognitive exam to assure that his level of cognition had not been affected. She needed to call Alex, and she needed to report to her crew.

"Hi Alex. Do you have a minute to talk? And you may as well grab Abbie, too, if she is not too busy."

"Sure, Sam. Hang on a second."

"Okay, Sam. We are both here. What's happening?"

"I wanted to tell you, Damon woke up for a minute or two. He first squeezed my hand, and I told him to open his eyes. He resisted at first. He said his head hurt. He also said he was tired."

"Sam, that's wonderful. Did he realize who you were?"

"Yes. He responded appropriately to me and asked where he was and what happened. He asked what day it was, and when the accident happened and what day it was now."

"That a great sign, Sam! I was concerned about his cognitive status, but it appears he is in better shaped than I expected."

"I bullied him into opening his eyes. I told him I was going to let go of his hand if he did not open his eyes and I was tired of having a one-sided conversation."

"He noticed his parents, and they spoke to him as well. the nurse gave him pain medication, and we returned to the house."

"Sam, do you have time for a call with the others? I will get it setup."

"Yes, Abbie. I'm aware they are waiting patiently for any updates. Pick a time that works for everyone. I'm too wound up to sleep. There are so many questions I want to ask him."

"Okay. Let me put the kids to bed and I will get the call set up. Sam, I am so happy for you. I realize there's still a long road ahead, but it's a great first step."

"Thanks, Abbie. Talk to you shortly."

Samantha spent the next few minutes with the Parkers discussing Damon's condition. His father was cautiously optimistic, but his mother considered this a miracle. Samantha tried not to smile when Abagail made this statement. John smiled at her, and she took this as a sign that he was being as cautious as she was, and that each day would give them a better idea of how his recovery would proceed.

Abbie sent an invitation to the zoom meeting, and she accepted. She logged in and everyone was talking over one another, speculating on Damon's recovery.

Kate was the first to speak. "Okay, Sam, let's have it. How are things going?"

Samantha filled them in on the past several days, and how she bullied Damon into responding to her. Kate cheered her determination to get a response out of him. Samantha laughed, and the tears started.

"What's wrong, Sam?" Julie asked.

"It is the stress of getting through the past few days. But he asked the right questions, and that tells me that his condition might not be as awful as I expected. I can't get the picture of him under that truck out of my mind. Now that he is waking up, perhaps I can get through the night without constant nightmares."

"Did the nurse call Tobin?"

"She said she was going to do that as soon as she gave Damon his medication."

"I'll call him and get his thoughts. I'm so glad that he is awake."

"Are you and Tobin a thing now, Julie?"

"I think Abbie is rubbing off on you, Sam."

"Oh, that's funny, you two. I can ignore you completely."

"That's not what we're saying, Abbie. We need to watch out for one another, but we don't always need to share every detail."

"I'm not asking for every detail. I want to see if you are doing okay, and how your relationship is going.?"

"Did you question Dana about her relationship with Conor?" asked Sam.

"Why do you assume there's a relationship? Can we not be friends? Why do you assume everyone is looking for more than a friendship?"

"If you pass on him, Dana, you are as crazy as Sam when Damon started asking her out." Said Abbie.

"Don't you have four kids to mother now, Abbie?" Sam asked. "You are making more of this than is necessary. Why Abbie?"

"Because." Abbie said. "These guys are a real catch and if you pass up the opportunity that is right in front of you, I am going to send you the phone number of my therapist."

"There you go," said Sam. "You're so put together that you need a therapist, and yet here you are trying to give us advice."

"I've learned a few things along the way."

"We appreciate your point of view, but we need to make decisions for ourselves."

"I understand, but I was trying to help."

"We understand that as well, but for now, I'm going to bed. I want to visit Damon tomorrow, and I want to be rested. I'm hoping I can get a complete sentence from him. Let's meet back up tomorrow evening. Is everyone free?"

They answered yes and agreed on a time after the visiting hours were over for their next call.

Samantha showered and let the dogs out. Once again, they followed her into her bedroom and lay on the floor. When did this become a routine? She needed to break this habit. If Damon came here to stay during his recovery and rehab, she did not want him getting up and tripping over dogs. He had a tough road ahead, and their instinct was to protect people. If they followed too closely, he could trip and fall. Koko and Kody loved him and always wanted to be near him. While Kohl liked him as well, she was still his favorite. She'd talk to Abbie, and they could figure out the best way to manage their training and work around Damon's recovery.

CHAPTER 13

Samantha set her alarm clock to wake her up early today. She wanted to be up, showered, dressed and in the kitchen before John came downstairs this morning. She needed to practice brewing the coffee the same way Damon prepared his brew.

Samantha let the dogs inside, gathered up her supplies and measured the exact volume of coffee beans and ground them with the current setting on Damon's grinder. When the water came to a boil, she added the water to the coffee press, and then let it brew for precisely four and a half minutes. She poured half a cup into her favorite mug, sat at the counter, and took her first sip.

"Not too shabby," Samantha uttered.

It tasted like Damon's and now she was eager to make him a thermos full of coffee and take it to him. But first, she needed to check with the staff and ask if she could bring coffee into the ICU. If not, she'd wait until they moved him to a general floor.

She heard the bottom stair creak, and John walked around the corner. He smiled when he caught her fixing the coffee.

"You're up early, Samantha."

"I'm trying to make this coffee like Damon's. Now that he's off the vent, talking, and able to open his eyes, I'm going to check with the ICU and ask if I can bring him in a thermos of coffee."

"He'll enjoy that, Samantha. And by the way, Abigail and I discussed today's visits with Damon, and we're going to do the morning and the afternoon visit, and we're going to leave the evening one just for the two of you. Hopefully, he'll be awake and able to talk to you for a while."

"That's unnecessary, John. I don't need time for myself."

"No, Samantha, Abigail and I have discussed it. We're giving you time to visit with him. We're able to go twice a day. And it's always hard for you to squeeze those visitations in with your busy schedule."

"I appreciate that, John. We'll see how today goes. I anticipate his tests will come back well, and they will transfer him out of the ICU soon into an ordinary room where visitation hours are longer."

"That will thrill his mother if that occurs. It's difficult for her to look at him lying in that bed in the ICU."

"It's difficult for every one of us, and I'm eager for him to be out of that room as well."

"I agree Samantha. They can't make that move soon enough for me. I'd be happy to just get him out of there and home. Wherever home might be for him. We can transfer him closer to our house, I suppose, but his doctors are here, and he will doubtless not be agreeable to the move."

"He's welcome to stay here, John, and so are you and Abigail. He's going to have long, painful days of therapy ahead. There are going to be hard days, and I expect him to not be happy with those arrangements. You realize he may not take the time to do the therapy that he needs to get that leg working properly."

"I understand Samantha. His mother and I have discussed that he's never been one to remain idle. So being told he can't do something will not be an easy pill for him to swallow."

"Well, let's get through the next few days and go from there, John. Let's hope he takes things one day at a time and does as he's told, which overall will get him where he needs to be sooner."

Samantha gathered the dogs and their leashes, got them ready, and walked across the street to the therapy building. As she entered the parking lot, Alex was getting out of his truck.

"Good morning, Sam."

"Good morning, Doc."

"How are you, Sam? Are you still having discomfort from the accident?"

"I'm better, Alex. The bruises are fading. They are still tender, but nothing a dose or two of ibuprofen won't fix."

"I'm glad you're feeling better. I'm going to check in the ER and if it's quiet, I'm going to check on Damon. I'll call you with an update."

"Thanks Alex. I appreciate it."

"No worries, Sam. You realize if I don't do this, Abby's going to be after me."

"No doubt, Alex. I'll check with you later."

Alex walked into the ER, checked in with the nurses, and looked at the patient board. Everything looked good. He told his staff he was going to the ICU to check on Dr. Montgomery.

When he arrived in the ICU, Damon's nurse was in the room with him. She waved to him and motioned him into the room.

"Dr. Parker. There's somebody here to visit you. Are you going to open your eyes again this morning?"

"Is it mandatory?"

Alex spoke. "No Damon, it's not mandatory, but since I'm here to check on you for Samantha, I'd prefer you open those eyes."

"Look Montgomery, my head still hurts. I don't want to talk to anybody."

"Well, that's just too bad, Parker, isn't it? At least open one eye and I won't tell her you refused to cooperate."

"Is she giving you a tough time through this Montgomery? I remember her telling me to open my eyes when I didn't want to, but she was darn persistent. So, I did what she wanted."

Alex chuckled.

"That's the best way to have a good relationship with that group of women, Parker. If you have not learned that yet, you need to get up out of this bed and take lessons."

"Funny, Montgomery. I don't imagine I'm going to be out of this bed soon."

"There's no rush Damon. You need to take your time. You had severe injuries. We did everything we could to put you back together, so my advice, as your friend and as a doctor, is to take your time and make sure that you're doing everything the right way."

"You are aware that I have never been good at taking orders, Montgomery. What makes you assume I'm going to start now?"

Alex chuckled again. "You may not have done it in the past, but this might be a good time to reconsider, Damon."

"Did you just come here to irritate me this morning, Montgomery, or was there something you wanted?"

"What I wanted is to check on you so that I can tell Samantha something good. It's been a long week for every one of us, Parker, and I'm tired of telling her as little as possible concerning your condition so that she doesn't worry more."

"What precisely happened to us, Alex? What happened that got me in here?"

"Do you remember any of it, Damon? Do you remember any events from that day?"

"Not actually, Alex. I remember I was at your house with Samantha and the next morning I took the dogs back to your place because we were going for a ride on the bike. I have a bit of recollection of getting up the next morning and making coffee to take on the ride, and I can remember being in Charleston. We ate lunch. But I don't remember much after that."

"That's not too shabby, Parker. When you left Charleston, the two of you headed back north. Samantha said you stopped at the beach and took a short walk and then decided it was time to head back to her place. When you got to the swing bridge, the light was green apparently, and you proceeded through the intersection. But there was a guy to your right in a truck that didn't stop for the red light. You pushed Samantha off the bike, so you apparently saw the truck coming, Damon. That's all anybody can surmise. Samantha landed on the road. A guy named Steve that was near the intersection helped her off the road. She noticed you under the truck, so of course, Samantha crawled under the truck with you, and the first thing she did was call me. I asked for a rundown of your injuries. Steve, the guy that helped her off the street, crawled under the truck and helped her take your belt off to use as a tourniquet, and applied it to your leg. The ambulance was already on the way, and the police were on their way. It wasn't long before they got you in here to me."

"Wow. That's a long story, Montgomery. I'm not sure if I'm going to remember that."

"Well, that'll be an excellent test of your cognition after the ding to your head. It's not good to be struck by a truck."

"You could be right. That might be a good test."

"Do you remember anything else, Damon?"

"That's about it. I remember when Samantha was telling me I needed to open my eyes the other night. But as far as the accident is concerned, I remember nothing after Charleston."

"That's okay Damon. It will come back to you. But for now, I'm going to let you rest and let the nurse finish what she needs to do. You have tests scheduled this morning, and your parents will be in to visit you later this morning."

"By the way, Alex, how long have they been here?"

"They got here Saturday afternoon. A couple of hours after the accident. Once I got you evaluated. I called them, and they got in the car and drove down to be here with you. They are staying at Samantha's."

"Well, all right then. I need to rest."

"That's exactly what you need to do. I'm going to head back to the ER, and I'll call Samantha and tell her you talked to me. That's going to make her happy, Damon."

"Thank you, Alex. I'll catch you later."

Dana was off today, and she decided it was time for her to call her mother. After she and Alex talked the other day, it was on her mind, and she realized she needed to reach out. She picked up her phone, found her mother's number, took a deep breath, and hit the send button. The phone rang three times when her mother answered.

"Hi Mom. It's me, Dana."

"Dana. What a surprise!"

"I realize it's been a while, but I have been missing you, and I wanted to check on you."

"I'm good. Dana. What are you up to these days?"

"Well, I left Memorial Hospital."

"When did you do that? Where are you now?"

"I'm just up the coast in North Myrtle Beach at Coastal hospital."

"What are you doing there?"

"I am still the nursing director for the ER. The doctor that I worked for at Memorial Hospital in Charleston married Abbie, Mom. You remember my friend Abby?"

"Of course, I remember Abbie."

"She married Dr. Alex Montgomery. He moved up here before they got married. I missed her, and I wanted to be at the same hospital with her again. I love it here, and I am glad to be working for Alex again."

"I thought Abbie was married to Tom. Did they get divorced?"

"No. Tom died in an accident that occurred while he was on a rescue call."

Dana relayed the story of Tom's accident, and how Abbie and Alex came to be together.

"I'm sorry to hear that, Dana. I realize he treated the four of you like the sisters he never had."

"You remember Samantha Mom?"

"Sure, Dana."

"Samantha works here as well. She's at the therapy department right next door to Coastal hospital. So, Samantha, Abbie, Alex, and I are here. Alex and Abbie just had triplets, and Alex has a seven-year-old son named Andy."

"Wow, that's a bunch of changes, Dana."

"It sure is, mom, but they were changes everybody needed. Everyone is happy here. You remember Julie and Kate as well?"

"Of course. The fabulous five, I called you."

"They are looking for homes here as well and searching for medical groups to join."

"Can you come for a visit, Dana?"

"Well, Mom, I wondered if you might come here. Then you can meet Dr. Montgomery, spend time with Abbie and the babies, and meet Alex's son, Andy. I rent a small place on the beach now, and we can relax and enjoy the beach. I haven't accumulated vacation time yet, but we have the evenings and the weekends. And Julie and Kate often decide to pop in for the weekend."

"I might do that, Dana. I'll check my schedule and get back to you on that. But I don't expect any problems with making plans."

"You're retired, Mom. How much of a schedule do you keep?"

"Not much, dear. Nothing that can't be moved. Are you dating anybody now?"

"Well, I took a break from that mess for a while, Mom, but I am dating someone. His name is Conor O'Brien, and he's a cardiothoracic surgeon here at Coastal hospital. He's originally from Ireland and came over to go to med school in Chicago. He got tired of the weather up there and took the position that was open here at Coastal."

"Are you two serious?"

"No, Mom. We're dating. We have only had just a handful of dates. Nothing serious at this point. Why does everybody think everything needs to be serious? You sound like Abby. I call her my mother. Samantha calls Abbie her mother because Abbie tries to mother everybody. She has four kids now. We hoped she might stop mothering us, but it doesn't appear as that's going to happen soon."

"I'm glad the five of you are still looking out for one another. I'll check the flights and get back to you soon, dear. Love you. I'm glad you called."

"Love you, too. Call me on the dates that are the best for you. I'll check with Abbie and maybe she can pick you up at the airport. She has a nanny to help with the kids, so any arrival time should be fine."

Dana called Abbie. "How would you feel about picking my mother up at the airport? I told her I'd check."

"Absolutely, Dana. When is she arriving?"

"She hasn't made any travel arrangements yet. She is going to check her calendar. She's retired. How busy can she be?"

"Funny, Dana. I was thinking the other day that I have not heard you or Sam mention your mothers lately. Now is the perfect time for Sam to call her mother. She could use the extra support."

"That might be more stress than she needs right now, Abbie. We drifted from our families, but with Damon's parents staying at her place, it might be too much for her."

"How long do you expect them to be there? It could be a while before Damon can move back to his own place and start living on his own."

"I'm not sure what the plan is, but Damon's mother strikes me as the kind of person that won't leave until she says it's time. Remember, Damon is an only child, and that has influence in how she might react."

"That's true, but they will not put Sam out for too long. Do you think Sam will have Damon move in with her since she is close to the hospital and therapy department? And how do you expect his therapy to go if he is not willing to listen to her?"

"I don't want to even consider that right now. I'm worried about the two of them. Too much time together might be a dangerous thing when they are both under the stress of him recovering, and when she is the one responsible for getting him back on his feet, there could be tension if his recovery does not go well."

"Well, let's hope for the best. How are things with you and Conor?"

"Going well so far. He is a genuinely nice guy. Not what I'm used to, but I built my past relationships on good looks and great sex. I understood those relationships were not going anywhere. Conor is intelligent, caring, funny, and just a decent person. I hope this last, Abbie."

"I hope so too, Dana. Are you settled into your new position?"

"Yes. It's not too much different from Memorial. The same responsibilities, but different layout. Dr. Parker is great to work with, and he and Alex portray this laid-back approach, and even when the tough cases arrive in the ER, they help keep everyone calm and things run smoothly. Even the cardiac arrests run smoothly. Their calm manner keeps everyone else calm, unlike things at Memorial. This was a good move for me, Abbie, and I am happy to be living near you again as well."

"You are only three houses away, yet I rarely get to visit with you."

"I realize that, and I don't hear from Sam as much as I prefer either, even though she is in the building right next door."

"I need to have the girls baptized. Send me the details of your mother's visit once you receive them from her. That might be a great time to have the baptism."

"I'll do that as soon as I get the dates. Talk to you soon, Abbie."

CHAPTER 14

Samantha's phone rang. She noticed Alex's name on the screen.

"Hey, Doc, what's going on?"

"Damon appears to be stronger today. Good enough to get his test completed. His frame of mind might not be the finest, but he's been through hell in the last week. Tobin is going to be in later today and check on those test results. Hopefully, we'll be able to get him moved to a general floor. Do you have any questions?"

"No, Alex. I appreciate the update."

The ER was busy this morning, not absurdly busy, but steady, busy. Around noon, his phone rang. It was the front desk calling.

"There's somebody here to visit you. Dr. Montgomery. He says his name is Steve. Should I send him back?"

"I'll be right out to get him. Thanks."

Alex opened the door and noticed Steve relaxing in the waiting room with a big grin on his face.

"Come on back, Steve. How are you doing?"

"I'm good. Dr. Montgomery. I was passing by and wanted to stop and ask how Dr. Parker and Sam were doing."

"I'm glad you stopped. Dr. Parker is awake now, but still in the ICU. His recovery is going well, and I'm sure he is going to love to meet you once he gets out of the ICU."

"That's great. I am having a tough time getting that picture of him under that truck out of my head."

"You're not the only one having trouble with that, Steve. Sam is experiencing that as well. But Damon is doing better now. The biggest challenge he's facing now is his therapy. Samantha is an excellent therapist, and I am positive she will get him back up and, on his feet, as soon as possible. If you want to stop over and say hi to Sam, I'll send her a quick text and ask her what her schedule is."

"That'd be great. I've been wanting to visit her. Is she okay?"

"She's doing well. Hold on a moment."

Alex sent Samantha a text to tell her who was in the ER with him and asked if she had time to meet with him.

"Absolutely. Send him over here."

"Okay, Steve. Go on over to the therapy building. Sam does not have a patient right now, so she has time to meet with you."

"Thanks, Dr. Montgomery. I appreciate it. And thanks again for letting me spend time with your group and sit in on part of the surgery for Dr. Parker. That was a fascinating look at medicine."

"No worries, Steve. If you ever need anything, call me. We'll see if we can help you out."

Samantha stood in the building's corridor as Steve walked through the door. She had a big grin on her face, and so did he, and she opened her arms and gave him a big hug.

"How are you doing, Sam? I have been thinking about you and Dr. Parker, and hoping you were both okay."

"I'm good Steve. How are you? And I'm sorry none of us called to give you an update. It has been a ridiculous week, but it looks as though we are going to be fine."

"How's Dr. Parker?"

"Well, he's been through so much in the last week, but he's awake now and off the ventilator. He can hold a brief conversation and we hope that he's going to be moved out to a general floor in the next couple of days."

"That's great. I'd love to meet him."

"Absolutely. I'm sure Dr. Parker will be grateful to meet you. Let me make sure I've got the correct phone number for you, and I will contact you as soon as he is out of that room in the ICU, and you can visit. I'll meet you and we'll visit him together. How's that sound?"

"That sounds good. I'm glad you're both doing better, and I'll wait for your phone call. I'm eager to meet him."

"I'm sure he'll be eager to meet you too, Steve. And thanks again for everything you did for us. I never would have been able to stop the bleeding on my own, and nobody else offered to help me that day. You helped save his life, and we can never repay you for your help."

"No worries, Sam. I'm glad I was there to help you. Tell Dr. Parker I'm glad he is on the road to recovery. Take care and I'll talk to you soon."

Tobin walked into the ICU and reviewed the test that Damon had completed earlier in the day. Everything looked good. His leg was improving, and his head CT showed that the injury was slowly resolving as well.

He walked into Damon's cubicle.

"Hey, Parker. What's happening? How are you doing?"

Damon kept his eyes closed.

"Who wants to know?"

"It's Tobin, Damon. Open your eyes."

"Why is everybody so interested in me opening my eyes? Can't I hold a conversation with people without looking at them?"

"Wow, aren't you in a great mood today, Parker? What's the problem?"

"I'm tired of my head hurting, and I'm tired of my leg hurting."

"Well, let's get that drain out of your leg. That'll help. I'll be right back. I need to grab equipment."

Tobin came back into the room.

"Alright, Parker, are you ready for this?"

"Listen, O'Brien. I'm not a three-year-old. Take the dang thing out."

"I should leave it in until I get back from Ireland in a couple of weeks, but I'm hoping removing it will improve your mood."

"There's nothing wrong with my mood."

"I think that's debatable, Parker. But I'll give you a pass for now. Let's make a deal. There is not going to be another episode of you under a truck, because I may pass on fixing you up if you're going to insist on acing like an ass. Keep in mind I was the only one available that afternoon, or you might not have pulled through this disaster."

"I am not being an ass. And what happened that you were the only choice?"

"The orthopedic surgeon on call was in the OR with a case that was going south. His partners were both out with COVID. Alex called the hospital CEO and the Board to get emergency approval for me to do the surgery, and lucky for you, they approved."

"I'm not trying to be an ass. I'm trying to figure out a way to get better and get out of this bed. Please tell me it will not be a long time before that happens."

"I don't think you're going to be in bed for a long time, Damon. Let me check your pain medicine. I can swap a couple of your medicines and that might help. Part of that headache might be a side-effect from the medicines you're taking."

"Alright, O'Brien, that sounds good, and thanks for your help. I'm glad you were in town when the accident happened."

Damon napped for a couple of hours, and his parents came in for the afternoon visitation. His mother took his hand in hers.

"Damon, are you awake? Can you understand me?"

"Yes, mother. I can understand you."

"Can you open your eyes for me?"

Damon sighed inwardly. Apparently, this is going to be the theme of all my conversations today.

CHAPTER 15

It was Saturday, and Alex's weekend off, so he brought Kohl, Koko, and Kody home from Samantha's to their house to be with them for the weekend. It had been days since Kohl was home with Andy, and they were missing one another. Koko and Kody were used to splitting time between the two houses and were comfortable with either location.

Abbie and Alex were up with the girls, and Andy and Kohl were asleep in Andy's room. Koko and Kody woke up with the girls and were outside playing in the backyard.

"Alex. I was hoping to have the girls baptized and wanted to learn how you felt. I talked to Dana on Thursday, and she has reached out to her mother, who she hadn't talked to for a while. Her mother is considering coming to town for vacation, and I thought it might be a suitable time to baptize the girls. Do you agree?"

"It's funny you mentioned doing that, Abbie. Dana and I were talking at work the other day and I asked her how long it had been since she talked to her mother. I have not heard her, or Sam mention their mothers recently. Neither Julie nor Kate have mentioned their families, either. I've considered calling my parents and Maria's parents as well. None of them have talked to or seen Andy for roughly four years, and I'm sure they'd love to visit him. I need to fix whatever's broken in this relationship. I am aware they weren't happy when I took him and started moving around the country. But it was exactly what he and I needed. They will be delighted to hear that he is walking again. My parents need to be informed they are now grandparents to three pretty granddaughters, too."

"That is a good idea, Alex."

"Since we met you, life has totally changed for all of us, and it's time for me to reach out to both sets of parents."

"I agree wholeheartedly, Alex. That is a wonderful idea. Samantha hasn't talked to her parents recently, either. But she has so much on her plate right now. I'm not sure if reaching out to her parents might help or hurt the situation with Damon. I'll talk to her and get her thoughts. Celebrating the birth and baptism of three little girls might be the key to bringing our families together."

"Damon is being moved to the general medical floor today. That should take stress off her knowing that he's well enough to be moved and that she can stop in and visit when she wants. Damon will need to attend therapy sessions for hours twice a day in the early weeks and she can visit if it does not interfere with his exercises."

"I understood she was doing the therapy. What changed?"

"Sam told me she is planning to do his therapy, but he still has an open wound on his leg from the surgery, and she doesn't allow him in the pool with any open wounds."

"Well, I wouldn't want to be in a pool with someone that has open wounds. That's disgusting."

"I agree. So, he needs to wait. His wounds are healing rapidly, but for now, he will get his therapy done at the hospital therapy department."

"Once we get everyone settled for their nap this morning, I'll call my mother. I hope we can patch things up after all this time."

"That's great, Alex. I'm sure Andy will love to reconnect with his grandparents. Let me know if there is anything I can do to help."

Tobin stopped in the ICU to check Damon and to release him to a general floor for additional care.

"You ready to get out of here, Parker?"

"How far out?"

"Not sure which floor has an empty bed, but at least out of the ICU?"

"If that's the best you can do, I guess I'll take it."

"Any relief from the headaches?"

"Yes, thank you. The pain has eased up and my eyes are not as sensitive to the light."

"Glad to hear. I accepted a position here at Costal with the ortho group. Do you think you can stand to have me around this place every day?"

"As long as you keep your fingers out of my body parts, we should be fine."

"Alright. Don't put your body under any more vehicles, and we should be good."

"Are you going to allow me to look at those films, O'Brien?"

"You sure you really want to see the before pictures?"

"I need to check out your work if you want me to refer any patients to you."

"Great excuse. Just tell me if you want to examine my handiwork. Hang on a moment and let me pull them up on my iPad. I'll show you the before and after films."

"On the left is the before, and the right is the after photo. Do you remember how to read x-rays.?"

"Give me a break. I didn't hit this head that dang hard."

"No Damon. It only got run over by a truck."

"Geez. Give me the dang iPad."

Damon looked at the films, studying every detail, then read the reports. He pulled up the operative report as well, then looked at the ER notes from his initial evaluation.

"Okay, O'Brien. I will push referrals your way, and if I can ever walk on this leg again, I'll own you one."

"I need to leave town for a couple of weeks. Try to stay out of trouble while I'm gone. You will not get that quality of work from a local."

"Where you headed?"

"Back to Ireland for a couple of weeks to close out personal business, then I'm heading back. If you get bored, find me a place to live."

"I own a place one street off the beach. You are welcome to stay until you find your own place."

"Thanks. I might take you up on that offer. Stay out of trouble while I'm gone."

"I understood you the first time you told me. I'm not too good at staying out of trouble, but I'll give it my best. Saft travels. And thanks again, Tobin."

The nurses from the second floor arrived in the ICU to take Damon to their unit and got him settled in his new room. The room was bright and had an unobstructed view toward the ocean. He couldn't see it from his room, but he realized it was there, and that was good enough for now. He wanted to call Samantha, so he pushed his nurse call button.

"Can I help you, Dr. Parker?"

"Can you find Dr. D'Alessandro's phone number for me please? I am not in possession of my phone, and I need to speak with her."

"I'll find the number and bring it to you. Do you want me to call your father and ask if he can bring your phone now that you are out of the ICU?"

"Yes, please. I appreciate your help."

The nurse brought in the number he needed, and he picked up the phone off his bedside stand and dialed the number.

Samantha's phone rang, and she picked up the phone.

"Good afternoon, Dr. D'Alessandro speaking. May I help you?"

"Good afternoon, darlin. I've moved up in the world. Just wanted to let you know where you can find me."

"Damon. How are you feeling today? Apparently, you have been moved to a new room since you called me. What's your room number?"

"I'm not sure, and I didn't look when they wheeled me in here, but I'm on the second floor. I asked the nurse to look up your number for me since my father has my phone. She's going to call him and ask him to bring it to me."

"That's great. We gave it to him in the ER. We used facial recognition to get your phone open so we could notify your parents. I hope that was okay for us to do, Damon."

"Yes, Samantha. It was precisely what you needed to do. And thank you for letting my parents stay at your place. Tobin changed my medicine, and my headache is practically resolved. Nothing I can't manage."

"I'm so glad."

"Why are you working on a Saturday, Samantha?"

"I'm putting information together for Abbie. She bought a piece of property at the intersection on Sea Mountain Highway just past North Myrtle High School. She wants me to make a list of the equipment we need, and I figured it might be easier to do if I were looking at the equipment I have. It's going to be a lengthy list."

"Can you take a break and visit me?"

"Yes. I will be there shortly. Is there anything you want?"

"Just yourself, darlin. That will be perfect."

Alex and Abbie laid the girls in their beds for their nap. He didn't realize how much he missed having babies. Andy was growing up so fast, and he was walking and getting around on his own. He could not say thank you enough to Abbie and Sam for the work they had done with him. Andy surprised him when he said he wanted to run with him. Full out running will take him time to achieve, but they could start with short, easy sprints and work their way up to short runs.

He picked up the phone, selected his mother's phone number, and waited for her to answer.

"Hello?"

"Mother, it's Alex. How are you?"

"Alex. It's good to hear from you."

"Do you have a few minutes to talk?"

"Absolutely. How's Andy?"

"He's good. He's walking again. I found the right therapy program for him, and he is doing great."

"We miss the two of you, Alex."

"We miss you as well. I have great news for you, Mother. I got married again a couple of months ago to a nurse I met at a hospital in Charleston, South Carolina. We had triplets about three weeks ago. They are identical. I'd like to fix whatever is broken with us, and I was hoping to introduce you and Dad to my new wife and babies."

"That's wonderful, Alex. What does Andy think of the changes in your lives?"

"He loves Abbie, and he can't get enough of his new sisters. We purchased a big house on the beach and our lives are full of love and laughter. There are days it's a baffling mess, but it's amazing, and I am totally in love with every one of them. Abbie has a close group of friends that I'd like you to meet as well. Can you and Dad find time to visit? We are getting the girls baptized, and we hoped that might be a perfect time for you to visit."

"I'm sure we can work that out, Alex."

"That's great. Do you think Maria's parents might like to come as well? I'm sure they miss Andy, too."

"We have not been as close as we were when Maria was alive, but maybe it's time to fix that as well. I'll call her. Are you sure your wife is willing to put up with everyone being there at the same time?"

"Abbie is good at doing crazy. You are going to love her. She is brilliant and gorgeous, and funny, and she loves this ridiculous household as much as I do."

"Can we do a FaceTime call so that I can talk to Andy and meet the rest of your family?"

"Sure. Give me a date and time that works best, and we can work around the girls' nap times. I am home around five every evening, and Abbie is around most days."

"I can't imagine that with three newborns, she would not be home."

"We hired a live-in nanny until the girls are bigger and we can settle into a routine. Abbie is working on a couple of extensive projects, but she plans her meetings around the girls' nap times. Let's do that call soon, Mother. Andy will be so happy to tell you every detail about his sisters."

"That sounds good, Alex. Call me when you settle on a date and time for the baptism so that we can make plans."

Dana's phone pinged with a message. It was Conor. "Are you free?"

"Yes."

Her phone rang. It was Conor calling.

"Hi Conor."

"Dana, Hi. Can I convince you to have dinner with Tobin and me tonight? He's headed back to Ireland for a couple of weeks, but we are celebrating his acceptance of a position with the orthopedic group here at Costal."

"You do not need to find a way to convince me to have dinner. I'd love to have dinner with the two of you. What time?"

"Is an hour enough time for you to get ready?"

"More than enough, Conor. I do not need time to primp in front of the mirror."

"Okay. I'll be there in forty-five minutes. Looking forward to seeing you."

"Ditto, Conor."

Conor knocked at Dana's door precisely forty-five minutes later. He was dressed casually in jeans and a dress shirt. Dana was glad she had put on a summer dress and low-heeled sandals. Conor hugged her and kissed her on the cheek. Tobin was yelling from the back seat that he was hungry and for the two of them to hurry. Conor rolled his eyes.

"If we are going to hang out together, you are going to need to learn how to ignore him. I'm not sure if it's a brother thing or a twin thing, but he's brutally competitive, so I'll apologize before we get in the car."

"Don't worry. I can hold my own. I am one of five children, and the other four are boys. And I mean that literally. They never matured enough to be called men. They were constantly running off anyone who tried to date me. My answer was to go away to college and never move back home. They still live near my mother, but I vowed to stay as far away from them as possible. Not that I don't love them, I do, but I got tired of them interfering with my life."

"Alright, let's go feed this beast so we can catch up later when I drop him off at home."

Dana had a wonderful time at dinner. It was interesting to watch the interactions of two highly intelligent physicians who were known internationally for their skills and proficiency. They reverted to their sibling rivalry and bickered like fourteen-year-olds.

"Are you two ready to go home?"

"What's your hurry, Tobin?"

"I need to call Julie. If I'm leaving for two weeks, she might want to know where I am."

"Are you two in a relationship?"

"No. That's hard to do since we don't live in the same town, but if she moves here, I'm going to convince her she can't live without me."

"When you get to Mom's house, tell her that Dana and I will try to visit when we both accumulate earned time off."

"I will tell her that for you, Conor. You will love Ireland, Dana, and my family is going to love you as well."

"Really, Conor? You are willing to take me with you? Ireland has always been on my list of must-see places."

"Absolutely. It's so gorgeous, and I miss it. However, there is more opportunity for me here in the United States."

"I appreciate your offer. Can I play the tourist and make a list of the places I want to visit?"

"Sure, but I will give you the local tour. That will include the places we do not tell the tourist."

"That sounds fantastic. I'm going to start my list tonight."

Tobin chuckled. "You are going to love our family as well. We are loud and fun, and we drive our mother bonkers, but she loves us anyway."

"Sounds comparable to what my brothers do to my mother."

"You should bring your mother too."

"Are you sure, Conor?"

"Sure. She will love our mother. We might need to wait to introduce your brothers, but my family will expect your mother to be with us. It's how things are done."

"She'd love it, but I'm not mentioning it to her until I accumulate enough vacation time. Then I will surprise her."

"We love surprises don't we, Conor?"

"I don't believe you jumping out from behind a wall and scaring the bejesus out of someone is the kind of surprise Dana is referring to, brother."

"Shucks. And here I assumed I had new victims."

"Alright, you two. Let's go. Is Julie aware of the surprises you prefer?"

"I can't tell her everything up front. But she appears to be easy going. Maybe I should buy her expensive surprises to start with and she will tolerate the other surprises along the way."

"We'll drop you off first, Tobin. Do you need a ride to the airport tomorrow?"

"No, I can grab an Uber."

"Ring me when you arrive."

"Will do. Love you, bro."

"Back at you."

CHAPTER 16

Samantha hung up the phone after talking with Damon and called John's cell number.

"Hi John, I'm coming over to grab Damon's iPhone if that is okay with you. He told me the nurse was going to call you. I want to make coffee and take it over and surprise him with that as well. Damon's on the second floor but he said he didn't look at the room number, so he's not sure of the room. The nurse gave him my number, and he called me. He would like one of us to bring his phone, and since I am taking coffee, I will be happy to take the phone as well."

"That's fine, Samantha. We have not received a call from the nurse. They're probably busy. We're just relaxing, so if you want to get the phone and deliver it with his coffee, we'll visit with him after dinner."

"That sounds great, John. I'll be there soon."

Samantha gathered her things and walked across the street to the house. John turned on the teapot for her to boil the water for the coffee. Samantha gathered the coffee ingredients, measured the coffee beans, and placed everything in the coffee press to steep. While the coffee was steeping, she poured boiling water into the thermos so that it would heat up while she waited for the coffee.

Damon would love the coffee surprise, and Samantha expected he might love a visit from the dogs, too. She had to check with Abby to find out if the dogs were certified to be in the hospital. If not, she'd check with Alex on the hospital requirements to allow them to visit.

She poured the coffee into the thermos and threw his phone into her purse and walked back across the street. Damon would be wondering what was taking her so long. She hid everything in her purse to hide the surprise.

Samantha got off the elevator on the second floor and asked the nurse for his room number.

"He's in room 221. I've not had time to call his father regarding his phone."

"No worries. I have it with me. And thanks for giving him my number."

"You're welcome, Dr. D'Alessandro."

"Knock, knock. Anybody home?"

Damon opened his eyes and grinned at her.

"Now you are somebody I want to open my eyes for today, darlin."

Samantha walked over and gave Damon a kiss. He wrapped her in his arms.

"Were you asleep?"

"No. Just resting. I haven't recovered my energy yet."

She reached into her purse, got his phone, and handed it to him, along with a charger.

"Here's your phone, but I brought another surprise for you as well."

"And what surprise might that be, darlin?"

"Well, I hoped you might appreciate an afternoon beverage."

Samantha reached into her bag and pulled out his thermos and set it on his bedside stand.

"Now that's what I'm talking about. Other than you, that's the best-looking thing I have seen all day."

Samantha smiled.

"Do you need help to pour the coffee? I'd be happy to do that for you."

"Let me try to do it myself."

Damon removed the cup from the thermos, but unscrewing the lid required more strength than he possessed. He realized he was weaker than he expected.

"It appears I'm going to be needing your help with this too, darlin."

Samantha unscrewed the top from the thermos and poured half a cup.

"I hope you're allowed to have coffee. I didn't check with the nurse on the way in, but I don't suppose a little coffee will hurt you."

"Well, this doctor says it's okay. So let me taste this coffee, and I'll let you know how well you did."

Damon picked up the cup, took a whiff, raised his eyebrow at Samantha, and took a sip.

"That's nearly as good as mine."

"Well, I had plenty of time to practice while you were asleep for five days."

"Are there snacks to go with that coffee?"

"Let's not push your luck, buddy. You just got out of the ICU earlier this morning. We'll consider this a clear liquid for now and I'll check with Tobin about snacks for you later this week. How are you feeling?"

"Not horrible. My chest isn't hurting as much today, but my leg is still throbbing. It's been better since Tobin removed the drain."

"That's great news, Damon. Your parents will be over this evening after dinner."

Samantha grabbed hold of the chair in the room and pulled it over next to Damien's bed.

"Why are you sitting in that chair darlin, why don't you just sit up here on the bed with me?"

"Damon, I don't want to sit on the bed and hurt you. Once you can move yourself in this bed and you have been up out of bed, I might think about sitting with you. Your leg is still fragile, so let's not rush things."

"Are you going to spoil my day, darlin?"

"I'm not spoiling everything, but I'm not going to take the chance of making your leg ache worse than it does."

"Alright, I'll forgive you this time, but I'm not giving out too many passes."

"You're awfully darn bossy for somebody who spent time under a truck."

"Did you notice the truck coming at us, Samantha?"

"I didn't see the truck coming, Damon. I realized you were going through the green light, and the next thing I realized, I was on the ground. I wasn't sure what happened. Steve helped me up, and I was not able to find you. When I turned around, I noticed the truck, and you were underneath it. I'm struggling with that image, Damon. Steve told me he was having the same problem. He just can't unsee the whole accident scene."

"I'm sorry, but I don't remember any of it, darlin. But I'm glad if anybody had to be hurt in the accident, it was me and not you."

"Neither of us wanted this, but here we are. Let's get through therapy. We will need to work on your muscle strength as well."

"How long do you expect it will take before the leg heals?"

"I'm going to say a good four to six months, Damon. What's your take on this?"

"I agree with you on that. Tobin let me see the films. I advised him that if he expected me to refer anybody to him, I needed to see his handiwork. He's going to be away for a couple of weeks."

"Where is he going?"

"Back to Ireland to settle up a couple of things before he starts here full time."

"Well, I wonder if he called Julie. She's going to be thrilled that he's going to be here full time. And I bet she pushes up her timeline to find a group to join here and finding a place to live."

"When did this take place?"

"After your accident. She and Kate both decided they're here all the time, so they should just find a place to stay. Alex offered to help Julie look for a practice to join. Abby's plan is to build a new medical building. She assumes maybe Julie might want to open her own practice, and Kate might want an actual office instead of working from home. If Kate needs specialized equipment for her experiments, I imagine it would be helpful for her to have access to an office instead of trying to work from home."

"Remind me again where this building is supposed to be?"

"She is looking at that large empty lot at the intersection of Sea Mountain Highway and route ninety, across from the gas station and the funeral home."

"Well, that'll interest the physicians in the area because of the proximity to the hospital."

"That is what she is hoping for, and she is planning to build a whole new therapy complex that includes multiple pools and general therapy suites. She is planning to put the pools on the ground floor and general therapy on the second floor. That's why I was working on the list when you called me earlier. She asked for a list of everything we are going to need and said to choose a couple of pieces of equipment that nobody else in the area uses that will drawl clients."

"Did she buy the property?"

"She asked me to go with her. But it's been a hectic week, and I did not hear from her, so she may have looked at it by herself. What do you know about constructing medical buildings, Damon?"

"Well, I have not been involved in building medical complexes before, but it shouldn't be too difficult to understand. I can investigate that for her in my spare time. How long do you think it will be before I am allowed to go back to work?"

"Well, I'm not sure, Damon. Your injuries were significant, so I say it's going to be months. You will spend your days in therapy. I won't be the only one doing your therapy, though, Damon. You and I can start in the pool once your leg heals, and we will work to get those muscles built up. You had muscle damage, but it was insignificant according to Tobin compared with the bone injury. I realize you're used to working, Damon, but you need to be careful you do not overdo your activity. You're aware that being confined to bed for five days is going to be one of the first hurdles you're going to need to overcome."

"I understand that darlin. But we're one step in the right direction. At least I'm out of the ICU."

"Do you want more coffee, love?"

"Yes, please, but I don't want to push the issue since I haven't had anything on my stomach in the last week, but any time you want to make coffee for me, I'll accepted it."

"That's a deal, love."

"Tell me something, darlin. I'm curious, when did you begin to use the term "love" when speaking to me? I was confused when I was in the ICU. I assumed I overheard your voice, and I smelled my dad's cologne. I assumed I was just at home, sick with the flu, and that was the reason I was aching and feverish. I was exhausted and could not get my eyes open."

"What else do you remember, Damon?"

"I remember smelling my mother's perfume and my dad's cologne, and it confused me because I didn't realize where I was, and then I heard your voice. But then I assumed it was my mother's, so I was confused. I remember feeling hot. I thought I was out in the blistering sun because I was so hot. Did I have a fever, Samantha?"

"You did Damon, you had a fever, and you were in pain. They took you off the vent once and you started having trouble breathing, so they had to put you back on the vent."

"I remember thinking I was in a tunnel, and I felt like it was sucking the breath out of me. All I can remember is that I was hurting everywhere, and I was exhausted. No matter how hard I tried, I couldn't figure out what was going on around me, and I was not able to open my eyes to see what was happening. However, that seems to have become the theme around here. People think they can't talk to me unless my eyes are open."

"But it makes it easier to talk to you if your eyes are open."

"I understand, but my head was hurting, and the light made it worse. It's better now, and I'm glad because I can look at your beautiful face here in front of me."

"Do you expect I'm going to need to go to a rehab center, Samantha?"

"I'm not sure, Damon; I hadn't considered that far ahead. That might be something they're going to suggest. But we're right across the street from the hospital. You can continue to stay at my place. Tobin will not suggest a rehabilitation center if you are staying with me, and once your surgical incision is healed, you can start the therapy lessons in the pool, so in my opinion, a rehab center is not necessary."

"Your father mentioned taking you up where they live, and you staying at their house, but then he assumed you'd fight his suggestion."

"He was right. I'm not moving back to my parents' house. I'm staying here. I have my own place, and since you suggested I continue to stay at your place, I agree that does make sense. I'm right here next to the therapy building instead of having to find somebody to drive me back and forth. I don't want to be an inconvenience to anybody."

"Your mother and dad will be happy to take you back and forth from our house to the therapy center."

"Well heck, darlin. I could walk that short distance."

"Right now, love, I don't expect you could make it to the bathroom and back. You might walk that eventually. If you fall on that leg, those bones are nowhere near healed enough to tolerate a fall. Tobin will never forgive you if you mess up his handiwork."

"I imagine he might rage at me all the way from Ireland."

"Damon, I'm going home. You're falling asleep."

"Stay until I fall asleep, please."

Barely a minute had passed, and Damon was sound asleep. She thanked the nurses on her way out and made a mental note to bring the nurses snacks on her next visit.

Alex came home with a surprise for Andy and found him and Kohl in the backyard, playing with the pups.

"Are you four ready to go in? I have a surprise for you, Andy."

"What's the surprise Dad?"

"It's not a surprise if I tell you!" Alex said, smiling, and continued his walk to the house.

Alex kissed Abbie and the girls, and Andy and the dogs were right on his heels.

"What's happening?"

"I have a surprise for Andy, and everyone followed me into the house."

"Can I have my surprise now, Dad?"

"Sure, Andy. Here you go!"

Andy opened the bag that his dad handed him. Reaching inside the bag, Andy pulled out a new pair of running shoes.

"Are these running shoes, Dad?"

"Yes, Andy. Are you ready to run?"

"Yes. And these shoes are so cool. Thanks, Dad."

"Abbie. Are you up to a run once the girls are taking their nap?"

"That's a yes from me too!"

Ms. Helen watched the interaction from the kitchen. "You can go now. I'll put the girls in their cribs for their nap."

"We can wait awhile, Ms. Helen. Andy needs to get changed and so do Abbie and I."

"Nonsense! Get ready. They will be asleep before you get out the door."

Andy grabbed his running shoes and went to his room to change. Alex and Abbie got changed as well and waited for Andy to finish changing his clothes.

"Okay, Dad. Are these clothes okay for running?"

"Perfect, Andy. We are ready."

They used the ramp off the back deck to get to the beach. Andy was smiling and talking a mile a minute. He was putting together his approach for his running schedule. Kohl walked beside Andy. Abbie smiled at Alex as Andy walked ahead of them on the beach. Alex advised Andy to pace himself and try running short, slow sprints.

Alex made a line in the sand for their starting point and walked approximately one hundred feet up the beach and made a second line in the sand as their ending point.

"Can you make it that far, Andy?"

"Sure, Dad. Can we move the line further if I can make it that far?"

"Let's see how this distance works, and then we can make adjustments once we see what you can tolerate."

"Okay. Mom, are you ready?"

"Let's go, Andy. I'm ready."

Kohl barked twice to show he was ready as well.

The three started off gradually and let Andy set the pace. Andy started haltingly but picked up the pace within seconds. Before he knew it, he was at the finish line.

"How did I do, Dad? Can we go again?"

"You did fantastic, Andy. What do you say, Abbie?"

"You did an amazing job Andy. You can run with me any time. Kohl and I need to spend more time running. We can run in the afternoons when you get home from school."

"That sounds fun, Mom."

"You can run with me in the mornings, Andy. I'd be happy to have you join me."

"Can I run sometimes by myself? Well, not by myself. Kohl can run with me."

"Let's run a mile or two every few days for at least two months, then we will decide if you and Kohl can run together. What do you say, Abbie?"

"I say that's perfect."

CHAPTER 17

The next morning, Abbie got Alex and Andy out the door and got ready for her doctor's appointment this morning with Dr. Andrea Jeffers, her obstetrician. She did not remind Alex of the appointment. She hoped everything went smoothly with the appointment, and she could surprise him later this evening when he came home with good news.

Miss Helen and the girls were going with Abby. Not only did she want to bring the girls so that Dr. Jeffers could see how well they were doing, but everyone needed a day out of the house. They were going to have lunch and do shopping before one of the three girls commenced screaming and the other two joined their sister. Abbie and Ms. Helen got everybody in the car and headed out for her doctor's appointment.

The waiting room had three other ladies waiting for their appointments. They admired the triplets, and asked Abbie how she managed three babies at a time. She introduced Ms. Helen and explained she was lucky to have her help.

Finally, it was her time to go back. Miss Helen wheeled the triple stroller and followed Abbie into the room. The nurses were fawning over the babies. Dr. Jeffers peeked into the room.

"Well, who do we have here? They've certainly grown since I delivered them."

"Yes, they have, and they're good sleepers."

"They're great sleepers," Miss Helen said.

Abbie introduced Ms. Helen to Dr. Jeffers.

"We appreciate you bringing them in, Abbie. I rarely get to visit the babies after I discharged them from the hospital. I get to look at pictures, but we enjoy seeing them in person."

"I'll take the girls out to the waiting room, Ms. Abbie. Let's leave girls, so mommy can have her exam with the doctor."

"Get changed, Abbie and I'll return in a couple of minutes."

Abbie changed into the exam gown and sat on the exam table.

Dr. Jeffers returned to the room.

"How are you feeling, Abbie?"

"I'm doing great. We are getting enough sleep. I'm eating my typical plant-based diet and walking. I ran a short distance yesterday because Andy asked if he could start running, so we marked off a short distance and we ran with him at a slow pace. And everybody looks to have adjusted to this big new family."

"And Alex? How's he doing? Did he not have the time to come with you today?"

"I didn't tell him I had my appointment. I'm hoping you give me good news and that I can surprise him this evening with a nice dinner and an intimate evening."

"Let's get your exam done and make sure nothing is troubling you."

Dr. Jeffers finished her exam.

"Everything looks wonderful, Abbie, and I am sure that will make Alex happy as well, but all activity in moderation for another four weeks."

"I understand."

"Do you need a refill on your birth control medication, or are you looking for an alternative method of birth control?"

"I'm good. I still have refills available and trust me when I say I will contact you, because I'm not sure our house is big enough for another set of triplets right now."

"Your body's not ready for another set of triplets right now, so be careful and take your medication for another six months, if you can."

"I believe we've learned our lesson on birth control methods." Abby chuckled. "Nothing better than a set of triplets to remind you that if you don't want another set, or another baby, make sure you're taking your pills as directed."

"I'll catch you back here in six months, Abby. I to prefer to check on my multi birth mothers in six months. If everything is good, then we can stretch it out for a year. Make your appointment on the way out."

Samantha planned to spend her lunch hour with Damon and walked up to the second floor to visit. He was sitting up in the recliner chair with lunch in front of him. He did not look happy.

"What's that face for this afternoon?"

"Did you look at this tray yet? What kind of food do they feed people here? I need to go to the board. This is disgusting."

"Did you not make your own selections from the menu?"

"Not today. They hadn't told me they had increased my diet and I could do that, so I just got what they sent me."

"Well, certainly you can use a phone. Call downstairs and turn your charm on the cafeteria staff, and you'll most likely have gourmet meals delivered starting this evening. If you can make the nursing staff grovel at your feet, surely the other staff members won't be as difficult."

"Do I detect jealousy, darlin?"

"Not one iota, Parker. I realize what your capabilities are. I can't imagine one meager meal is taking you out."

"It'll be fine. For now. I'll choose something for dinner. And it's not the food. It's the whole accident thing. I'm tired of hurting and being at the mercy of others, and I miss work, and I miss the dogs. I want to hold Abbie's babies and walk on the beach with you. And finally, I want to take a ride on my bike. Do you realize how long it will be before I can do those things again?"

"Yes, Damon. I realize how long it will be before we can do those things again. But we are lucky to be alive, and fortunate that the injuries we sustained are not lifelong nor life changing. I'm sorry you had to take the brunt of the accident, but I'm so thankful you are alive and able to complain."

Damon chuckled. "I sound like a spoiled brat, don't I?"

"You sound like a frustrated patient, but there may be a lesson to be learned."

"And what lesson might that be, darlin?"

"Empathy, Damon. You are a caring physician, but the ER is so fast-paced, and you run from one patient to another, and the more serious the case, the faster paced the day becomes. Unfortunately, being on the other side of the bed can be eye opening."

"Do you feel better sitting up in the recliner?"

"Sitting in the recliner doesn't differ from sitting in the bed, but at least I get a different view of the room."

"Have they mentioned any therapy yet?"

"I asked this morning. Apparently, Tobin checked the latest X-rays from abroad, and he's decided that I need to be in a long leg cast for at least three weeks. Not what I wanted to hear today."

"I'm sorry, love, but we can't rush this recovery. Everyone wants you to get better, but we need to avoid any relapses."

"I need to rest. Maybe they got me up on the wrong side of the bed this morning. Do you mind if I recline the chair and rest?"

"I don't mind, love. I'll bring dinner this evening. That will give you something to look forward to and we can have dinner together. Any request for dinner?"

"Whatever you decide will be fine with me. I don't have my appetite back yet."

"Okay, love. I'll see you this evening for dinner."

Samantha kissed Damon and walked back toward the therapy department. She stopped in the ER and asked for Alex.

"Check his office, Dr. D'Alessandro."

Alex's door was closed two-thirds of the way. Samantha noticed him sitting at his desk, reading a medical journal.

"Hello! Anybody home?"

Alex looked up from his magazine.

"Hey, Sam. Come in. This is a surprise."

"Hey, Alex. I was upstairs visiting with Damon, and I have a question for you."

"Sure. How's he doing? I haven't been up to look at him for a couple of days."

"According to him, it's not a good day. He's contemplating how long it's going to be before he can do what he is used to doing every day. He misses work, and the dogs, and riding his bike. So, my question is, what do I need to do to bring the dogs in to visit?"

"Nothing. They are therapy dogs; so, they can visit on the units if they behave and do not interfere with any of the medical procedures or emergencies."

"That's great. He misses your babies and wants to hold them. Mostly, he is missing his interactions with his patients. If holding babies and having the three dogs visit keeps him from spiraling into a deep depression, then I will do whatever it takes to make him contented. Except for riding his bike. That I can't stomach right now."

"I'll talk to Abbie this evening and I'm sure she'll make time this week to visit. Did they start his therapy?"

"No. Tobin logged in remotely and looked at his leg films and wants him in a long leg cast for three weeks. I imagine the ortho team will do that later today or tomorrow."

"Well, that sucks, but it doesn't surprise me. I'll talk to Abbie this evening. She and Ms. Helen can bring the girls in to visit and discuss the new buildings with him. That will give him something constructive to do, and we are aware Abbie will question him to death and keep him busier than he ever imagined."

"So true. Thanks, Doc."

"I'll stop by after work and check on him."

Abbie's phone dinged with a text message. It was Alex, telling her he was stopping in to check on Damon. She sent him the thumbs up icon, followed by a heart icon. Perfect. She wanted to shower and change before he got home. Andy was occupying himself by finishing homework, and the girls were resting in their playpen, so everyone was busy.

She checked on dinner and set the dining room table. She added flowers and candles. It was time for them to get back to their normal routine. The girls were growing, and they needed more organization in their lives.

She recently purchased the property for the new medical complex and needed to start concentrating on that project or it was never going to be completed. Sam still had the dogs, and

Andy was missing them, so she needed to bring them to their house for the weekend. Maybe Kohl could come home with Alex in the afternoon and go back to the hospital with him in the morning. That should keep Andy happy.

Alex finished his shift and took the stairs up to the second floor. He walked into Damon's room and noticed they had indeed added a cast to his leg. He was looking out the window and did not hear Alex walk into the room.

"Hey, Parker. How are you?"

"I was great until they buried me under this cement. Now I am fantastic."

"Great perspective, Parker. We need to find you something to keep you occupied."

"How fast can you push a wheelchair?"

Alex rolled his eyes. "Where are we going so fast?"

"Anywhere outside this building. I noticed one sitting in the corridor when they brought me up from the ortho clinic."

"Look, Parker. I went out on a limb for you when I begged the hospital board to let Tobin do your surgery. I am not breaking you out of here. You are aware of the hassle and the paperwork when a patient goes missing. I'm going to send you more work than you want because my wife has another project on which she is working. If you survive the project, you're stronger than anyone realizes."

"I told you not to let her spend time together with Samantha. Those two produce more projects than anyone I've ever known."

Alex chuckled. "I agree. But they are doing remarkable things, so I'll give them a chance to prove they have not completely lost their minds."

Damon smiled. "I miss working. Maybe taking on Abbie's project will help me get through the worst of this. Thanks, Alex."

"No worries. I've got to run, though. I want to do a quick run with Andy before dinner."

"That kid is amazing. I'm so proud of his accomplishments, and it's great to learn he advanced to running. Enjoy, man. I'll see you later."

Alex got off the elevator at home and walked into the house with his left hand placed behind his back. He smiled at Abbie and walked toward her. She was holding Annabella, and he kissed them both.

"What's happening Montgomery? That smile makes me suspect you are up to something."

"Not up to anything, Mrs. Montgomery. But these are for you!"

Alex held out the flowers.

"Thank you, Alex. These are lovely. Did you do something wrong, or did I forget a special date?"

"Neither. Can't I just do something nice for my wife?"

"Thanks again. Hold Annabella, please, while I find a vase."

"Where are the other children?"

"Ms. Helen took Isabella and Gabriella for a walk, and Andy is with them. They should be returning soon. I kept Annabella. She's been fussy this afternoon, and it was easier to keep her here."

"Do you suspect she is coming down with something, or is she just having a fussy spell? I'll check her. Let me grab my medical bag."

"Okay, Dr. Daddy. Let's not overreact. It's possible she needs the attention. If she is still fussy after dinner, then check her. Take her out on the deck for fresh air and daddy snuggles, and I'm sure she will be fine. I'll bring you something to drink."

"That sounds great. Anything special go on today?"

"No. Just our normal day."

Alex turned and walked out the door with Annabella and smiled. He knew she had an appointment today with Dr. Jeffers, but she was not telling him about the visit. He'd be patient until the kids were asleep, then ask her how it went. Alex had only been outside with Annabella for twenty minutes when Ms. Helen returned with the rest of his brood. Everyone joined him outside, and he was a happy daddy.

"Dinner is in fifteen minutes, everyone. I'll meet you in the dining room."

Abbie added the vase of flowers to the table and lit battery-operated candles. Not as fancy as she'd prefer, but she did not trust real candles with the babies. She was afraid one of them might grab the tablecloth and knock a candle over, causing a fire on the table. She tossed the salad and plated the rest of the meal.

"Okay, everyone. Dinner is served."

Andy was the first one to sit at the table.

"Mom, what is going on now? Are we having a fancy dinner again?"

"Nothing special, Andy. Everyone has been working so hard, and I figured we deserved a special dinner."

Alex raised his eyebrows at Abbie. She smiled at him. He smiled back.

"What's with you today, Montgomery? Are you sure you did not do something wrong?"

"Nothing wrong with me. Are you okay?"

"I'm fine, but I can't claim the same for you."

Ms. Helen and Andy watched the interaction between Alex and Abbie. Andy shrugged his shoulders at Ms. Helen, but Ms. Helen was having trouble hiding her grin. She realized precisely what Mr. Alex was referring to, and that Ms. Abbie was trying to pull one over on him. She loved working for the Montgomery family. They were fun and loving and kind to everyone around them, and Andy was the same. She was glad to be part of their family.

They played with the kids after dinner, then Alex helped with bath time while Abbie cleaned up the kitchen and prepped lunches for the next day. Alex walked into the kitchen just as Abbie finished her tasks. He picked her up and set her on the counter.

"Hum, this feels familiar, Montgomery. If I remember correctly, this exact behavior started this house full of little girls."

"And I am so thankful for every one of you. Do you have something you want to tell me, Mrs. Montgomery?"

Alex started kissing her neck and jawline.

"Why do you keep asking that question, Alex?"

"Because Abbie. I remember you had an appointment today with Andrea Jeffers. How did that go?"

"It was fine. I took the girls and Ms. Helen with me. Dr. Jeffers was happy to look at them. She said that she usually gets photos, but she enjoys seeing them in person."

"What else did she have to say?" Alex continued kissing her neck, and Abbie was trying to ignore him, but was failing.

"She said everything looked good."

"Was that all she said?"

"She asked if I had enough birth control medication or if I wanted to try an alternative method."

"And your answer?"

"I told her I was good with the prescription, and that we had learned our lesson because the house is not big enough for another set of triplets."

"I'm sure we could fit another set of triplets here. What else did she say, Abbie?"

"She said my body was not ready for another set of triplets."

"Did she give you any other advice, Abbie?"

Abbie had enough of his teasing, and she began mimicking his movements.

"She did Alex."

"And what advice did she give you, Abbie?"

"She said everything in moderation, Alex."

Alex groaned. "I can do moderation, Abbie. Can you?"

"I think we have an abundance of time to make up for, Alex."

"And when do you think we need to make up for lost time, Abbie?"

"I was thinking we should have started when you walked in the door with the flowers, Alex, but we had little ones to feed."

"They're all fed and tucked in, Abbie."

"Then quit wasting time, Montgomery!"

And he scooped her up and carried her into their bed.

CHAPTER 18

Samantha finished work and walked home. She called Damon to tell him it would be 7:00 p.m. before she could be there for dinner. She told him to ask the nurse for a snack if he got too hungry before she arrived. When she arrived at her house, she took a pan of veggie lasagna that Abbie had prepared after the accident out of the freezer.

She told John and Abagail Parker of her plan to take the dogs to visit and have dinner with Damon. They agreed that was an excellent idea and John sent Damon a text stating that his mother had a migraine, and they were going to pass on visiting this evening.

Samantha brushed and trimmed the dogs and took a shower. She put on a summer dress and fixed her hair. If she and Damon could not go out on a date, she'd take the date to him. She missed him at her place but was thankful that he was out of the ICU.

Samantha filled a backpack with placemats, plates, silverware, and a thermos of Damon's special brew of coffee. There were brownies for dessert. When the lasagna finished baking, she added garlic bread as well. There was enough for John and Abagail to enjoy for dinner, and she thanked them again for allowing her the time to spend with Damon.

She leashed Koko and Kody and let Kohl walk free to cross the street. The younger dogs obeyed her, but she had to ensure they paid attention, even with distractions. If the public reacted to the three dogs as they reacted to Kohl, she needed them to react on command. Once they got used to walking through the hospital, she'd try them off the leash.

Visitors stopped Samantha and the dogs three times, but she explained they had an appointment and needed to continue. They arrived on the second floor, and the nurses waved as they exited the elevator.

"Damon is up in the recliner chair, Dr. D'Alessandro. He said you were bringing him dinner. He didn't mention the dogs."

"I did not tell him the dogs are visiting as well. I hope to surprise him. Thanks for getting him up, and please call me Samantha."

They approached Damon's room.

"Okay, you three. Sit. Now, there will be no running and no jumping at Damon. Do you understand?"

Kohl huffed at Samantha, and the other two did the same. Wonderful, Samantha muttered aloud. Abbie will be delighted to learn that Koko and Kody had picked up the ability to huff just like Kohl. I better stop that behavior, or there will be trouble for everyone.

Samantha unclipped the dog's leashes and told them to walk ahead. They entered the room, and Damon looked up from the magazine he was reading. Someone had brought him a stack of medical journals and he lost himself in an article when they entered the room.

"Well, look at this surprise. How are my guys?"

The dogs sat next to Damon's chair. Koko and Kody looked nervous, but they behaved. Damon reached over to the side of his chair and spoke to the dogs.

"Thank you, Samantha. I missed seeing them." Samantha leaned over and kissed him.

"Are you ready for our date?"

"Definitely."

Samantha reached into the backpack and took out the supplies. She added a battery-operated candle at the last minute and set everything up on his over the bed stand. She told the dogs to lie on the other side of the room so that she could set the over-bed table. Damon was chucking as he watched her take stuff out of the backpack.

"Watching you empty your backpack reminds me of Mary Poppins, darlin. I'm not sure what is coming out of there next."

"Only good things in this backpack. No clowns or other silly things, Damon. We have our meal, drinks, and dessert, so pace yourself. I brought enough so that the nurses can put the leftovers in the refrigerator for your lunch tomorrow."

"It smells amazing. Did you make this?"

"No. Abbie, Kate, and Julie filled my refrigerator and freezer with enough meals to last for a month. This is Abbie's plant-based adaptation of veggie lasagna. It is amazing. Your parents love it too. If she weren't so busy having babies, and building medical programs, she could be a Michelin Star chef."

"Thank you for doing this, darlin. It gave me something to look forward to today. I'm so used to the fast pace of the ER; I'm having trouble adjusting to this sedentary life."

"I'll remind you that you said that when they drag your tired body up here from therapy this week. You should strengthen your muscles and improve your balance to prevent falling until the cast comes off. Then the actual work begins."

"I sent my dad a text to bring my computer. If I'm going to help Abbie with this project, I need to do research on building codes. He's going to pick it up at my apartment tomorrow. I need to pay my rent and other bills as well. My mother is going to clean out the refrigerator. I told them they're welcome to stay at the apartment if they want."

"They prefer staying at the house. It is close for them to visit."

"It may be, but it is infringing on your lifestyle."

"Let me tell you a secret. Until I met you, my lifestyle was boring."

Damon took two or three bites of the lasagna and bread and laid down his fork.

"Is something wrong with your food, Damon?"

"No, darlin. I don't have an appetite. The food was fantastic, and I saved room for one of your brownies and more coffee. Everything was amazing. Thank you again."

"You're welcome, Damon. Is there something you'd like me to bring you tomorrow?"

"Just yourself. I'm going to ring the nurse to help me get back into bed. I'm getting tired. Can you stay longer?"

"Sure. I'll clean this up and take the dogs out while they help you get into bed. We'll return in ten minutes."

Samantha returned to Damon's room, and he was nearly asleep.

"I'm going to go home, love. You are nearly asleep."

"Can you crawl up here with me for a little while?"

"Sure. I'll get in on the right side of the bed, so I don't hurt your leg."

She climbed onto the bed, and Damon put his arm around her. He was snoring quietly within seconds. Samantha reached into her pocket for her phone and called the nurse's station.

"It's Dr. D'Alessandro. I'm going to lie with Damon for a couple of hours. Can you wake me at 10:00 p.m. if I fall asleep? The dogs will be fine. They will go nowhere without me."

"Sure. Dr. D'Alessandro. There is nothing we need to do for him for a while. Relax and enjoy your time together."

"Thanks. Damon is already asleep. I want to stay with him for a while."

The nurse walked quietly into the room and turned off the lights. Samantha and the dogs fell asleep as well. Two hours later, the nurse woke her, and Damon never stirred. She kissed him and gathered her belongings. The dogs were groggy as well, and she leashed the two young ones, and they walked home.

John met them when they entered the kitchen.

"Everything go okay this evening, Samantha?"

"Yes. Damon enjoyed his dinner, although he ate extraordinarily little. He asked the nurse to put him back into bed, and I stayed with him for a couple of hours. I put the leftovers in the fridge on the unit for him for lunch tomorrow. Thanks again for giving me time with him this evening. We both needed the time together. He was happy to see the dogs."

"His mother and I can visit him during the day, Samantha. I can't express how grateful we are that you have allowed us to stay here."

"I'm not sure I could have gotten through this accident without the two of you here, John. I'll see you in the morning. Good night."

"Good night, Samantha."

Abbie was awake and up out of bed, well before Alex and the rest of the household. She set up a call with the crew. It had been a while since they had talked. She gathered her computer and made a list of the things she wanted Damon to help her with on this project, and she hoped he had the stamina to help. She'd ask Alex to check on Damon's therapy schedule and she told him she planned to visit before his therapy session. Ms. Helen was going with her to help with the girls. Alex said Damon wanted to hold the girls. She'd accomplish one of Damon's goals, and one of hers today as well.

Abbie heard Alex get up and heard the shower turn on. She waited until she heard the water turn off, then poured a cup of coffee for him and walked into their room and stood in the doorway with his coffee. He smiled at her, and she held out the coffee.

"I thoroughly enjoyed last night. Thank you, gorgeous. Why are you up so early?"

"I woke up and had the construction project on my mind. I want to take the girls to visit Damon later today. If I don't get this project underway, we'll never get it completed."

"Not planning any panic attack today, are you?"

"Funny, Montgomery. I'll save those for a day you're so busy with your patients you're not sure which direction to turn next."

"Thanks for the warning."

"Can you bring Kohl home with you today? I miss him and Andy does, too. I'll call Sam and ask her if she is okay with him coming home with you. If she needs him tomorrow, I can run him up to the hospital and check on Damon, too."

"Sure. I'll pick him up after work. Text me if plans change. I'll see you later today. Stop in when you are done with Damon so that I can show off our babies."

Andy came out of his room. It still took Abbie by surprise that he no longer needed his wheelchair. He was thriving in school and making friends.

"Mom, I miss Kohl."

"I just asked your dad to bring him home after work today. If Sam needs him tomorrow, I'll drop him off after I drop you off at school."

"Woo-hoo! Can he run with me this afternoon? Can we get him this weekend? We should take the girls to the zoo. Kohl and I love the zoo. Can take them to the zoo, Dad?"

"That sounds great, Andy. We need a trip to the zoo, but let's just take Kohl on this trip. We can take Koko and Kody the next time we go. They'd like the zoo, but we need to see if we trained them well enough to take them to places where there are crowds of people. The zoo is the perfect place."

"Who's taking me to school today?"

"Your dad is taking you today. I'll take you to school tomorrow. Have an enjoyable day! Any request for dinner tonight?"

"I love your meatloaf. Can we have that tonight?"

"Yes, Andy. And would you like mac and cheese to go with it?"

"I'm hungry for dinner now."

"Here, love. I made you a breakfast burrito to take in the car with you. Make sure you eat lunch today. You are getting so tall. You need to feed that growing body."

Abbie gathered the information for her meeting with Damon and placed it in the outside pocket of the diaper bag. She had a list of items she wanted him to check. She had to become knowledgeable on building codes, technology, materials, and acoustic requirements.

"I lied to Alex," she mumbled aloud. "I may have to schedule a couple of panic attacks before I get through this construction. Thank goodness Damon is available to help."

"Did you say something, Ms. Abbie?"

"No, Ms. Helen. Just muttering to myself."

She contacted Sam to confirm Damon's therapy schedule. Samantha informed her Damon's therapy was at 2:00 p.m. and before lunch was a suitable time to visit. She agreed Kohl should have time at home for two days and he was free for the weekend, while she would keep Koko and Kody to visit Damon.

Abbie decided they would visit Damon after morning nap time. She and Ms. Helen got everyone in their seats and packed the diaper bag and stroller into the back of the van. She called Alex when they pulled into the lot, and he came outside to meet them.

"Damon has therapy at 2:00 p.m. today, so I planned to visit before that time."

"It's perfect. I'm hoping we can get the three of them through the corridors without too many distractions. I'm not sure who gets more attention, three massive dogs, or three indistinguishable little girls. I'll help you manage the chaos."

Dana was the first one to stop them.

"Oh my, look how much they've grown. I am sorry I haven't been over to see you, but I've been busy with work, and Conor. Sorry, Abbie. I will do better."

"No worries, Dana. They're only two months old. How's Conor?"

"He's good, Abbie. We see each other regularly. I'm so glad I met him."

"I'm happy for you, Dana. But now we are off to see Damon."

"Tell him Conor and I will stop in to visit soon."

Alex walked upstairs to Damon's room with Abbie and Ms. Helen. He carried Isabella. She snuggled into Alex's arms and stared up at him. Abbie smiled. It still amazed her every day how her life had changed.

"Are you decent, Parker? I don't want my girls being exposed to something they are too young to see."

"Hush, Montgomery, and hand me those babies."

"Let's start with one baby and go from there."

Ms. Helen took Gabriella from the stroller. "Here Dr. Parker. Ms. Gabriella is the quietest one of the three today. Perhaps we should see if you have the energy to put up with one before we hand you three."

"Well, hello, Gabriella. You are a bright spot in my uneventful day, and your sisters are lovely as well. I could get used to seeing you more often. By the time your mother gets the medical building built, you'll be walking, and talking, and getting ready to go to pre-school."

"Could I enjoy them as infants, Parker, before you get them married off at the tender age of three?"

"Listen, Montgomery. These are three of the cutest girls I have ever seen. At least until I have my own. And I am not surprised. Look at their mother, and I suppose the ladies might call you handsome. The two of you are the perfect example of good DNA."

"I'm supposed to say thank you, but I'm going to say goodbye. I need to get back to the ER."

"I'd go with you, but certain people might frown at that idea."

Alex kissed Abbie and the girls and thanked Ms. Helen for her help.

"Damon, I made a list of things we need to review. Do you have a computer? If not, I can buy one for you."

"Yes. It's in the top drawer of the bedside stand, and I hear you worship list."

"And let me guess. Was it my handsome husband, or your charming girlfriend who told you I worship lists?"

"To be honest, I heard it from both of them." Damon looked over the list.

"Did you consider any of this before you planned to build a new building?"

"We don't need to learn every word of every regulation that goes into building this place. We hire experts. And an adviser. That's where you come in, Damon. I recognize you are an intelligent physician and that you will let no one steer us in the wrong direction. The public needs this building. My former husband gave me the means, and Kohl will not live forever. Andy is the perfect example of how this program works. And unfortunately, you will learn first-hand how water therapy works. By the time you are done with your therapy, you will have intimate knowledge of how muscles work and recovery times. Any tips and tricks you pick up during therapy may help others overcome their hesitancy to adopt this program."

"Montgomery told me you and your friends were brilliant. I expect I'm about to find out what he was referring to when he made that statement."

"So, Damon. Are you in or out?"

Damon paused before answering the question, read the list again, and looked up the information on his phone. Abbie was getting nervous. If he said no, it would devastate her. She needed help, and since he wasn't working right now, this was the perfect job to fill that void.

"Alright, Abbie. I'm in, but if this project takes a toll on our friendship, or the friendship between any of us, we agree to call this partnership quits. Do you agree?"

"I agree. That is a brilliant plan, Damon. Thank you. And I promise to not have too many panic attacks."

Damon chuckled. "Honestly, Abbie, I'm not sure where you find the time or energy for the things you do, but I feel I'm about to find out."

CHAPTER 19

Abbie logged into the Zoom meeting the next morning after dropping Andy at school. She placed the girls in their bouncy chairs in the living room and sat on the floor next to them, positioning the computer so everyone was in view. Abbie hadn't heard from Julie and Kate recently. They kept occupied with finding a house and Julie was searching for a job in Myrtle Beach.

Julie and Kate joined the meeting, and Dana a joined few minutes later. They were talking over one another, and the girls were smiling at them. Julie was asking how they were eating and sleeping, and every other question her pediatric physician's brain could conjure up this morning.

Kate looked at her watch and realized fifteen minutes had gone by and Sam had not joined the meeting.

"Abbie, did Sam decline the Zoom meeting for this morning?"

"No, Kate. She accepted. Although she's not usually late. Maybe she had a last-minute session come up, but she usually texts me if she can't make it. Let me shoot her a text."

Before she finished sending the text, Sam joined the meeting.

"Sorry I'm late. I did not sleep well last night, and I slept through my alarm. Thankfully, Koko woke me up."

"Are you feeling alright Sam?"

"I'm fine Julie. I had a couple of nightmares in the middle of the night, that's all."

"Are you losing weight Sam?"

"Not that I'm aware of, Kate. I'm busy trying to work, and keep up with Damon, and the dogs. I don't have time to worry over losing a couple of pounds."

"Sam, if you need Alex and I to take the dogs, he can bring them home with him in the afternoon when he finishes his shift in the ER."

"No thanks, Abbie. I want to have Koko and Kody here to visit with Damon. He enjoys seeing them and it gives him something to look forward to each day."

"That's good, Sam. Tobin said they put a long leg cast on for three weeks. How's he doing in therapy?"

"According to him, it's torture. He's been grumbling about most things this week. He is not used to being sedentary, and he misses work. He's doing this research for Abbie, but it's still not enough to keep him occupied."

"I can give him more work, Sam, if you expect he needs more to do."

"How is that project coming, Abbie? We've not had any information from you. Did you get the property you wanted?"

"Yes, I did, and the price was better than I expected. I hired an architect to do the designs, and Damon is learning the building requirements, so we stay up to date on the codes. I asked Sam to give me a list of the things she needs, and I've been in touch with the city to make sure we do not miss a step in getting permits and everything else we need. When are you and Kate, coming to visit?"

"We discussed that yesterday. Tobin will be returning to the country in two weeks, and we were contemplating the week after he returns. Can we drive by the property you purchased while we're there?"

"Absolutely, Julie. By that time, Damon may be out of the hospital and allowed to take a ride in the car. That might improve his mood and Sam can get a better night's sleep."

"Abbie, you worry too much. And let me remind you that you are still not my mother. I can manage the stuff going on right now."

"Sam, I am not trying to mother you. I was just saying that once Damon gets out of the hospital and can do more, it will make his recovery easier on everyone."

"Abbie's right, Sam. We worry about you. That accident took us by surprise, and when any of us is having a problem, it affects the rest of us more than you realize."

"I understand you're concerned for us, but we are doing better every day."

"Are Damon's parents still staying with you, Sam?"

"Yes. They are still here. This accident is taking a toll on them, too. They're restless and haven't been visiting Damon as frequently. They have been skipping the evening visits."

"That may be your sign that it is time for them to go home."

"They don't bother me, Julie. I am working or visiting with Damon. After I get back from visiting with him, I play with the dogs outside, then go to bed. It's a busy, but boring routine."

"That settles it. When we get to town, we need a girl's night together."

"We can use my place, so we don't get thrown out of a restaurant or bar. It's only three doors from Abbie, and if Alex or Ms. Helen need help with the girls, we are close."

"How long has it been since the five of us went out together without husbands and boyfriends?"

"Way too long." they said in unison.

"It's a date then, ladies. I can't wait. Alex and Ms. Helen can surely manage the kids. Text us when you're coming to town so we can make plans."

Samantha's day flew by, and she was exhausted. Her appointments were non-stop today. The dogs were tired by the end of the day as well. They trudged across the street and the dogs stretched out in the living room and fell asleep. Samantha showered and decided she was too tired to cook dinner tonight. Damon depended on her bringing food, but tonight she planned to order pizza.

"How are you this evening, Samantha? We haven't seen too much of you this week."

"Hi, John. A little tired this evening. The dogs are tired, too. I'm leaving them here this evening. Is that okay with you?"

"We enjoy spending time with them, Samantha. Would it be all right if Abagail and I take them for a short walk?"

"They'll enjoy that, John. Be ready to get questioned to death by the tourist and locals."

"We'll do our best. I thought Damon looked tired this afternoon, too. I imagine the therapy is more taxing than he planned."

"I'm aware he is restless, and he is nowhere close to his usual energy level. He'll figure that out quickly. I'm ordering pizza for us tonight. What are his favorite toppings?"

"Get what you want on the pizza. That boy will eat whatever you put on a pizza. It's one of his favorite meals."

"Great. I'll see the two of you later this evening."

Samantha trudged back across the street. She waved at the staff as she arrived on the second floor and planned to order pizza for them as well. Damon was resting in his chair and did not hear her come in, so she turned around and walked into the corridor, and called the local pizza shop. They took Damon's room number and the pizza she wanted, and she asked them to leave the rest of the pizza at the nurse's station. She went back downstairs to the snack shop and purchased two sodas, grabbed extra napkins to use as plates, and returned to Damon's room.

Samantha leaned over his chair and kissed his cheek. He smiled but did not open his eyes.

"I hope you're Samantha, or I'll be in trouble."

Damon opened one eye and smiled at Samantha.

"I don't own you, Damon. We've only been together a brief time, and much of that time has been inside these walls. If you want to see other people, I can adjust. I'm not sure I'll be happy, but I do not dictate your life."

"Hey, darlin. What's going on? There is nobody else I want kissing me or doing anything else with either. Are you okay?"

"I'm sorry. I'm tired and slept poorly last night."

"Come here, darlin. Let's try that kiss again, shall we?"

Samantha walked over and kissed him again. The kiss lasted longer than she had expected.

"That was much better, darlin. Hey, why the tears? Grab a chair and sit next to me. Tell me what's wrong! Is it something my mother said or did?"

"Nothing is wrong, love. I had an exhausting day, and so did the dogs. That's why they are not here with me."

"What if I told you I am being discharged tomorrow? Would that help?"

"That's wonderful news! Your parents will be happy with that news, too."

"It's time they go home, Samantha. They've been here too long."

"They love you, Damon. You're their only child. I'd do the same if this happened to a child of mine, no matter what age he or she might be."

"Do you want children?"

"When the time is right. I see how happy Alex and Abbie are and the love that shines from their faces when they are with their children, and sometimes I feel meaningless. I have done nothing meaningful with my life."

The tears started flowing again, and Samantha turned her face away from Damon's.

"Look at me, Samantha!"

Samantha turned her head, and Damon reached up and wiped the tears from her face.

"I'm sorry we are going through this mess, darlin. I promise to make it up to you."

"You do not have to make up for anything. I'd not be alive if it weren't for you, Damon. I'm still having trouble getting the image of you under that truck from my mind. When I'm tired it is even harder for me. But I will be fine. I ordered pizza for us for dinner tonight. I hope that is okay."

"Samantha, I appreciate you bringing dinner in the evenings, but if it's adding to this exhaustion, I am certainly fine eating hospital food. At first, I was uncertain if the patients could survive and get discharged after eating the hospital food, but they have proven me wrong."

Samantha chuckled and wiped more tears from her face. The pizza delivery person knocked at the door, just then, and Samantha stood to give him a tip.

"The nurses appreciated the pizza, miss. Thank you for the generous tip."

Samantha grabbed a handful of napkins and laid them on the over the bed table she had placed in front of him.

"We are using the good plates today."

"Thank goodness. I assumed I was going to have to give up my bachelor ways. Nothing better than eating pizza right out of the box. Hot dogs are great, too. Just put one on the bun. No condiments."

"Oh dear, Damon. Do not say the word hot dog in front of Abbie. She may faint and bruise that lovely face of hers."

"We can't have that now, can we!" Said Damon while taking a huge bite of pizza.

"Do you want to stay at my place after your discharge?"

"Are you okay with that arrangement? I will need home Health staff to help for a while. I do not want you to feel you are responsible for taking care of me."

"Do you have any details on the Home Health's plan for your care?"

"I was told they will stop sometime tomorrow morning. The hospital will discharge me after I've finished my afternoon therapy session."

"How do you expect your mother to react to that, Damon? She's extremely interested in your care."

"I am too old for my mother to take care of me. She is too old to take on that challenge as well. I'm okay with her and my father providing transportation back and forth to my therapy appointments, but I can get myself there in my wheelchair if the weather is good."

"That will certainly help you maintain your upper body strength."

"It should, but I better make transportation arrangements until I gain my strength. Amazing how fast you can lose muscle strength."

"True, but you will gain it back rapidly. I'll give you the downstairs bedroom, and I'll stay in a room upstairs."

"Why can't we sleep together, Samantha?"

"We can, but I do not want to disturb you or accidentally bump your leg during the night. In addition, you will need help if you need to get up during the night for pain medication, or to use the bathroom. I can help on the weekends, but I need to work, love, and I cannot be up frequently during the night, or I will be useless to my patients."

"I understand, and I suppose the dogs will be up and useless as well if they do not get adequate rest."

"I imagine they will be concerned when you come home. I don't want them in and out of the bedroom. I'm worried they might get in your way and cause you to fall. That would be disastrous. I saw the films of your leg, too, love, and I am not sure Tobin or anyone else will be able to repair that leg again."

"You make a valid point, but I am disappointed, darlin. I enjoyed sleeping with you before the accident occurred."

"And I enjoyed it as well. We have time for that when we get you back up and walking again. It feels like it will take forever until that happens, but you will be returning to work before you realize, and eventually this will just be a nightmare we can try to forget."

"There are things I am going to have to get used to doing differently. But on the bright side, I'll see you in the mornings before you leave, and again in the evenings."

"We both need to get used to a new routine. Do you want more pizza? If not, I'll clean up this mess, and head across the street to get our rooms setup."

"I'm finished, and thanks for the meals. I'd prefer you to stay longer, but I understand you want to get things organized. I'll work on the items on Abbie's list this evening."

"Keep in mind that won't be the only list she hands you, but I give her credit for seeking help, and realizing she can't do this project without help from others."

"Thanks for the warning."

Samantha left the hospital less teary than when she arrived but was still exhausted. She sat in the living room and talked with John and Abagail.

"Damon is being discharged tomorrow. Did he tell you, Abagail?"

"Damon informed us this afternoon but asked us not to tell you. He wanted to tell you himself."

"It's good news, and he is excited he's getting out of the hospital. I am giving him the downstairs bedroom and I'll make up one for myself upstairs. I'll set up the den for the home Health staff. Damon did not have information on what that schedule will be, but I want them to be comfortable while they are here. Can you stop in my office tomorrow and give me the details on his care?"

"Yes, Samantha. We will fill you in on the details. Do you need help with the rooms? Abagail and I can help."

"I'm fine. It will only take me a minute, then I will go to bed. I'll see you in the morning."

CHAPTER 20

Samantha prepared her bedroom for Damon's arrival, but then wondered if the home health company might recommend a hospital bed. It would certainly make it easier for him to get in and out of bed, but she expected him to refuse. She learned that if the idea was not his, then he would protest. Her bedroom was on the main floor and could easily hold a twin-sized hospital bed beside her king-sized bed. She sighed. She needed to concentrate on her day and quit worrying over things she could not control.

Samantha called Damon to say good morning. He said he slept well through the night and had less pain as well. She wished she could say the same for herself. She woke up twice in a cold sweat and needed to get up and change nightgowns. Hopefully, the nightmares would stop when Damon settled into her place.

She decided she needed to ask John and Abagail to help fix meals. Damon liked to cook. Maybe they could all pitch in with the cooking and other responsibilities. She was looking forward to sitting on the front porch and relaxing in the evenings instead of running back and forth between the house and the hospital.

Damon was determined to do things on his own. She was glad to see him asserting independence, but she worried he might try to do things too soon and re-injure his leg. His cognitive status appeared to be intact. Other than the loss of memory of the accident, he appeared fine.

Samantha and the three dogs had a light schedule today, and no hydrotherapy was scheduled after lunch. She contemplated bringing the dogs back to the house at lunchtime, then worried they might impede Damon's arrival. Why did she feel everything was out of her control? Alex suggested therapy after the accident. She needed to look for that number. It was likely on her desk at work. She'd look for the number after her last appointment today.

Damon called his father and asked him to go to his apartment and grab shorts and T-shirts from his closet. It was impossible for him to wear regular pants or jeans while he was in the leg cast, and he suspected Tobin would recommend a brace after the cast.

He despised wearing sweatpants. Why did people feel they were appropriate to wear everywhere these days? Sweatpants were only to be worn at the gym. The weather remained warm enough in the winter in Myrtle Beach to wear shorts year-round. In the ER, he either wore scrubs, or dress pants, dress shirts, and ties.

The orderly helped with his sponge bath and dressing in a hospital gown and scrub shorts until his father arrived. He was expecting the Home Health agency nurse to arrive this morning and wanted out of this room and out of the hospital. This place was suffocating him. It was fine while he was working, but it had been nearly two weeks since the accident, and he needed to sit outside on Samantha's porch and enjoy the fresh air. He needed to be near her, his parents, and his friends. He missed driving and riding his bike, and he realized it could be a long time before he would have the opportunity to do those things again.

Damon was concerned about Samantha. She appeared thinner than he remembered, and she was teary and exhausted. They still had a lot to get through before life returned to normalcy. He still faced weeks of therapy and attorney visits related to the accident. He suspected she had not considered that far ahead. They'd recall this accident for a long time, and since he did not remember what happened, others would rely on her memory to build a case.

He needed an attorney but would ask for recommendations from his colleagues while Samantha was working. His parents offered to take him where he needed to go. He needed to ask the therapist to teach him the best way to get in and out of a vehicle.

Damon's insurance company had paid him for the bike, but he was planning to sue the drunk that caused the accident. To his understanding, there were witnesses, and it should be an open and shut case. He needed to do his own research on the driver and wanted to know if the driver had any earlier accidents that involved being intoxicated. And he wanted to know his blood alcohol level. He would ask the attorney if he should include the bar owner, too. They should train staff on alcohol consumption and never let an impaired customer drive away.

He needed to convince Samantha she should sue as well. He was thankful her physical injuries had been minor, but it remained to be seen how she did emotionally. She had told him three or four times that she couldn't unsee him lying under the truck. She was correct when she said they had not had enough time together to know each other well, and he was hoping she could tolerate the legal battle they faced.

Damon wanted his parents to go home, but knew he still had to rely on them for a while longer. He and Samantha needed time alone to manage everything that had occurred. He knew his mother. She would hover over him every minute of the day. He was thankful to have loving parents, but he did not want to be smothered by their concern. There were reasons to be thankful to be an only child, and others that could drive a man insane. His father had always given him the space he needed to make his own decisions. Many of those decisions were not the best, but he allowed him the space to learn from his mistakes.

There was a knock at the door. Damon looked up from the notes he was writing.

"Good morning, Dr. Parker. I'm Gloria, your Home Health nurse. Is this a good time to discuss our program?"

"Yes. Perfect timing. Come in. Sorry, but you'll need to grab your own chair. I'm still useless at being a gentleman."

"No worries, Dr. Parker. Are you ready to get out of here?"

"I lack the words to describe how much I want out of here right now."

"I understand you have an apartment. Do you have steps going into the apartment?"

"I'll be staying with my girlfriend, Dr. Samantha D'Alessandro. She lives directly across the street from the hospital. She has two to four steps for me to maneuver depending on the entrance I use."

"You should be able to manage a few steps. And is the shower a standalone or is there a tub? Is there a built-in seat, or will you be needing one?"

"There is no tub in the primary bath. I might need a temporary seat to bathe at the sink until Dr. O'Brien removes the cast. The shower already has a seat. And I cannot wait to get into a shower."

"I hear that frequently. And the bedroom? Is there one on the main floor, or do you need to climb steps?"

"No steps other than the ones to get into the house. The primary suite is on the main floor."

"That's perfect. We can deliver a hospital bed for you if you think it will make getting in and out of the bed easier. Instead of the hospital bed, we can add a rail to the bed you will use to help in getting in and out."

"Let's go with the rail. If I find it too difficult, I will let you know. What other equipment might I be needing?"

"The usual dressing and grooming equipment. The aid assigned to help you will assist with bathing and dressing. They will help with making the bed but will teach you how to complete your daily tasks until you are released to put weight on your leg. The therapist will work on your balance. The goal is for you to complete your own bathing, dressing, cooking, and light housekeeping task."

"Is there someone available during the night to help with getting in and out of bed until I regain my strength?"

"Your insurance does not cover that service, but you can pay for the night staff yourself if you are financially able to cover the cost."

"I will cover the cost, but I will not expect them to be awake the entire night. I will arrange a room for them and give them my phone number so that I can communicate with them if I need something. They will have a private bath available as well."

"I will schedule a nighttime aide, per your request. Is there anything else you were expecting?"

"Not right now, but there may be by the time I get home and attempt to settle into some kind of routine."

"No problem. We can adjust as we go. I will see you later this afternoon, and we can work on a schedule."

Damon took a quick nap, ate lunch, then left the unit for his therapy session. When he returned, he discovered his father had left clothing for him to put on, and the nurse encouraged him to dress and pack up his belongings. The transport service arrived to take him across the street.

Damon arrived to find his parents waiting on the porch. He used the handrail and one crutch to go up the stairs. He gave them both a hug and took a seat in the rocking chair. His father moved a footstool over for him to rest his leg upon.

"Thank you, Father. I am going to sit here and wait for Samantha. It feels amazing to get out of the hospital and breath in fresh air."

"We are glad to have you here, Damon. Can I get you something to drink? I made iced tea."

"Iced tea sounds great. Any snacks to go with the tea, Mother?"

"I might have something."

Abagail walked into the kitchen and returned to the porch with freshly baked chocolate-chip cookies.

"Here you go, sweetheart. Enjoy your snack."

Damon sighed. "I better pace myself or I'm going to be sick."

Damon devoured three cookies and half a glass of tea and started nodding off to sleep.

"Damon, let me help you into bed."

"Thanks, Father, but I'm staying right here for now. I'll take a light blanket if you can find one. I believe Samantha has one on the back of the sofa."

Damon was snoring lightly by the time his father returned with the blanket. John covered him and arranged a pillow under his foot. Damon never moved. He was still dozing when Samantha and the dogs arrived at home.

Kohl stepped onto the porch and walked over to Damon. He looked at Samantha, and she nodded in his direction. Kohl huffed quietly at Damon and licked his face.

Damon opened one eye and smiled at Kohl. He reached over and gave Kohl a hug.

"Come here, you two."

Koko and Kody looked at Samantha.

"You can sit next to Damon. Do not bump his leg."

With tails wagging, they walked over to Damon, and he gave them both a hug as well.

"I have one hug left for you, darlin, but you need to help me stand."

"No need for you to stand. I can accept my hug sitting next to you. I'll sit on the empty side of the footstool. How long have you been asleep out here?"

"Since I arrived from the hospital." He gave Samantha a hug and a kiss.

"Are you ready to go inside? I need to start dinner."

"Let's call out for something. I just want to sit by your side this evening. No cooking or cleaning. Besides, I am waiting for the nurse to arrive."

"That sounds good. Let's go in and decide what to order. I need to feed the dogs and let them out in the backyard for exercise."

Samantha helped Damon to his feet and passed him the crutches. She opened the door and told the dogs to go in first. Samantha walked beside Damon to the bathroom and told him to yell for her if he needed help.

Samantha walked into the kitchen and searched for her folder with the takeout menus. She handed them to Abagail and told her to choose. Samantha saw the dogs run toward the door and saw the nurse had arrived. She let her in and introduced herself.

"It's nice to meet you, Dr. D'Alessandro. I've been hearing wonderful things from the physicians about your therapy program. What an innovative way to help patients recover. I assume these are the dogs that help you get the results you are seeing."

"Call me Samantha, please, and yes. This is Kohl. He was a coast guard rescue dog. Dr. Montgomery's wife, Abbie, and I developed the program based on Kohl's rescue skills. This is Koko and Kody. They came from the same breeder as Kohl and have similar competences. We're happy with the way the program is going."

Damon came out of the bedroom and recognized Gloria.

"Are you okay, love? This is Gloria. You met earlier."

"Hi, Gloria. Let's sit. That short walk did me in."

"You'll regain your strength quicker at home, Damon. Why don't you rest, and Samantha can show me where you will be staying."

"That's a good idea."

Samantha showed Gloria the bedroom where Damon planned to sleep, then walked to the study to show Gloria the room where the staff would sleep.

"I am having a bed delivered tomorrow, Gloria, but the bedroom upstairs has a private bathroom and a sitting room your staff can use tonight."

"It will be me tonight since it was short notice. Thanks for the offer. I'll give Damon my phone number and he can call during the night if he needs anything. I will check on him every two hours to make sure he is okay but will not wake him unless he needs pain medication or help with transfer or repositioning in bed. As a physician, you know the importance of staying ahead of the pain."

"That's perfect. I will leave lights on for you so that you don't have to search for the lights in the dark. You're not afraid of the dogs, are you?"

"Not at all, and I will assign staff who are not afraid of them, either."

"I'll put the dogs in my room tonight. Let me show you where you will sleep, and where everything is. Please help yourself to any snacks and drinks from the kitchen."

Samantha and Gloria came back to the main floor. Gloria said she'd return around 10:00 p.m. and planned to leave around 6:00 a.m. Samantha told her she was always up early in the morning, and she'd check with her to see how Damon made it through the night.

The food delivery arrived as soon as Gloria left. They ate dinner in the living room, where Damon was comfortable. Abagail cleaned up after dinner and John offered to stay up and let Gloria into the house when she arrived.

Samantha helped Damon get ready for bed. He had done more since arriving at the house than he had done in the past few weeks. Samantha helped Damon get into bed, then she lay on the bed, and they talked for a while until both began falling asleep. Samantha kissed him good night, gave him pain medication, and wrote a note for the nurse on his medication time in case he needed medicated through the night. She let the dogs out, then the four of them climbed the stairs and crawled into bed.

John let Gloria into the house at 10:00 p.m. and he turned in as well. Gloria peeked in at Damon and he was sleeping. She took her things up to the room Samantha had shown her and made her first nurse's note for the night.

Samantha fell asleep at once. She woke twice in the night, but vowed to let the nurse check on Damon, and rolled over and fell back asleep. She woke to the alarm the next morning, showered, dressed, and walked downstairs. Gloria was sitting on a stool at the kitchen island, finishing her notes.

"How did he do through the night?"

"He did great. I supported him to walk to the bathroom once and gave him pain medication as well. I just peeked in, and he was still sleeping. I'll call you later today with the name of the staff who will be here tonight."

"Thank you, Gloria. I'll be awake tonight when they arrive."

"Our night staff typically works 7:00 p.m. to 7:00 a.m. They can help Damon with his bath if he is up that early, or they can assist with bathing in the evening if that is his preference."

"I'll discuss it with him today and he can decide. Thanks again."

Samantha closed the door and leaned against it. They had made it through the first night.

CHAPTER 21

Samantha brewed a pot of Damon's special brew and poured two cups. She carried them into the bedroom. Damon was still sleeping. She placed the cups on the bedside stand and leaned over to kiss him.

"Wake up, Dr. Parker."

"Humm. Why?"

"I have coffee you might be interested in drinking before it gets cool."

"Is that my coffee beans I smell coming from that cup?

"Could be. Sit up and I'll hand you a cup."

"That's a perfect way for me to wake up in the morning."

Damon opened his eyes and smiled at Samantha.

"Drink up, Parker. I need to go to work this morning."

"Call in sick and stay here with me."

"Impossible. I have multiple clients today. Let me get the dogs. They are eager to say good morning."

Samantha opened the door and Kohl was the first one to enter the room. He went to the opposite side of the bed and climbed up on the mattress. He lay next to Damon and put his paw on Damon's uninjured leg. Koko and Kody stood next to the left side of the bed.

"How are my boys this morning?"

Kohl huffed gently, and Koko and Kody did the same.

Damon smiled. "Abbie is not going to be happy when she finds out the three of them are huffing at things. How do we correct this, Samantha?"

"I'm not sure, but maybe it is a common behavior of the breed, and she is not aware that other dogs are behaving the same way."

"I'll check the internet. Perhaps I can find information about this habit. If we find a common trait, they might not be in trouble."

"Your aide will be here soon. Do you want me to help you with any tasks before I leave for work?"

"Another coffee would be great, darlin."

"I overheard your father in the kitchen. He doubtless has more brewed."

"Do you both understand how to prepare my brew?"

"I think your father has been on to this secret for a long time. He helped me to get it perfected."

"I was not aware he was paying attention to my methods."

"Let me get you more coffee. Do you need help to get to the bathroom?

"I'll try to do it by myself. I'll holler if I need you. I'll come out to the kitchen for my second coffee."

John and Abagail were both up and in the kitchen.

"How's Damon doing this morning, Samantha?"

"Good. He's in the bathroom. He'll be out in a minute for another cup of coffee."

Damon came out of the bathroom in his wheelchair and said good morning to his parents.

"What's on your agenda today, son?"

"I have therapy at 11:00 A.M., then I am going to call an attorney regarding the accident. I need to get a copy of the police report as well."

"Why do you need a police report, sweetheart?"

"Because, Mother, the guy who put me in this chair was drunk. I'm not going to let him walk away from his responsibility in this accident. The insurance company may have paid for my bike, but there will be outstanding medical bills that need paid, and his insurance will be responsible. Father has been in medicine long enough for you to appreciate the astronomical bills that are mounting. My insurance company will pay initially, but they will go after his insurance to pay them back. Unfortunately, it's a cutthroat game that is played by the insurance companies."

Damon glanced over at Samantha and noticed her hands were shaking. She lifted her cup to her lips, trying hard not to let him catch her shaking.

"Samantha, darlin. You need to consider talking to an attorney as well. I'm aware your bills are minor compared to mine, but you should not be paying out of your pocket."

"I'll consider it, Damon. The dogs and I are heading to work. I'd love for you to stop by, but I have no free time in my schedule today."

Samantha kissed him goodbye, thanked John for the coffee, and called for the dogs to put on their leash. She said hello to nurses in the parking lot. They asked how Damon was doing, and she told them he'd been discharged yesterday and was improving daily.

Damon's aide arrived and helped get him started with his care. He decided he wanted to wheel himself to therapy, but there was no ramp available for his wheelchair.

"Father, can you lift my wheelchair? I want to take myself to therapy, but I can't manage the wheelchair and my crutches at the same time."

"Do you have the stamina for that, Damon?"

"I'm not sure, but we are going to find out. I want to stop in the ER and talk to Alex before my therapy session."

"I'll take care of your wheelchair. We should be here this afternoon when you return."

"Let's see how I manage this today, if you don't mind helping."

"Damon, why don't I push you? I'm concerned you'll overdo it and then you'll be exhausted before therapy."

"I'll be great, Mother. You and Father should do something fun today. Go shopping and have lunch. It's time to stop sitting around here worrying about me."

"That's a little hard to do. Your father and I have been extremely worried about your ability to recover from this accident."

"I'm going to be fine in time. You need to go home, Mother."

"Does Samantha want us to leave?"

"Samantha says you are welcome to stay here as long as you want. You have given up three weeks of your time to sit here and wait for me to recover. I'll be completely fine soon. You need to get back to your friends, and golf, and your card club."

"Nonsense Damon. Those things don't matter to us. You matter, and we'll be here until you are up on your feet again."

"Okay, Mother. We will finish this conversation another time. I'm leaving. I'll see you later this afternoon."

Alex heard a commotion coming from the corridor and walked out of the office. He noticed Damon sitting in a wheelchair talking to the staff. Good for him, thought Alex. He wasn't sitting around moping about being encased in a cast and depending on others to help him get through the day.

Damon looked up and noticed Alex watching his interaction with the staff. He gave him a two-finger salute, and Alex laughed. That knock on the head did not affect him, either. He was happy for him and Samantha. When they wheeled Damon into the ER three weeks ago, he was not sure of Damon's long-term outcome.

Alex returned to his office and Damon arrived two minutes later.

"Great to find you up and around, Parker."

"Thanks, Montgomery. It's good to be out of that hospital bed. I thought I'd catch up on ER happenings while I wait for my therapy session."

"How's that going?"

"Good, so far. If Tobin ever gets back from his trip abroad, I may be able to get this cast off and get into Samantha's program. The other thing I need is to stay awake more than four or five hours at a time. I'm exhausted by lunch."

"Patience, Damon. It will be good to have you back at work. I asked the board to hold your position. I told them you'll do chart audits and paperwork to get you back in the office at least part-time."

"I think I can manage that before too long. I'm not used to sitting around doing nothing."

"Let's not push it, Parker. When you come back, I need you to be back, and not in and out, because you are overdoing everything. Just pace yourself."

"You, and your beautiful wife are both pretty bossy, Montgomery."

"Look, Parker. You agreed to help her, so don't throw that back at me. I have nothing to do with that decision. You are on your own with her. I'm not getting into the middle of that construction project. If she asks for my help, I'll be happy to assist, but I'm not volunteering."

"Understood. I've got to run."

By the time Damon finished his therapy he nearly had to crawl into bed. He was exhausted and in severe pain. He took a pain pill and refused the lunch his mother had made. He pacified her by telling her he would have the food she made for a snack when he woke up."

Kohl woke him up by huffing at him again. He spoke to the dogs and looked at the clock. How had it gotten to be 5:00 P.M. so quickly? He had crashed hard. He used the side rail to move to a sitting position, and the room spun. He needed food. He sent Samantha a text message, and she came through the door seconds later.

"How are you Sleeping Beauty?"

"Okay, so I admit I overdid it today. I've learned my lesson. I'm starving and the room was spinning when I sat up. Can you grab me a snack before I pass out?"

"I'll be right back. Do you want your wheelchair?"

"Yes, please. Can you have my father grab it for me?"

Samantha stood by Damon while he transferred to his wheelchair. She pushed him to the kitchen table. She had prepared crackers, cheese, and an apple coated in peanut butter.

"Did you eat breakfast, Parker?"

"No."

"Lesson number one, Parker. Eat breakfast. Lesson number two, carbs, and protein immediately after you finish your therapy session. You are burning calories and will be lying flat on your face on the floor if you don't eat. No more lunch refusals."

"I swear I'm going to send my mother back to her own home."

"Well, you better send your father, too, because he was the one who told me you did not eat lunch today."

"Okay! I got the message.",

"You're a doctor, Damon. You are aware of what a body needs. Quit trying to prove you are fine, and prove you are educated enough to take care of yourself without a relapse."

"If you're done yelling at me, can I get a kiss? And thanks for the food."

Samantha leaned toward him and kissed him.

"You better eat your mother's dinner, or she is going to be highly irritated with you. Not only did you ask her to go home, but you refused her lunch. If you refuse her dinner, she might just swoon."

Damon chuckled. "Do they tell you everything, darlin?"

"You are the only thing they need to worry about. And by the way, we are eating your favorite childhood comfort foods for dinner, so bring your appetite or figure out a way to sneak the food to the dogs without her seeing you."

"Dear Lord. I am never going to survive this rehabilitation."

"Before you succumb to the rehab, you should find a way to eat some of her fried catfish, mac and cheese, some veggie I've never ever heard of, and a piece of key lime pie."

"Dear Lord. I've never liked any of that food, so I'm not sure how she decided they were my favorite dishes."

"Find a way to eat a little bit of everything she made so you don't offend her again today. They'll be leaving here soon enough."

Samantha helped Damon to sit on a chair at the dining room table. She tried not to laugh when Damon noticed all the food on the table.

"Mother, this is entirely too much food. I'm not used to eating much, so we need to take this slowly."

"You need your strength to get through therapy, dear. You can't do that unless you eat."

"I appreciate the trouble you went to, Mother, but I need smaller meals, or I will be puking my guts out in therapy and undoing all your hard work."

"I'll consult with your father, and produce options for you to choose from, dear. You need food to heal and get back to your normal routine."

"Mother, this is going to take months. You do not need to be here that entire time. I can call you daily if you want, but we have encroached on Samantha's hospitality for long enough. Alex is going to let me come back to work part-time to do chart audits and other paperwork until I'm released to examine patients. There's no reason for you to sit around here the entire time."

"Do you want pie, dear?"

"I'll have a very small piece, and I will take it out on the front porch. Hand me my coffee stuff and I'll make us coffee to go with it."

Damon had another quiet night, and the dogs woke him the next morning. Samantha made coffee, and he got up and sat at the table in his wheelchair for breakfast.

"I have an appointment with my attorney this afternoon. My father will take me to his office. I may not be here when you get done with work."

"I have nothing planned this evening, love. Let's plan to watch a movie."

"That sounds great. I'm going to take a nap before Father, and I head to the attorney's office this afternoon. Hopefully, I can stay awake through a move."

Samantha's phone pinged with a text message from Abbie.

"Kate and Julie will be in town in two weeks. We are going to get together at Dana's house that weekend. Kate and Julie want to look at the property on Friday afternoon after they arrive. Can you ask Damon if he wants to view the property as well? Looking forward to all of us being together."

Samantha sent Abbie the thumbs up emoji.

"That was Abbie. Kate and Julie will be arriving here in two weeks, so that means Tobin will be back soon as well. They want to view the property Abbie purchased on Friday after they arrive. She asked if you wanted to join them."

"Yes. If Tobin comes back, then I might get out of this long leg cast. That would be wonderful."

"It would make it easier for you to get around, and we can begin hydrotherapy on your leg. That should speed up the recovery process. I need to head across the street. Have a good day, love."

Damon pulled himself to a standing position and reached for Samantha. He leaned against the kitchen counter and balanced himself on one leg while he kissed Samantha. He wrapped her in a hug.

"It won't be long before we are through this, darlin. Just hang in there."

Damon stopped by the therapy building when he was finished with his session. The dogs had completed their sessions for the day, and he asked to take them home with him.

"How are you going to manage them, Parker?"

"Wrap Koko, and Kody's leashed to the armrest on the wheelchair, and they can walk beside me. Kohl will be fine. You realize he is not going to wander off."

"Fine. But I will watch the four of you from outside while you make your way across the road. If they get tangled up, you are all going to be in a pile in the middle of the road."

"Give these pups the credit they deserve. They are wonderful dogs, and they listen to everything they are told."

"And they are still pups, Damon. I'm not sure I can trust them yet. They are fine in the pool. We need to practice a little more off leash and evaluate how they do before we turn them loose."

"I agree with that plan, darlin. If you don't give them a chance, you will never know what they are capable of."

The five of them walked outside. Damon called his father to meet him in the driveway to get the chair. Samantha watched from the sidewalk next to the therapy building and was relieved when the four of them arrived at the steps to the front porch. Damon turned to her and waved. She waved back, and Kohl turned toward her and barked.

Damon napped, met with the attorney, and was waiting for Samantha on the porch, when she arrived home. Abagail started dinner and refused Samantha's and Damon's offer of help. Samantha cleaned up the kitchen after dinner and told Damon she would meet him in the bedroom for the movie they had agreed to watch.

Kohl climbed up onto the bed and lay next to Samantha, while Koko and Kody settled onto the rug next to Damon. They were barely thirty minutes into the movie when Samantha listened to the sounds of soft snoring coming from Damon's side of the bed. She turned to look at Damon, who was sound asleep.

She was exhausted as well and did not really want to climb the steps to the bedroom upstairs. She reached for her phone and set her alarm for 5:30 A.M. Chances were, she would be awake before Damon and could turn her alarm off before it woke him up in the morning.

She got up and got ready for bed, then climbed in next to Damon. She snuggled up to his side and his arm went around her. Right now, she felt safer than she had since the accident.

Her thoughts were all over the place lately, and she realized she needed to make an appointment with the therapist Alex had recommended. She had done wonders for Alex and Abbie when they were struggling with their relationship, but there never seemed to be enough time in her day to squeeze in an appointment with anyone else.

She was looking forward to the ladies' weekend at Dana's place. The last time she remembered the five of them being alone together was right after Tom and died.

She felt guilty about leaving Damon with his parents, but she needed time with her crew. She realized he would understand and would encourage her to take time for herself. He was a good guy, and his father reminded her Damon would always do the right thing. She snuggled closer to his side and fell into a deep sleep.

CHAPTER 22

Damon and Samantha fell into a daily routine of coffee in the mornings, dinner that his mother prepared, and sitting on the front porch relaxing before bed. They were discussing Abbie's construction project when Damon's phone pinged with a text message.

"Flight arriving tomorrow. I hope you are staying out of trouble. I ordered an x-ray of your leg. Get that done tomorrow, and if it looks good, we can get the cast removed. Plan on an air cast for a couple more weeks and ask that lovely girl of yours if she has room in her schedule for you to start water therapy."

Damon let out a resounding woohoo!

"Must be good news. Who was that?"

"That darlin, was Tobin. He's on his way back to the states tomorrow, and he ordered an x-ray to be done. If it looks good, he'll remove this annoying cast. He asked if you have room in your schedule to set up my water therapy."

"My schedule is completely full, love. I may need to refer you to another therapy company. I understand there's one in Columbia. I'd be happy to call them for you."

"What? That's nearly three hours from here. How am I going to get there and back and still get work done?"

"I'm sure your parents will chauffeur you back and forth, or you might consider getting a hotel room in town until you complete therapy. Your mother did say she was here to make sure you get better."

Samantha was trying not to laugh at Damon.

"Are you serious? Can't you discharge someone?"

"I can't just throw people out because you might be ready for therapy."

John, and Abagail were also trying to keep a straight face.

"Damon. We can drive you. Your father and I have nothing else to do. We want you to get back on your feet. How long do you expect the therapy to last? We can get an apartment in town. We have nothing to rush home to, Damon."

"Does the Columbia facility use dogs like you do in your program?"

"No, love. We are unique in this field. You will receive standard water therapy if they have an opening in their schedule."

"You can stay at our house Damon if you are going to do standard water therapy. Charlotte is an hour from us and a much quicker commute every day. I'm sure we can find you a program that has an opening that is located near our house."

"Am I dreaming this? I must be. When I was in the ICU, I couldn't understand the sounds and smells going on around me. Apparently, I'm dreaming again. This cannot be real. I just hope I wake up and don't find myself in that ICU again."

"You are not dreaming, love. We are sitting on the front porch. Life doesn't always go the way we plan. Once Tobin gets back and we know the results of your x-ray, I will look at my schedule. Perhaps there will be a spot open for you."

Samantha, John, and Abagail started laughing.

"You are messing with me, aren't you?"

Samantha raised her eyebrows but said nothing.

"Not funny, Samantha. I may search for a program in California, and I'll return when I want to come back. And I'll take the dogs with me."

"They belong to me and Abbie, Damon. They won't go with you."

"They'd go with me. Well, at least Koko and Kody would go. Kohl assumes that you and Abbie are the only ones in charge because you brainwashed him."

"Tom was the one who trained Kohl, and the six of us raised him. He will always defer to us and protect us first. Everyone else is secondary. If we are fine, then you become his primary concern. It's just the way he is. Newfoundland dogs are loyal to a fault. Koko and Kody may defer to you because you've been around since we got them, but Kohl's allegiances lie with the five of us."

Kohl watched the interaction from his spot at Samantha's feet. He turned his head to Damon and huffed.

Samantha chuckled. "I rest my case, Parker."

Damon stared back at Kohl. "You are a dang traitor, Kohl. We're men. We must stick together."

Kohl stood and huffed at Damon, turned his back to him, and laid his big head on Samantha's lap.

Everyone laughed, including Damon.

"Dang traitor. Is there something here for dessert, Mother? And don't give Kohl any."

"There is ice cream or cookies, or both. Which one would you prefer?"

"Both please, and can you bring three biscuits for the dogs please? I need to try to sweeten up that traitor draped across Samantha's lap."

"Good luck with that, Parker. He'll take that biscuit and be back on my lap in a heartbeat. It took him a long time before he trusted Alex, but he will always defer to Abbie. Face it. You will always be second fiddle."

"As long as I am first in your eyes, I will tolerate second place with the traitor."

Samantha slept downstairs with Damon again. They were both exhausted and rarely moved once they fell asleep. There was no fear of her accidentally bumping Damon's leg during the night.

Damon woke up as Samantha turned on the shower. He prayed today was the last day with the cast because he wanted to take a shower, even if it meant he did it from a chair. He needed to ask his father to drive him to the barber once the cast was removed.

Damon grabbed his crutches and walked out to the kitchen, and gathered the supplies needed to make coffee. He wanted to treat Samantha and his parents to coffee this morning.

He needed to do more of the daily activities he was used to doing. He was finally feeling rested and if he did not overdo his daily activities; he would be able to take on more tasks.

He left the dogs outside and found the thermos in the kitchen. He grabbed two cups and poured a cup for Samantha just as she was entering the kitchen. The remainder he poured into the thermos for later.

"Good morning, darlin. Here is your coffee. I decided it was time I tried to tackle more tasks around here. I let the dogs out, but I don't believe I can manage their food and water yet."

"Thanks for the coffee, love, and I will get the food and water. Don't push yourself, Damon."

"I'm good. I feel like I have energy to do more things today. I'm going to head to the x-ray department and talk my way into getting on the schedule this morning."

"Oh, I don't doubt that you can charm your way into whatever time you want. The female staff at the hospital are doubtless going through withdrawal because you have not been at work. Take time to visit everyone. I'm sure they are missing you."

"I'll stop in and visit with you before my therapy. What is your schedule like, Samantha? Do you have room for me if Tobin removes the cast?"

"Are you seriously worried about getting on my schedule, Damon?"

"A little. I know you are in great demand."

"It's not me that is in demand, it's the dogs. Funny how adding animals to therapy can get people to show up when expected."

Damon reached out and grabbed Samantha around the waist and pulled her to him.

"If I get out of this cast, we can get back to spending quality time together."

"That sounds great, but let's get you out of the cast first. I'll look for you later this morning."

Damon charmed his way through the hospital and got his x-ray completed within thirty minutes of his arrival. He spent just under two hours visiting with the nurses and other staff. Eventually he made his way over to Samantha's building.

"I brought us snacks to enjoy before I go to therapy. I want you to realize that I am listening to your advice."

Damon reached into a bag and brought out a turkey sandwich with lettuce and tomato to share, along with peanut butter crackers.

"I bought cheese sticks and more crackers to eat after my session. Do I pass the test?"

Samantha chuckled.

"Yes, love. You passed the test. Can you manage to go out to dinner somewhere this evening? It's Friday, and your mother has been cooking every night, and she needs a break."

"I can manage dinner out. I'll ask Father to drive. Nothing fancy, I hope. I can't get this leg into pants. Anywhere particular you want to go?"

"I wanted to try The Black Drum at Kingston Resort. I know they are geared to tourists, but they are on the beach and have a nice outdoor patio with dining. I'll make reservations. They serve everything from pizzas to steaks and fish, and this evening there is music on the terrace as well."

"That sounds fantastic. I'll rest after therapy so that I don't fall asleep on my food. Can you text my father the address, and details after you make the reservations?"

"I've already given him the details. I couldn't imagine you would say no."

Damon got quiet and lowered his head.

"What's wrong, Damon?"

"Nothing's wrong, Samantha. I know you said this relationship between us cannot go anywhere. But you're wrong. You need to give us a chance. There is nobody else but you for me."

"I'm aware of what I told you, Damon. So much has happened in the past few weeks. We need to take our time and get through the next day. We were on a high from a new relationship, then immediately switched to fighting to save your life. We need to pace ourselves. We need to learn about each other separate from hospitals, therapy, and surviving. I trust we can do this, but let's not rush. I know more information about your parents than I know about you. I promise we will get through this and get back to a normal routine before long. Are you all right with that plan?"

"I'm good with it, darlin. I'm not always a patient person but I can be for you."

"Good. Now finish your sandwich and say goodbye to the dogs. I have a client in ten minutes. Get a nap and I will meet you this evening. We should leave the house at six. And by the way, I saw Hummingbird Cake on the dessert menu at The Black Drum to satisfy your sweet tooth."

Damon groaned. "You're killing me, darlin. Did you know it's one of my favorite desserts?"

"Your mother told me you loved it."

"Well, at least she got one right."

Samantha slipped quietly into the bedroom. Damon was still sleeping. She was quiet as she stepped into the shower, dressed, applied makeup, and dried her hair. He was sitting up in bed when she entered the bedroom.

"How is it that you appear more appealing every time I see you?"

"It may have something to do with the pain medication you are taking."

"I'm serious, Samantha."

"Thank you, Damon. I appreciate the compliment. Now, get out of that bed so we can take your parents to dinner."

"Send my parents to dinner and get into bed with me."

"Get out of the cast, and we can discuss. For tonight, you need to get ready for dinner."

"Remind me to throttle that idiot who hit us. He's robbing me of the one person who gives me pleasure."

It was a perfect night for dinner on the terrace at the beach. Samantha had called early in the week to make reservations but did not tell anyone what she had done. It was easy to cancel reservations, but difficult to get them in this town. Damon appeared well rested, and his color was improving. They all needed a night to relax and enjoy decent food and music. She reserved a table on the corner of the terrace and had explained that Damon needed the additional room for his leg that was in a cast.

"This is lovely, Samantha. John and I appreciate the offer of dinner. The weather is perfect this evening."

"We all needed an evening out. It's my first time here, but I've heard their food and service are great. I'm glad tomorrow is Saturday. We all need a morning to sleep late, and if Damon's x-ray looks good, perhaps I can bribe Tobin to remove that cast tomorrow. Did you review your results, Damon?"

"No. I considered it, but then decided I did not want to be in a lousy mood if the results were less than I hoped. I'll check them later tonight."

Samantha reached out and took Damon's hand in hers.

"Let's not worry about your x-ray this evening. Tobin will text you with the results once he has looked at the films. Tonight, we need to relax and have an excellent dinner. Do you want a glass of wine or a beer, love?"

"I did not take any pain medication this afternoon, so a glass of wine would be perfect. Father is driving. Mother, would you care for wine?"

"I would love a glass of wine, dear. We can get a bottle and take the leftovers home with us."

Damon ordered a bottle of wine, and they settled on the Smoked Black Drum Dip for an appetizer for the table. Samantha took a deep breath and relaxed. It was the first time since the accident. If she did not glance down at Damon's leg, she could ignore what had happened.

She sipped her wine and enjoyed the warm breeze coming off the ocean. She liked the convenience of living across the street from the hospital, but she was happiest when she was able to see and smell the ocean.

Her dream was to buy a small house on the beach. For years she had saved and was aware that if she kept up her savings, she might make it happen soon.

They talked about Damon and what he was like as a child. He tried to change the subject at every opportunity. Samantha laughed at the stories his mother insisted on telling. Damon ordered another bottle of wine, hoping that his mother would mellow out if she had another glass or two of wine, but it did not work. She was happy to have him out in public and continued to tell story after story.

The music started, and Damon insisted he and Samantha dance.

"How do you propose we accomplish that task, Damon?"

"I've one good leg and a crutch. We don't need to do circles on the dance floor darlin. I just want a chance to show you off."

"If you drop on the floor from pain or exhaustion, I am going to leave you lie there, and walk away. I hope you have friends in this crowd to pick you up. Your father told me you were a daredevil. Apparently, he was not wrong."

"Are you sure you should be dancing, dear?"

"Let's go. I will prove you wrong. I can stand on my own two feet. Well, my one good foot, and a crutch, but I can still dance with a beautiful woman."

He took Samantha's hand and used one crutch to walk to the dance floor. The other people moved out of his way to make room for them on the dance floor. He balanced himself on his good leg and put his arm around Samantha. The band watched the two of them walk onto the floor and immediately switched to a slow song. They barely moved their feet, but Samantha was proud of him for trying to stay upright, and she held tight to him so he would not fall. This was as close to normal as they had come in the past four weeks.

There were people in the crowd who recognized Damon and called out his name, but he concentrated solely on Samantha. They managed to dance to two songs before Damon admitted to Samantha that he needed to immediately return to his seat before he fell on the floor.

They returned to the table, and Damon gulped down two glasses of water. His phone rang, and he noticed Tobin's name.

"Excuse me, but I need to take this call."

"O'Brien, I hope you're calling with good news."

"Hello to you too, Parker. And what are you up to this splendid evening?"

"I'm drinking wine and dancing with a beautiful woman. Probably not what you expected to hear, is it?"

"Not exactly, but that tells me it is time to take that cast off your leg if you want to get rid of it. We can always leave it for another month."

"Try it. I know how to use a saw to remove a cast, remember?"

"Meet me in the ortho clinic tomorrow at 11:00 a.m. and we will switch it for an air cast. Don't drink too much and ruin all my work. Tell Samantha I said hello."

"Thanks O'Brien. Glad you're back."

CHAPTER 23

Tobin rolled over in bed and put his arm around Julie's waist. She turned to face him.

"Good morning. You are awake early this morning."

"It's a habit that's hard to break, but that doesn't mean we are getting out of this bed early."

"That invitation is one I'll willingly accept."

"Are you telling your friends you are here, or can I keep you hidden and to myself for the week?"

"I'm yours. Even if they find out, I'm here, it doesn't change the plans we made."

"Good. If I can keep Conor out of the apartment this week, nobody will find out. I believe I can talk him into staying with Dana for the week."

"I can always call her and make that suggestion. She won't notice if I call from here or my place. If they find out I'm here, I'll say I was house shopping and wanted to do it by myself. They have enough to keep them busy this week, but that Abbie has this innate ability to recognize when something is happening."

"Are you sure you are good with us moving in together? You can tell me no. It might hurt my feelings, but I will adjust."

"You sound as though you are having second thoughts. If so, just tell me Tobin."

"No second thoughts from me. I know what I want. I want you with me every day. I don't care what anyone else thinks."

"What time are you meeting Damon today?"

"I told him to meet me at the clinic at 11:00 a.m."

"Great. That gives me time to take you up on your lovely offer of staying in bed."

Damon woke up early, but Samanta was still sleeping. He stayed in bed and quietly looked at the news on his phone. He wanted to let her sleep. Even though he had home health aides, Samantha tried to help before they arrived. Once he got the cast off today, he would end his contract with the agency. He'd manage on his own without the heavy, long leg cast.

Damon was ready to send his mother and father home, and to take Alex up on his offer to go back to work part-time. He was getting bored, but he still needed to rest after his therapy. He'd talk to Alex regarding working the early morning shift, then he could still make his therapy appointments in the afternoon. When Samantha woke up, he'd discuss his plan with her and see if she had an open early afternoon slot for his therapy.

Damon quietly slid out of bed and looked for the dogs. Samantha closed the door to the bedroom, so the dogs did not wander in during the night and pose a tripping hazard for him. They were standing at the door to the bedroom with their tails wagging as soon as they heard him. He said hello and let the dogs outside. He stood at the door and watched them wandering around the backyard.

His home health aide said good morning, and Damon told her he was getting his cast off today and no longer needed someone available during the night. He planned to call the office later this morning and cancel the services. He gave the aide a large tip and thanked her for putting up with him and the dogs.

Damon walked into the kitchen and made coffee. He wanted to treat Samantha to breakfast this morning. Dinner last night was wonderful, and he wanted to return the favor. He searched for ingredients to make pancakes and lined everything up on the counter. Pancakes were his mother's favorite breakfast food, so he could treat her as well.

He heard Samantha open the door to the bedroom. She walked out wearing a pair of sleep shorts and a tank top, and Damon groaned. He needed this cast off, and soon. He was having trouble keeping his hands off Samantha, and he wanted her more than the air he breathed.

"What are you doing up so early, love?"

"I've spent too much time in bed, and I need to find something to keep me occupied. I made coffee for you. I'm planning to make breakfast as well."

"I'll help you, Damon. I appreciate the offer, but you are still in that long leg cast. Take your time for a couple of weeks before attempting too much."

"I can manage this, darlin. I told my aide I'd not be needing their services any longer. I'll call the office soon."

"What are you doing, Damon? Just because you are converting to an air cast today, does not mean they released you to do everything you want. Your leg is still fragile. Be careful with activities. I'm going to feed the dogs and take a shower. I'll have coffee once I'm dressed. Do you want me to go to your appointment this morning?"

"Yes, please. It will give you a chance to talk to Tobin about my therapy. Did he submit a request for me?"

"No Damon. Tobin has been away. I will fit you into my schedule. Why are you trying to rush everything today?"

"I'm not trying to rush. I'm eager to take a shower and get out of the cast. When was the last time you went a month without a shower? I can't stand the smell of myself. I don't blame you for staying away from me."

"Whoa! Do not start projecting your insecurities on me. In three hours, you can shower. Did you ask your father to take you for a haircut? If not, ask him. But I have never given you any sign that I don't want to be near you for any reason other than a shattered leg. You need to consider your next words carefully, Damon."

John walked into the kitchen. "Everything okay in here?"

"Everything is fine, John. I'm going to get into the shower, and Damon wants to talk to you about a haircut."

Samantha walked toward the bedroom and locked the door. She was fuming over Damon's ridiculous idea, and right now, she did not want to be near him. She grabbed her phone and sent her crew a text.

"Need a call with all of you this morning to help me regain my balance. Are you free at 10:00 a.m.?"

Everyone immediately said yes. Samantha took a deep cleansing breath and stepped into the shower. What had happened to Damon overnight? In her opinion, he was being reckless. What was he trying to prove?

"Everything okay, son? Samantha looked upset."

"She blamed me of projecting my insecurities on to her."

"Was there a good reason for her saying something like that, Damon?"

Damon sighed. "I'm an idiot Father. I accused her of not wanting to be near me because I've not been able to take a shower for a month."

"Did she give you a reason to say something that stupid?"

"No. It is my guilt. I'm tired of depending on everyone else and I'm tired of being exhausted all the time. I fired my home health aide this morning as well."

"Why would you do something like that?"

"I need to be more independent, Father. I am a physician. It's my job to take care of people. I don't want people taking care of me."

"It is because of other people you are still breathing. Did you forget that already?"

"No. I need to go apologize to Samantha."

"Give her time to herself, Damon. She is not going to listen to anything else you have to say for a while. Sit down and drink a cup of coffee with me. We need time to catch up. We've been preoccupied with you, and your recovery. It's time we talk about everyday stuff."

"I'm not sure I recognize how to do that any longer. I need to call Alex about going back to work."

"I agree. We need to invite Alex, Conor, and Tobin for an evening of wings and a couple of beers. I'll drive or we can hire a driver."

"I'll talk to Tobin this morning and call the others. That's a good idea. The girls are planning their girls' weekend at Dana's next weekend. I'll make sure Samantha plans to go. She needs time away from my crazy ideas."

Samantha walked out of the bedroom and went straight to the kitchen for a cup of coffee. She avoided looking at Damon.

He shuffled to the other side of the island and took the coffee cup from her hands and placed it on the countertop. She dropped her arms to her side and continued to avoid looking at Damon. John walked out to the front porch to give them their privacy.

"I'm sorry, Samantha. I had no right to accuse you of anything. I am wallowing in my own self-pity, and I did not mean to hurt you."

He wrapped his arms around her and balanced his good hip against the island. "Can you forgive me?"

Samantha nodded, but otherwise did not move.

"Can you look at me, please?"

She shook her head no.

"Samantha, I'm an idiot, and my father has confirmed that for me. I'm going to call Alex and ask if I can go back to work because I need something to do. I'm so angry at that guy for putting us in this situation. Then I get angry because I cannot take care of everything on my own. I need Alex's therapist."

Samantha nodded her head but refused to look at him.

"I'll go to my appointment on my own. Why don't you call Abbie and spend time with her and the babies today? You deserve a break. I promise to get my head on straight and make this up to you. I realize how much you sacrificed for me."

Samantha nodded her head and wrapped her arms around him. They stood until she noticed he was getting tired of standing on his feet.

"Sit down, Damon. I'm going to call Abbie."

Samantha walked out onto the back porch and sat down on the step. She sent Abbie a text asking if she was free. Her phone rang almost before she hit the send button.

"Hey Sam. What going on?"

"Are you busy today? I need a break from Damon and was hoping you were free."

"Are you okay? Are you crying? What's happening, Sam? Of course, you can come over here. Never think I'm turning people away with three babies in this house."

"I do not wish to intrude, but I need a break."

"Get your stuff and get over here. You can stay the night."

"I don't need to stay the night, but I'll hold and change babies. They are much easier to deal with than adults. Is Andy at home too?"

"Andy's here. Can you bring Kohl?"

"I will bring Kohl. Damon can keep the other two. I'll be there shortly."

Samantha walked into her bedroom to gather her things. She might stay the night. Right now, she was angry with Damon and not thinking clearly. But he deserved an explanation of where she was going and what she planned to do.

Damon was sitting in the kitchen with his mother. They were sipping coffee. His father was outside with the dogs. She opened the door and called for Kohl to come back indoors.

"I'm going to Abbie's house and taking Kohl with me so he can see Andy. I'm not sure if we will be home tonight. I'll text you and update you on my plans. Lock up please if you are going to be away."

"Can we talk before you leave, Samantha?"

"Not right now, Damon. I need to leave. We'll talk tomorrow. Good luck with your cast removal this morning. Tell Tobin to submit the paperwork for your therapy."

Kohl noticed the tension between Samantha and Damon and leaned against her side. She turned and walked away. Kohl walked out the door, turned, huffed at Damon, walked next to Samantha, and got into the car.

Andy was waiting in the yard for them when Sam pulled into the driveway. Kohl nearly knocked her over, trying to get out of the car and see Andy. Within seconds, they were rolling around on the ground together. Kohl was licking Andy's face, and Andy was giggling.

Abbie and Alex walked outside and carried the girls, and they started giggling, too. She reached for Isabella, and breathed in the baby smell that was so contagious. She was good until Abbie hugged her, and the tears started. When she noticed Isabella's bottom lip form a pout, she dried her tears and said hello to all the others, and they all walked inside. It was just before 10:00 a.m.

"Do you still want to do our call, Sam?"

"Yes, but I don't need the others to realize anything other than I am visiting for today."

"I'm good with that idea. We will discuss what we are doing next weekend."

They logged into the call while Alex and Ms. Helen put the girls down for their morning naps. Kohl and Andy were back outside playing.

"Hey, what are you two doing together?"

"Hanging out with Abbie and the kids. Kohl and Andy needed a play date, and I needed baby time."

"How's Damon doing?"

"Damon is good. He is getting his long leg cast off today and going into an air cast. He's beginning to get his strength back. We went to dinner last night and were on the dance floor for five minutes. We did little dancing, but it was nice to do something besides sit at the house."

"What are we doing next weekend? Anybody have recommendations?"

"Beach time, alcohol, good food, and wonderful music." Kate said, laughing.

"I think that sounds perfect." Sam said. "I need all the above listed items."

"I'll hire us a driver so we can have a couple drinks if we want, and I'm paying for our shopping splurge as well. We will use the driver for shopping and lunch. No responsibilities next weekend other than having fun."

"Abbie. We can pitch in for the limo. You are not paying for everything."

"You guys can leave the tip. I'm paying for our weekend. We've not had an opportunity to get together for a long time. And don't forget, Julie, Kate, Damon, and I are doing a quick tour of the property Friday afternoon. We will pick Damon up at Sam's since he does not have clearance to drive. When we are done, I'll drop Damon off and drive us all to Dana's. I've ordered food and snacks to be delivered, so we don't need to lift a finger all weekend."

"You realize we work, Abbie. We can help pay for things."

"Tom would not want it any other way. He always wanted to pay for things when we were together. Little did any of us know he had a private stash, but that doesn't change the fact that we are still using his money to pay for our weekends."

"Well, then we will spend our money spoiling Andy and the girls."

"Perfect. We will see you girl's next weekend. Samantha and I are going to relax on the deck while the three girl's sleep. Travel safe, Kate and Julie. Can't wait to see you next week."

"Mom, can Kohl and I play in the water? We will stay in front of the house. We won't go too far in. It's hot outside, and the water will help keep us cool."

"Sure. Sam and I are going to be sitting on the deck. If you hear me blow the whistle that means you need to return to the house."

"Thanks, we won't be too long."

Abbie poured iced tea, and they sat in the rocking chairs on the deck.

"Okay, Sam. Spill it. What is going on with you and Damon?"

"He blamed me for not wanting to be near him because he has not had a shower in a month, which is a complete lie. It made me extremely angry, and I walked away. He's bored out of his mind, but if he thinks he is going to accuse me of something I haven't done, he better pack his bags. Do not accuse me of things I haven't done.

"Wow. That surprises me. He does not seem the type of person who would pull something like that. Perhaps that knock on the head affected him more than we realize."

"It could be a result of the head injury. But I was so angry I couldn't speak. I was so close to tears, and I was determined not to show him how his accusation affected me. He suggested I call you, so I did. I've bent over backwards, and done everything to keep him safe and comfortable, and he is concentrating on suing the drunk guy who hit him. He thinks I should sue too, but I am not sure I want to get into a legal battle."

"Did his parents make plans to leave?"

"Not that I am aware of, but it's time. His mother is on a mission to feed him his favorite foods but none of them are foods he likes. It is a battle with every meal."

"You need to put your foot down and send them home. The two of you have enough to worry about. Let him call them with updates."

"Damon told her it was time for them to go home. He wants Alex to let him come back to work. If you have any pull with Alex, please tell him to give Damon work. It may be the only thing that saves this relationship."

"Do you love him, Sam?"

"I'm not sure, Abbie. Right now, I'm so angry I don't even want to look at him."

"Let's get through today then tomorrow you two can talk, and sort this out. You are perfect for one another, but the stress of his extensive injuries is taking a toll on both of you. You can always reach out to Alex and me for help."

"Thanks, Abbie. I'm so glad we are friends."

CHAPTER 24

Damon ambled across the street to his appointment at 11:00 a.m. and Tobin was waiting for him in the ortho clinic.

"It's about time you appeared, Parker. I assumed you'd be here early, so here I sit waiting. Not having seconds thoughts about getting that cast off, are you?"

"No. Get the saw in motion so that I can increase my mobility, please. This inactivity is killing me, and it may be the ruination of my relationship with Samantha."

"Oh no. What's going on with the two of you?"

"It's not her, it's me. I accused her of something she did not do, and she left to stay overnight at Abbie's. She would not even glance at me, and she isn't talking to me either."

"You know that group of girls will take you out at the knees. You won't need to worry about this minor injury when they get done with you. Wow, Parker, you better produce a good apology."

"I don't expect grand standing will affect Samanta. To tell you the truth, I don't assume it will affect any of them. They were all cut from the same cloth. Montgomery warned me not to get involved with any of them, and I did not have the brains to take his advice."

"Ha! Like he knows everything. He married one of them and has triplets."

"Didn't I pick up your name mentioned in connection to Julie's? You better run while you can."

"I'm not running anywhere. My Irish mother raised me. Apparently, I've had more sense beat into me than the rest of you. I know how far I can push things. And my mother's still living, so there will be no shenanigans from me, or Conor. That ocean is not deep enough or far enough away to escape her wrath if we mess up, especially if it involves a lady."

"Samantha said right off the bat that I was a player, and this could not go anywhere. We were on a great path until the accident."

"Is she still going to do your therapy? I'll put the order in for you."

"Samantha said to tell you to write the order and send the paperwork, but Kohl was huffing at me when they left yesterday. He'll doubtless just drag me under and hold me there to get back at me for upsetting her."

Tobin laughed. "They trained him. What else do you expect? And I'd watch my back if I were you. Those dogs can pull a boat full of people through turbulent seas. If you screw up again, no telling what he might do."

"Do you think those dogs are vindictive?"

"You need to have Montgomery tell you about his first run in with Kohl, then decide what your next move is."

"Get this cast off this leg. I need a shower and a haircut, then I need to figure out a way to get back in her good graces. Apparently, that woman is going to keep me on my toes. And if it helps, my father called me an idiot, so there will be no help from him."

"Good luck with that and take it easy on this leg. I can't repair it again, and your mother has previously informed me, plainly, there will be no amputation of your body parts. You need to check her heritage. There must be Irish in her somewhere."

Damon showered, dressed, and offered to take his parents to lunch if his father drove. His mother shopped while he was getting a haircut, and Damon found a jewelry store where he picked out a necklace for Samantha. The blue-colored stone matched her eyes. He knew this gesture would not sway her one way or the other, but he wanted to let her know he was sorry for his recent behavior.

Damon spent the rest of the afternoon playing with the dogs and napping on the front porch. He ordered a pizza for dinner and wondered if Samantha would come home tomorrow. His parents left to go out for dinner. His mother was worried, but his father reminded her Damon was independent and a college graduate.

What he needed was to get back to his usual routine, and that meant returning to work. He wanted to talk to Alex, but if he called now, Samantha would assume he was checking on her. It was precisely what he wanted to do, but knowing Alex, he'd tell him to mind his own business.

Damon planned to text her in the morning, apologizing once more and asking her to have dinner with him. No parents, no friends. Somewhere on the beach where they could sit outside and have the privacy they needed.

Damon turned in early and set his alarm so that he could let the dogs out in the morning. He overheard his parents come in shortly after he climbed into the bed. He needed to talk to them, too. It was time for them to leave. He would allow them to stay until next weekend, so that his mother could understand that he could get around better with the air cast and his crutches. But he was not extending the time. If he and Samantha needed to work this out, they needed time to be alone.

Damon was up with the alarm. His father was in the kitchen and had let the dogs out. Damon cleaned the dogs' food dishes and used a pitcher he found in the cabinet to pour water into their water bowls. Samantha kept a scoop in the food storage container, and he used it to fill their food bowls.

Damon had a cup of coffee with his father and mother and fixed breakfast for the three of them. The more he did, the easier it might be to convince his mother that he could manage on his own.

He showered and dressed and took his computer out onto the front porch to do research for Abbie. The regulations she asked him to study were straightforward, and they should be able to break ground on the therapy site soon. The lot was empty except for weeds and that would reduce the time needed to prepare the land. Abbie was going to explain the architect's rendering on Friday afternoon when they saw the property.

He glanced up when he heard Samantha's car pull into the driveway. He waved, and she waved back.

"Well, that's a good start. Who knows where it goes from here?"

Samantha left the car outside of the garage and walked over to the porch. Kohl bound up the stairs and stood by Damon. Damon said hello, then reached for his crutches and stood to greet Samantha. They both spoke at once.

"May I go first, Samantha?"

Samantha nodded her head.

"I'm sorry, and I don't have the words to apologize to you properly. I'm miserable because of the accident and not working, but I'm miserable when I am without you. Can we start over today and go to the same bar where we had our first date? I need to reset every part of me and I'm hoping that might help me get back on track."

"I'm sorry for overreacting to your comment. Normally, I'd roll my eyes at you and move on, but this accident has me out of sorts as well. I'd love to start over today. Can we start with a hug because I can honestly use one?"

Damon walked over to her and hugged her. Samantha got weepy again. Damon kissed her forehead. "Please don't weep, darlin. I'm not worth the energy it takes to shed tears."

Samantha wiped her face on her sleeve. "I'm going to take a shower and lay down on the bed for a while. What time do you want to leave?"

"How's 2:00 p.m.? We can have a late lunch, or early dinner and enjoy the afternoon by the water. The crowds should be gone by then and we'll have more privacy."

"That sounds good. Let me go say hello to your parents and the other dogs. I want to rest for a bit before we leave. I'll be back shortly."

Damon had called an Uber, and the car was waiting for them when Samantha came out of the bedroom.

"I decided we should have a driver. I don't plan to do shots like the ones we had the last time, but a glass of wine might be suitable for the afternoon."

"I agree, and I don't want to drive, so I appreciate your forethought."

They chose a high table on the covered deck. Damon pulled his chair closer to Samanta so they could talk without yelling at one another. They ordered a bottle of wine, and salmon topped salads. They were both hesitant at first but kept their conversation general and did not bring up the accident. It was an unspoken agreement between them.

"Are you still having your get together next weekend?"

"Yes. We haven't been together as a group since Tom died. Abbie hired a limo, catered food to be delivered at Dana's beach house, and planned a shopping spree to top off the weekend. And there's no sense fighting it. Tom always paid for our weekends together. Abbie assumed he just saved up money for us, but now we realize money was no object. Abbie intends to stick to that routine."

"Has she figured out who he is, and who left that enormous sum of money?"

"Not yet, but she'll make an announcement one day that will most likely shock every one of us. She and Alex did research, but they could never trace him anywhere."

"That's amazing. How does one just show up, or disappear as the case might be?"

"I'm not sure, but she deserves every penny. She had a tough life until she met the Wilsons. I suggested she make a list of the items we need for the therapy building like the ones shown in Santa Claus pictures. She told me she never made a Christmas list. Her foster families never considered her part of their families, so she was alone during the holidays. I hope she buys everything she wants now that she can."

"She doesn't seem to be one that will do that for herself."

"She's not. I assume she forgets she has that money. She treats other people, though. The community is lucky to have her creative ideas and Kohl's skills."

Samantha took another drink of her wine and Damon noticed she hardly ate any of her food.

"Are you okay, darlin? You have barely touched your food and you appear thinner than I remember."

"It's the stress of everything. And I don't want to appear rude, but it's time for your parents to go home, Damon. We need time to ourselves."

"I made that decision earlier today. I'll tell them tomorrow. I want to give them to the weekend so that my mother can understand I am more mobile with this cast, and I can fill them in on my therapy. If you can tolerate them watching my therapy one day, that may help satisfy her curiosity."

"I'm cool with that, Damon, and let's start with three days of water therapy for you this week. I have openings on Tuesday, Wednesday, and Thursday. That will give you a few days to recover from the basic eval and exercises. I planned to knock off work around 3:00 p.m. on Friday. I want to have time to get my stuff together before we head to Dana's and Alex is going to take the dogs. Andy is asking for the three of them, and this is the perfect opportunity."

"Abbie said she'd be at the house to pick me up around 3:30 p.m. When we get back, you can head to Dana's. I assume Alex will pick up the dogs when he is done with his shift."

Samantha and Damon crawled into bed early. Samantha snuggled up to his right side and fell asleep instantly. Damon lay awake for a while, struggling to find a comfortable position without waking Samantha. Finally, his pain medication took over, and he fell asleep.

The alarm woke up both of them the next morning. Samantha groaned and crawled out of bed. She let the dogs out, showered, and Damon greeted her with coffee when she entered the kitchen.

"This definitely tastes better when you make it."

"I don't think you or my father have perfected it yet. You are close, though."

"Okay, I'm out of here. I have a client this morning."

The week flew by quickly. Samantha insisted she and Damon keep a professional behavior during therapy in the pool. He stood by her request, and his mother and father were present for his session on Wednesday.

Damon talked to his parents regarding their return to their own house. His mother was not happy. After encouragement from his father, she agreed to leave if he and Samantha allowed them to visit or if they came to North Carolina to visit.

Friday rolled around, and Damon helped his parents pack their vehicle. They asked to wait until Samantha got home from work before leaving so, they could say goodbye. They went upstairs to rest and set their alarm so they could get on the road and be home before dusk.

Damon was restless and wandered around the house. He walked out to the garage and started his truck. He'd not run it for several weeks and he wanted to take it for a quick drive toward the coast. His right leg was okay, and Tobin had said nothing to him about driving. He raised the garage door and backed out. Traffic was thin, and he drove across the swing bridge and turned around in the parking lot at the beach but did not get out. He possessed the sense to realize maneuvering on the sand with crutches and one good leg was not a decent decision. He stopped and put gas in the truck and returned to the house and parked the truck in the garage.

He checked Samantha's bike. He adjusted the tire pressure, filled the gas tank, checked the oil, and cleaned the mirrors. The bike had not been ridden either since the accident. The garage door was still up, so he pushed the bike out of the garage. He closed the garage, pushed the bike to the porch, and left his crutches leaning against the railing. The bike started with one quick kick. He'd never been on Samantha's bike. They always took his bike when they rode together.

Turning left out of the driveway, he made his way over to route thirty-one. He missed the freedom of the bike. He knew he needed to be careful of the surrounding vehicles. Another accident, and he was likely to lose his leg.

He traveled past three exits on route thirty-one before exiting and took the ramp back onto thirty-one and returned to the house.

Samantha walked into the house with the dogs and did not notice Damon anywhere. John came down the steps with a suitcase.

"Have you seen, Damon? I was looking for him, but I can't find him."

"I overheard him start the truck earlier. I don't believe it's been run since the accident. Maybe he took it to fill the gas tank. Now that he is out of the cast, he can probably start driving small distances."

"Okay. I'll wait on the porch for him. Abbie should be here soon."

"Abagail and I will be out in just a moment. This is the last of our things."

Samantha watched, stunned, as Damon pulled into the driveway on her bike. He got off the bike in the driveway and smiled at her. John and Abagail walked out the door as Damon walked toward the house.

Samantha stood. "What are you doing, Damon?"

"I took the bike for a ride. It's been sitting in the garage for weeks. I also took the truck for a drive and put gas in it."

"Why are you on the bike, Damon.?"

"I just told you why, Samantha."

Samantha turned and walked into the house. She was gone just long enough for Damon to make his way to the porch.

Samantha came out of the house but did not notice Abbie, Kate, and Julie pulling into the driveway. She ran down the stairs with a baseball bat in her hand, kicked the bike to the ground, lifted the bat, and began destroying her bike.

Abbie gasped. "Dear Lord, Julie, what is she doing?"

"Stop the car, Abbie. Stop the car." Julie said as she jumped from the vehicle.

"Sam put the bat down on the ground. Stop hitting the bike."

Abbie and Kate both tried to get her attention, but she was oblivious to everyone and everything. Damon was pleading with her to stop, but his father stopped him from leaving the porch. Kohl was snarling from the doorway, but even that did not stop her. Bike parts were flying everywhere.

Abbie grabbed her phone. "I'm going to call Alex."

He answered on the first ring. "Hey love."

"Alex, Sam is using a bat and destroying her bike. She kicked the bike over as we drove into the driveway. We're trying to get her to stop, but she doesn't realize we exist."

Alex ran out of the ambulance entrance. "I'm on my way, love. Stay back until I get there. Where's Damon?"

"He's on the porch. His father has restrained him and won't let him leave the porch or go near her."

"I'm outside, Abbie. Call Dana and tell her to meet me in the parking lot with a gurney. She was getting ready to leave."

Abbie made the call to Dana.

Alex approached Sam without saying a word and waited until the next swing of the bat. As she lifted the bat for the next swing, Alex grabbed it from her hands and threw it to the ground. Samantha spun on him, appearing dazed.

"Sam. It's Alex. I'm going to pick you up and take you with me to the ER. Dana will be there, and Abbie, Kate, and Julie will be there too. You're okay. You just need to come with me."

Alex did not give her time to respond. He scooped her up and began walking back down the driveway, and back across the street to the ER. He talked to her the entire way. Dana was running across the parking lot with the gurney and met Alex. They ran with Sam into the ER and into the first trauma room.

Julie stomped up the steps and stood with her hands fisted on her hips, staring at Damon.

"What the hell went on here, Parker?"

Damon was shaking and pasty white. "I took her bike for a run since we had not run it for weeks. When I got off the bike and came up on the porch, she walked inside the house and came back out with the bat. I assume you observed the rest of what occurred."

"You don't deserve her, Parker. Pack you stuff and leave."

Julie walked back down the steps, got in the front seat, blew the horn at Kate and Abbie, and shouted, "Let's go!"

CHAPTER 25

"What in the world happened, dear?"

"Mother, you, and Father need to go home. I suspect Samantha has PTSD. I was aware she was not eating well, but she told me she was tired. I remember her hands shaking occasionally, but I was so wrapped up in my own misery, I didn't pay attention to the signs until today when everything broke. I'm not sure I can fix this, but I am going to spend every minute trying."

"Let's go Abagail. Damon will keep us informed. He's right. He needs to make sure Samantha is okay. They still have a bunch of healing to do, and they do not need the two of us in the middle of their suffering."

"Thanks, Father. I'll call later this evening and update you on her condition. If Julie assumes she can keep me from her, she might want to prepare to battle. Samantha is the only thing in this world I can't live without, and I'll do whatever it takes to fix her and fix this relationship."

"I believe in the two of you, son. Give her time to heal. None of us realized how this accident affected her, or we would have stepped in before now. I'm sorry I didn't recognize it either. Give her our love, son."

Alex took Sam's hand. "Sam, can you open your eyes for me?"

Samantha blinked. "Alex? Where am I? What happened?"

"You are in the ER with me and Dana. I suspect you are suffering from PTSD related to the accident, Sam, and I'm sorry I didn't notice it earlier. You had somewhat of a breakdown a while ago. I called Jillian Taylor, the psychiatrist I recommend to you. She'll be in to examine you shortly. Do you remember anything that happened?"

"No, Alex."

"What is the last thing you remember, Sam? Either from today or yesterday? Perhaps, even before that?"

"I was on the porch waiting for Abbie to get there. I looked for Damon but couldn't find him. I thought he might be with Abbie. I left work early, but apparently not early enough to go with them."

"Okay, Sam. That's good. How do you feel right now?"

"Okay, but to be completely honest with you, Alex, I've not been sleeping well. I keep having nightmares about Damon under that truck. I just can't unsee it."

"That's okay, Sam. That's difficult to forget. How is your appetite lately?"

"Not so great. I'm anxious and shaky and get sick if I think about eating. Damon has been telling me I look as though I'm losing weight, but I haven't weighed myself lately. Do you know where he is?"

"I understand he was assisting his parents to pack their belongings in the car. They were going home this afternoon. I'll call him. Do you want him to stop in and visit you?

"Yes, please. I'd prefer him to be here if he is not tired or in too much pain."

"Okay, Sam. I'll find him. Do you want something to drink?"

"No. Thanks though, Alex. I'll just close my eyes and take a nap if that's okay."

"That's fine with me. Let me get you a blanket."

Alex tucked two warm blankets around Sam and reached for his phone. Abbie and the others were in the private waiting room. He would update them after he talked to Parker.

Damon sat on the front porch of Samantha's house, staring into space. He didn't care what Julie said. It was not her house, and she had no right to tell him to leave. He and Samantha had an agreement that he could stay here. He was not leaving until she told him to leave. The dogs were laying at his feet, but Kohl was giving him the side eye, and he could not figure out why. He did nothing to him, nor said anything to upset him.

He leaned back in the chair and put his foot up on the footstool. His phone rang, and he realized it was Alex calling. He didn't bother to say hello.

"How is she, Montgomery?"

"Awake, but she is not aware of the incident that occurred."

"PTSD?"

"That's my guess, Parker. Did you not realize this was coming?"

"I asked her four or five times if she was okay. She wasn't eating well and complained she was tired. I caught her hands shaking at times, but assumed it was because of things my mother said to her. Please tell me she is okay."

"I called Jillian Taylor to examine her. She is on her way into the ER. I suggest you make an appointment with her as well. And I am sorry none of us noticed her symptoms. In retrospect, Dana and I both noted she'd change the conversation if the accident came up while we were talking with her. I don't get to see her often enough anymore to notice her weight loss, but I recognized it today once I picked her up in the driveway. She is asking for you, but that group of women who are in the waiting room may want to scratch your eyes out."

"Thanks for the warning."

"I'll talk with them. I realize this was not your direct fault, but what were you expecting when you got on that bike?"

"I just wanted to make sure it was okay for her to get on if she decided she wanted to go for a ride. It never occurred to me it would be the catalyst for her finally breaking over this accident. How am I going to apologize to her for this?"

"You are going to do what the rest of us are doing and take it one day at a time."

"I'll be over shortly. I'm going to feed the dogs and get a shower so that I can stay the night if she wants me there."

"I'll grab the dogs on my way home, Parker. You've got enough on your plate for now."

"Thanks, man. And can you get me back on the schedule, so I don't lose my mind, and need to be admitted to the psych ward?"

"Let's give Sam a few days to recover, and I will put you on the schedule part-time."

"Thanks man. I'm never going to find a way to repay you."

"No need for repayment. That's what friends are for Parker. Get over here and I will talk to the other four."

Alex walked to the private waiting room, and the four of them stood when he entered the room.

"How is she, love?"

"She is sleeping right now, Abbie. I called Jillian Taylor. I figured she was able to help us. She can help her and Damon, too."

"I told him to leave, and that he didn't' deserve her. What did he do that caused her to behave like that, Alex?"

"Well, Dr. Baxter, I assume you might have some understanding of PTSD?"

"Are you serious, Alex? How did I miss that?"

"We are all healthcare professionals. None of us caught it. It was the first words out of Damon's mouth when I called him. He said he suspected it a couple times, and he quizzed her, but she claimed she was tired. He said she was weepy, not eating well, not sleeping well, and appeared to be losing weight. Dana and I both caught her changing the conversation when we asked certain questions, and specifically when she glanced at photos of Damon's bike. I gave her Jillian's contact information, but never followed up with her. Every one of us is at fault this time."

"What can we do, Alex?"

"Kate, you, and the others can start by letting Damon realize you will not scratch his eyes out. He's on his way over here because he's the one Sam asked for right before she fell asleep. She doesn't remember what happened. It may come back to her, but looking at Damon on her bike apparently triggered her behavior. I'm going to keep her overnight. Sorry to ruin your girl's weekend."

"I've a confession to make?"

Abbie turned in her chair. "What type of confession?"

"I've been in town this week." Before she got another word out, Abbie turned on her.

"Do you mean the entire week? And where have you been?"

"I've been at Tobin's."

Abbie stood. "And you are just now telling us?"

"I just wanted time with Tobin. What's wrong with that, Abbie? And please don't assume you are going to mother me!"

"Alright, ladies. Let's concentrate on what's important here today. You should spend your weekend together. It sounds as though you need to discuss what's missing from your relationships. I'm going to pick up the dogs from Sam's and take them home. Argue between yourselves as much as you want, but find a slight bit of compassion for Damon and Sam. If we discharged her tomorrow, she could join the four of you."

"Perhaps we should cancel until Sam is better? What do the rest of you think? Dana, what do you want to do?"

"We should do things we had planned. I'd prefer to wait here for a while until we know how Sam and Damon are doing. And I realize we need to regroup and decide how to get back to the routine Zoom meetings or at least meet up on a more routine basis. We're busy, but we are not too busy for one another."

"Agreed!" they answered at once.

Damon let himself in through the ambulance entrance and nodded to the staff as he made his way to the cubicle where Samantha was resting. He sent his mother and father home, and there was no argument from his mother this time. He informed them he would keep them updated on both his condition and Samantha's condition.

Damon stopped at the entrance to Samantha's exam room. She was curled up on her left side and sleeping soundly. There was a slight smile on her face, and Damon wondered about the content of her dream. She appeared peaceful. And completely different from the woman who easily destroyed a five-hundred-pound motorcycle just a brief time ago. He leaned against the door frame and balanced himself with his crutches.

Damon's heart was breaking, and tears shined in his eyes. How had he fallen hopelessly in love with this fascinating woman who he had broken? No matter what it took, he would figure out a way to fix what was broken and make her realize he would go to the ends of the earth to make everything right again.

Damon groaned. Were they meant to be together? He was feeling like every time things went right, something or someone was determined to destroy everything and make them start again. He vowed to start over a million times if it meant she would be the one waiting there when everything came to rest.

Abbie walked out of the private waiting room to call Ms. Helen and check on the girls. She found Damon leaning against the door frame and walked over to where he was standing. She glanced at the tears on his face, and she reached for Damon's hand.

"How do I fix this, Abbie?"

"Why do you assume it's you who needs to fix things, Damon?"

"If I had not been on that bike, this would not have happened."

"I appreciate how you're thinking, Damon, but you're wrong. She was good at hiding things from us. She loves you, Damon."

"I wouldn't be too sure about that, Abbie."

"Sam told me herself, Damon. The problem is she can't get the image of you lying injured under the truck out of her mind. She's convinced you sacrificed your life for her. She can't understand why you did that for her."

"I love her, Abbie. She is the only person in this world I want, and I can't figure out what to do."

"Did you tell her that you love her, Damon?"

"No."

"You might reconsider."

"Do you think she will talk to me?"

"According to Alex, she has no memory of what happened, so I'm positive she will still talk to you."

"How do I fix this?"

"You need to take a step back, Damon. Take on your physician role. If she were your patient, what advice would you have for her family members?"

"Are you mad at me, Abbie? Julie told me I don't deserve her. Are Kate and Dana angry with me, too?"

"No, Damon. We are blaming ourselves because we missed the signs. We are usually so good at understanding one another. But we screwed up this time. And to top everything off, Julie has been here with Tobin this week and told none of us."

"Wow. I didn't realize she was here."

"Exactly what we said. Every one of us needs to do better, Damon. You need to concentrate on getting through therapy and going back to work. That will help both of you. Are your parents still here?"

"No. I sent them home. Samantha and I need to find our own way through this disaster without them living in the same house. Will she want me to leave?"

"I cannot fathom she will ask you to leave. When Alex and I split up, I chose to walk away. I needed to work on myself. I suspect Sam wants you by her side."

"Alex told me you walked away from him and Andy. He told me you didn't speak to him for weeks. Will she do the same thing to me?"

"She's different from me, Damon. I grew up in foster homes and had to fight my way through everything. I didn't trust anyone, so I learned to walk away, and figure out things on my own. That's not Sam's personality."

"I hope not. What would I do without her?"

"Can I get you anything, Damon? I need to call Ms. Helen and check on the kids, tell her where Alex and I are, and when Alex will be home."

"I was planning to stay the night if the psychiatrist allows me. Jillian should be here soon. I just needed to see her. I'll stop in the waiting room shortly."

As Abbie turned to leave, Jillian Taylor came around the corner, and toward Abbie and Damon.

"Hi Abbie. How's your family?"

"We are doing well, Jillian. Everyone is healthy and growing, and Alex and I are doing great."

"I'm glad Abbie. Damon let's walk to the doctor's lounge and talk. Samantha looks comfortable right now. Let's let her rest for a while longer."

"Sounds good, Jillian. Abbie, I'll talk to you shortly."

Damon and Jillian made their way to the doctor's lounge.

"Take a seat, Damon, and tell me what happened today."

Damon filled her in on the day's events and relayed the signs he recognized leading up to Samantha taking a baseball bat to her bike. Jillian questioned him for thirty minutes, then told him she needed to talk to Samantha.

"May I stay with her tonight, Jillian?"

"I'm not so sure that is a good idea. Let me talk to Samantha first and I will get back to you. It sounds as though she is suffering from PTSD, and I'm not surprised you did not recognize it sooner. You're busy trying to survive, so don't punish yourself over this event. It's not surprising for survivors of a major accident to suffer PTSD symptoms. She will be fine. I'll get her on the right medications, and you both need to make appointments with me."

"I'll do whatever it takes to make this right. I didn't mean to cause this, Jillian."

"Damon, listen to me. If it were not for this event today, it eventually would have been something. She was showing the signs. It could have been anything to set off a reaction. It was just a matter of time. Now we work to get her back to her baseline, and I understand she is a great person. I overheard the nurses talking about the two of you when she was by your side the past few weeks. They like both of you, and Samantha was generous to them for taking care of you."

"Thanks Jillian. Text me if I can talk to her once she is awake. I'll be in the private waiting room with her friends."

"You're welcome, Damon. I'll talk to you shortly."

CHAPTER 26

Jillian walked back to the exam room where Samantha slept.

"Samantha, it's Jillian Taylor. Can you open your eyes for me, please?"

Samantha opened her eyes at once. "Hi, Dr. Taylor. Thanks for stopping by."

"Call me Jillian. Do you mind if I put the head of the gurney up so we can talk?"

"That will be fine. Nice to meet you. I have seen you around the hospital but have not had a proper introduction."

"It's nice to meet you as well. How are you doing, Samantha?

"Well, I'm lying in the ER, and I do not realize how I got here, so I assume I'm not doing as well as I should be."

"I'll agree with you on your observation. Can you tell me about your day?"

Samantha filled her in on the day up to the point of waking up in the ER.

"You're a physician, Samantha, so I presume you have knowledge of Post Traumatic Stress Disorder. You suffered an incident earlier today, and that is why you are here. Do you remember the incident?"

"Alex asked me the same question, but honestly, I'm not sure what happened. Can you fill me in on the pieces that I can't remember?"

"I will do that but tell me how you've been feeling."

"I'm not sleeping well and I'm having nightmares. I do not have an appetite. I'm anxious, and I just can't unsee Damon under the truck that struck us during the accident."

"Damon says you appear to have lost weight. Do you think that is a valid statement?"

"I'm sure I've lost weight. It's been tough trying to get Damon healed and back on his feet. He is needy and sometimes obstinate and claims he can do everything himself. To tell you the truth, it's been exhausting."

"Were you concerned he might not survive his injuries?"

"Yes, but it wasn't until I looked at photos of the bike after the accident that I realized there was no reason he should have survived. Damon pushed me off the bike before the truck struck us. My guess is that he saw the truck coming. He put himself in harm's way to save me. I'm not sure how to live with that, Jillian."

"Do you think he might have done that because he cares deeply for you, or because he is a decent person?"

"He's a player. If you work here, you're surely aware of his reputation. He said I'm different from the other women he's dated, but I'm not sure what to believe. We just started spending time with one another when the accident happened, but I do believe he is the one for me."

"I'm aware of his reputation, Samantha. But I realize that people exaggerate. Do you want to continue your relationship with Damon?"

"Yes. I want to continue our relationship. He is a terrific guy, who is thoughtful and funny. He loves my dogs, and they love him."

"I'm aware of the success of the program you and Abbie put together. Congratulations."

"Thank you. We are amid expansion. There are days I feel overwhelmed. But Abbie somehow seems to keep everything under control."

"I understand you are part of a close group of friends. Can you depend on them to help you when you need a hand?"

"Yes. We've been busy lately. Dana moved here from Charleston several months ago, and Julie and Kate are moving here as well, so we'll be in the same town again."

"It sounds as though you are very tight with your inner circle."

"I am. We try to meet via Zoom meetings often if we can't meet in person. I guess we have not been great at that lately, but Abbie is busy with the babies and Andy, and I'm busy with Damon. We had a girl's weekend planned for this weekend, but I'm not sure I'm going to make it."

"Well, you won't make it today. I'm going to keep you overnight, and get you started on medications to help with the nightmares and your anxiousness. But I encourage you to join your friends tomorrow when I release you. It will perhaps put Damon out, but he will get over it. We need our best friends. Spend the rest of the weekend catching up with them."

"Thanks, Jillian. Can Damon visit this evening?"

"Samantha, do you live alone, or is Damon staying at your place?"

"Damon has been staying with me since the accident. We started dating around two weeks before the accident occurred. After the accident, I made an offer to him and his parents to stay at my place, since it was just across the street."

"Are you safe at home with Damon?"

"Yes, Jillian. I've no reason to be afraid of Damon."

"I'm glad to hear that, Samantha. Damon is in the private waiting room. I spoke with him earlier, and he wanted to spend the night with you. I think it will be okay if he sees you for ten or fifteen minutes, but I want you to get rest tonight, so I suggest he go home, or go back to your place."

"Thanks. I appreciate it. I will be sure to send him home tonight. Can I see Abbie and my other friends for a couple of minutes as well?"

"I'll tell Abbie, and your friends, they can visit you here in the ER for ten minutes, then they need to go start their weekend plans. Damon can visit you once you get upstairs. I'll let the ER nurse give you the first dose of medication here, so you will not be awake too long for Damon to visit. You need sleep, Samantha. That starts tonight."

"Thank you for seeing me, Jillian. I appreciate you helping us to get through this mess."

"Get rest, Samantha. We have work ahead of us."

Dana, Kate, Julie, and Abbie tiptoed into the room. Sam grinned at them and put her arms out for a hug. After the group hug, everyone settled down.

"How are you feeling, Sam?"

"I'm okay. I'm tired, but Jillian is giving me medicine that will help me sleep. I'm sorry I am going to miss tonight, but Jillian said I need to be with you tomorrow when she sends me home."

"Believe me, we plan to save the fun stuff, which includes spending loads of Tom's money, until tomorrow when you can help us support the local businesses."

"I'll dream of the things I want to spend money on tomorrow."

Abbie grinned. "Make a list, and if we don't get everything this trip, we can plan another one."

Sam grinned at her friends. "I love you ladies. Thanks for being here for me."

"We are always here for you. And I had to confess to Abbie, Kate, and Dana that I've been here the entire week and staying with Tobin. So, I'm confessing to you as well."

"I wondered how long it might take the two of you to get together."

Dana chuckled. "He's absolutely nuts over her. He's been talking for weeks about how she cannot live without him. I think it may be the other way around, but we'll let him keep his manhood."

They were giggling when Damon knocked on the door.

"Is it safe to come in here, darlin? Or do I need to find reinforcements?"

"Get in here, Damon. I'm sorry I was angry at you earlier this evening. We are leaving. Our ten minutes are done. They are going to take her upstairs."

Damon walked over and kissed Samantha on the forehead. "I'll meet you upstairs shortly. Alex is going to stop and get the dogs. I'll go with him and lock up after he leaves. By that time, the nurses will have gotten you settled. I'll return to tuck you in and kiss you goodnight."

"We are heading out as well. See you tomorrow. Give us another hug."

The nurse came through the door.

"Okay everyone, out! Dr. D'Alessandro is going upstairs now. Dr. Parker, you can visit for fifteen minutes, but give us thirty minutes to get her settled into her room upstairs."

"Understood. I'll return to you soon, darlin."

Damon and Alex picked up the parts to Samantha's motorcycle. They placed them in the back of the garage, then Damon sent the dogs home with Alex and made his way back across the street to the hospital. He took the elevator to Samantha's unit and made his way to her room. He paused in the doorway and observed her resting with her eyes closed. The nurse had dimmed the lights to prepare for her to fall asleep. Damon's eyes teared up again. The nurse watched him from her seat at the nurse's station. She stood and walked over to him.

"You haven't told her, have you, Damon?"

"Hi Susan. I did not notice you standing here. What are you talking about?"

"Just tell her, Dr. Parker!"

Damon turned to glance at the nurse with a puzzled expression on his face.

"Tell her you are in love with her, Damon. The rest of us in the hospital can see it on your faces. Don't tell me you don't realize that when you look into her eyes. You're an idiot. Tell her before she walks away, and you never see her again. The rest of us that dated you if that is even what it was called, we have never seen you this committed. She is a great person. Don't screw this up, Dr. Parker!"

"Thanks. I'll do that, but not here."

Damon walked over and sat on the left side of the bed. Samantha turned to him, and he wrapped her in his arms. He was terrified earlier today. Samantha's behavior this afternoon terrified him. His father had done the right thing by holding him back while she took out her frustrations on the motorcycle. He was glad she could not remember, but she needed to face it soon. She needed to remember so that she could heal and realize that not every action he made put him at risk of death. They were in the wrong place at the wrong time. He was recovering, and she'd recover as well. He looked forward to spending his days loving her and any children they might have together, but that was his dream, and he was not sure if she dreamed of the same life as him.

They lay quietly together, and Samantha finally asked him if he was staying with her through the night.

"I'd love to stay, but Jillian said no. She wants you to sleep tonight uninterrupted. I apologize for not recognizing that you were sleeping poorly. I was caught up with my own exhaustion."

"It's not your fault, love. I realized I needed to call Jillian, but I did not take the time to do what I needed to do. I recognized the symptoms in myself, but was trying to ignore them, and apparently, I waited too long."

"That doesn't matter now, darling. We will work with Jillian. This accident has affected both of us."

"We need to call Steve, love. He told me he was having trouble unseeing you beneath the truck. I want to make sure he is okay as well, and if not, we can recommend Jillian for him, too."

"I will contact him, darlin. Remind me again where he works."

"He's a bartender at the restaurant at the swing bride."

"I'll check on him this evening. In the meantime, I'm heading out of here so you can sleep. I'll pick you up in the morning and take you to Dana's so that you can finish the weekend with your crew."

"Thank you. I appreciate that, love. I'd rather spend the day with you, but Jillian said I need my friends right now, too."

"The two of us have the rest of our lives to spend together, darlin."

"Yes, we do."

Damon made his way across the street and got into his truck. He drove to the restaurant and took a seat at the bar. There were two people working behind the bar. The male bartender waked over to Damon.

"Hey there. What can I get for you?"

"I'm looking for Steve. Are you Steve?"

"Depends on who's asking?"

"I'm Dr. Damon Parker. You met my girlfriend, Dr. Samantha D'Alessandro. She may have introduced herself to you as Sam."

"Are you kidding, man? How are you? So great to find you up and moving. How's Sam?"

"Samantha's the reason I'm here. She asked me to check on you. She is being treated for PTSD related to the accident. She said you told her you were having trouble unseeing me lying under the truck. That's why I'm here. And, I'll take a blood orange brew and a menu, too, please."

"Let me grab that beer and menu, then we can talk."

Steve grabbed a coaster, put Damon's beer and menu on the bar, and walked around the bar, and sat beside Damon.

"Look, Doc. I've been having trouble sleeping and possibly have had too many drinks as well. I've never observed an accident of that type before, but I'm glad I could help."

"Are you drinking and driving, Steve?"

"Nah, I just grab three or four drinks after I get back to my apartment. It helps me sleep."

"Here is the card of a therapist friend of mine. Samantha and I are seeing her too. I'm going to suggest you consider the amount of alcohol you are consuming and give Jillian a call. If you need someone to talk to in the meantime, here is my number."

"Thanks, man. I'll call her."

"And thank you for helping Samantha and I at the accident scene. I understand nobody else offered to help. We'll always be there for you, so pick up the phone if you need a ride home, or just someone to talk to if you are having a rough day."

"We're cool, man. Glad I could help. Let me get your order. Tell Sam hi for me."

Damon finished his burger and beer, then drove to his apartment to check on everything. He glanced around and decided his life before Samantha was devoid of life. He chuckled at the décor of the apartment. Classic bachelor pad.

He grabbed additional clothes out of his closet and packed them in a backpack. The last weeks had been difficult on both of them, but he was making plans to change everything, including Samantha's opinion of him being a player. Damon grabbed the backpack and made his way back to the truck. Tomorrow he'd put the plans in motion and cross his fingers hoping Samantha could see things the same way.

CHAPTER 27

Damon decided he and Samantha needed a complete do over of their dates up to the time of the accident. He had time off work right now, and Samantha had the weekends, so he could plan to replicate their dates, minus the motorcycle. It might give them time to get to know one another again. Samantha said they didn't know each other very well. He wanted to give them another chance. His gut told him she was the one, but he needed her to admit that she felt the same way.

Damon spent the next day preparing her room at his place and making reservations at the place they had eaten lunch at on their trip to Wilmington. He wanted to show her they were able to make a life together that did not involve motorcycles and risk. Hitting the road on the bike used to be therapy, but he will give it up to keep her happy.

He planned to keep separation in their lives, which could make his physical therapy sessions more difficult. Samantha had an assistant that was trained to take over his water therapy sessions, which would give them time away from each other throughout the day. Koko, Kody, and Kohl would still be involved in his care.

Damon did not realize why Kohl was giving him the side eye after Samantha was admitted to the hospital. Then he remembered Kohl was inside the house and began barking and snarling when Samantha destroyed the bike. Apparently, he blamed Damon for Samantha's breakdown as well.

Damon spent most of the day Sunday cleaning up his apartment and finding more ways to lure Samantha comfortably back into his life. He felt good and had gained back his energy. Although he'd been on crutches long enough to do any task he needed to complete, he still needed to be careful he did not re-injure his leg. The cleaning service he hired was still coming every other week, so there was little he needed to do. He washed bedding and towels and brought a few breakfast items into the apartment, including enough coffee beans to make pot after pot of coffee.

Samantha would be home later this afternoon. He planned to stop by but did not plan to stay the night unless she did not want to be in the house alone. He worried that if he stayed, she might think she had to feed him and care for him. If they did not take a step back, they might be risking their future.

Samantha arrived home from her day with her crew, carrying more bags than she had planned. Abbie helped her tote everything into the house, gave her a hug, and told her she was going home to Alex and the kids.

Samantha called for Damon, but he did not answer. She looked in the garage and noticed his truck was missing. She looked for her phone amongst the bags, found his number, and hit send.

"Hey, darlin. How was your day?"

"Good. We bought more stuff than we planned, but Abbie did not take no for an answer. She blamed it on Tom, but I expect she likes to spoil us occasionally."

"I'm glad you had fun. I considered bringing a light dinner to your place. Do you feel like eating?"

"Can you bring something that is more of an appetizer than a meal? We were snacking throughout the day, and I'm not super hungry."

"Absolutely. Any desires, or do you want me to surprise you?"

"Make it a surprise."

"Sounds good. I'll see you soon."

Damon stopped at Boulineau's store in Cherry Grove and purchased steamed shrimp, cocktail sauce, and fresh vegetables for them to munch. His plan was to propose the idea of a do over to Samantha. He carried everything into the house while Samantha showered and changed. He set up the food and drinks on the coffee table so they could relax on the sofa while they talked. Damon was nervous, Samantha might think his idea was irrational.

"What's all this love?"

"We deserve to relax on the sofa and munch on shrimp and veggies and catch up with each other. Are you doing, okay?"

"I'm weary after the shopping spree, but I'll sleep good tonight."

"I understand. Our lives have been busy lately, and I thought maybe we should consider a do over."

"A do over? What are you talking about? Are you breaking up with me?"

Samantha stood and started pacing around the room.

"No, darlin. I wondered if you want to start over again. I understand you feel we've spent very little time together before the accident and I want to start over again. With you!"

Samantha stopped and stared at him.

"I'm not positive I'm as all right as I assumed I was. What brought this on, Damon?"

"Samantha. There is no doubt in my mind that you are the one I want to be with, but I want to make sure you are sure of this relationship, too."

"Right now, I'm sure I'm confused about what you are asking!"

"Can you sit, please? It's difficult for me to chase you around the house on crutches. If Tobin doesn't get me out of these orthopedic contraptions soon, I swear I am removing it myself."

"What do you want from me, Damon?"

"Samantha, take a breath and listen to me, please. I am not breaking up with you. I didn't want to admit this to you in what is now beginning to feel like an argument, but I am in love with you. I don't have any fancy words to describe my feelings. You've completely stolen my heart. I have seen people fall in love and break up, which made me question if any long-lasting relationships exist. I realize it has been tough lately, and you've spent many nights in tears. I wish I could change that for both of us. I promise to fix what I've broken. I love you, Samantha. I've been so alone for years and did not know if I could ever find someone to love. I can't imagine what I would do without you in my life. I want you forever. I'm not sure if that is what you want, but I want you! I want babies with you if that is what you want. I want more outrageous dogs who act like Kohl, who give me the side eye and huff just because I looked at you the wrong way. Life hasn't been easy for us, but that will change. It is you that mended my heart and made it possible to find love. When I'm with you, there's nothing missing in my life."

Samantha stared at Damon and wiped tears from her face with her sleeve. Damon stared back and got nervous when she did not reply at once. Samantha wiped her tears one more time and moved closer to Damon.

"I love you, too, Damon. I realized it since that fateful ride that nearly took you from me. I told Abbie you were perfect. I'm sorry I've been such a mess lately, but it took a long time to find the right person as well, and you are that person. I, too, watched so many friends and colleagues get into and out of a relationship that meant so little. They did not even try to work it out."

Samantha chuckled.

"I yelled at Abbie so many times to call Alex and work things out. Abbie and Alex were meant to be together, but she was not able to see it from the craziness in her life. I'm so glad we survived the accident. We'll both mend from our wounds, and I want to be right beside you when we come out of this mess. As for babies and dogs, well, I'm in for that too. There will never be another Kohl, but each of the dogs has their special personality. Apparently, each one of them has learned to huff at us as well."

Samanta was still wiping tears on her sleeve.

"I understand your do over now. I assumed you didn't want me, and that made me angry, and sad, at the same time. Can we be a boring, normal couple soon? I need boring and normal to survive."

"I will cheerfully do boring and normal things with you if it helps us heal and stay together. I looked around my apartment today and shook my head. It was so empty, and I realized that was my life before you."

"I can barely remember mine. This house is so amazing. Abbie could not have found a better place. But I might love to live on the beach one day."

"Really, Samantha? I love being near the beach. We can look for a place when you are ready. If I am with you, I don't care where we live. This is a great house, though."

"It is, but it's empty without you and the dogs."

"Do you want to sleep alone tonight?"

"Why do you assume I want to do that, love?"

"I know you've been having trouble sleeping, and I hope the medicine Jillian gave you will help you get the rest you need. But I do not want you to assume you need to do everything for me. I can take care of myself."

"I enjoy doing things for you."

"I understand that darlin, and I enjoy doing things for you as well. But I do not want you to think I expect you to do everything."

"I understand."

"Great. And I bought something for you the other day when I was out with my parents."

Damon handed her the box from the jewelry store.

"Damon! Thank you.!"

"It made me think of you."

Samantha opened the box and smiled. Nestled in the box was a six-carat aquamarine dangle pendant with a circular bale in white gold.

"Damon, it's gorgeous and way too extravagant."

"It reminds me of your eyes. It's the same color. Come here and I will put it on for you."

Damon took the necklace from the box and placed it around her neck. Samantha jumped up and took off for the nearest mirror.

"I'm speechless, love. It is so pretty."

"So are you, Samantha. Will this do until we decide to pick an engagement ring?"

"Damon, I don't require expensive jewelry. This is way too much."

"Do you want to give it back?"

"Umm, no. I believe I will keep it and enjoy it. Thank you, love!"

"You are welcome, darlin."

Samantha walked over to Damon and kissed him.

"I love you, Damon. I'm glad we finally got that out in the open. I've wanted to tell you, but I was afraid to scare you off."

"I'm not going anywhere unless you are right beside me, darlin. Can we officially say we are together?"

"Here we go, again! Didn't we have this conversation over titles? When we first started hanging out together, you wanted to call it dating, correct? So, what do you want to call this now?"

"How about we call us pre-engaged?"

"Lordy, Parker! Your obsession for titles just might make me reevaluate this relationship!"